SEA GLASS INN

Visit us at www.boldstrokesbooks.com

By the Author

Harmony

Worth the Risk

Sea Glass Inn

SEA GLASS INN

by

Karis Walsh

2013

ISBN 10: 1-60282-771-0
ISBN 13: 978-1-60282-771-4

THIS TRADE PAPERBACK ORIGINAL IS PUBLISHED BY
BOLD STROKES BOOKS, INC.
P.O. BOX 249
VALLEY FALLS, NY 12185

FIRST EDITION: JANUARY 2013

CREDITS
EDITOR: RUTH STERNGLANTZ
PRODUCTION DESIGN: SUSAN RAMUNDO
COVER DESIGN BY SHERI (GRAPHICARTIST2020@HOTMAIL.COM)

Acknowledgments

Writing the words is the easy part. I humbly thank the people who do the hard work behind taking a manuscript and turning it into a quality book. A grateful thank you to Radclyffe, for creating this amazing company, filling it with dedicated and talented people, and inviting me to be part of it. To Cindy and Toni and our eagle-eyed proofreaders, for turning out beautiful print and electronic books. To Sheri, for designing such a lovely cover that captures the essence of my book—this one is going in a frame on my wall. Finally, to Ruth, my editor. From idea to proposal to completed manuscript, this book has her fingerprints all over it. And I wouldn't have it any other way.

On a personal level, this book was inspired by a deep love of the ocean and by the friends and family who share this love. Thank you to Mom, Dad, Staci, Brad, Madison, and Morgan. And to my grandparents who are missed so dearly. I'm thankful for our cherished memories from the shores of Washington and Mexico and Hawaii. To Corina, for lounging on the beaches with me in sunny Spain. And to Colette, for spending days scrubbing oil-covered birds with me at Ocean Shores. All of you are with me every time I stand on a shore and watch the waves.

Dedication

With love, for my dad.
Because he taught me to notice.

CHAPTER ONE

Melinda Andrews clicked the windshield wipers to their highest setting as yet another logging truck sailed past in the oncoming lane and sprayed her car with muddy water. She fought to keep her spirits lifted as she drove along the rain-soaked winding road that led from Salem to her new home on the Oregon coast, but she lost another inch of ground in the battle at every turn. Growing up, she had spent vacations on the coast with her family, and somehow the area had been frozen in endless summer in her memory. The signs that winter was fast approaching the ocean communities caught her by surprise. The spruce and firs lining the highway were still green and full, but the deciduous trees had dropped their leaves after an early cold snap. The side of the road was covered with a blackish slime as the leaves decayed on the forest floor, and a depressing gray sky loomed through the bare branches.

Mel allowed her memories to resurface and color the drab October afternoon. The August sun. The promise of adventure. The summer day when she had first looked at Pamela Whitford's painting of the ocean and had the crazy idea she wanted to live there, be part of the coastal community.

Her son, Danny, had been at football camp and her divorce had just been finalized, so Mel had escaped to the only place she had ever felt alive and happy. She had come to the ocean alone and wandered the busy streets with a welcomed sense of anonymity. She could still hear the distant chime that sounded as she'd pushed through the

Seascape Art Gallery's door and entered the brightly lit space. She had stood there in awe, immersed in a maze of panels zigzagging through the room, each covered with a different artist's vision of ocean life. From watercolors to collages, a swell of waves and beaches enticed tourists to pay ridiculous prices and take home a small piece of their vacation experience. Mel had fallen under the same nostalgic spell as she stood in front of an oil painting and watched the light glistening off the mosaic of sea glass that accented the sweeping brushstrokes. It spoke to her of broken pieces made whole again, and Mel knew she had to own it.

The decision to buy the painting had everything to do with its beauty and the hope it inspired as Mel started her new life. It had nothing to do with the gallery owner who'd come up behind Mel as she stood transfixed in front of the painting. Mel could still recall her voice, so husky and soft, and how it managed to stir to life all the feelings and desires Mel thought she had shut down long ago.

"You like this one?" the owner had asked, her voice hesitant as if she didn't want to push for a sale. She smelled like an ocean breeze, salty and fresh and alive.

"It's beautiful," Mel had said, turning away from the picture to face the woman. She was tall and casually dressed, in long cargo shorts and a faded polo shirt. Her sandy-brown hair was cut short on the sides but was long enough on the top so Mel could see its tendency to curl. She looked windblown and confident, more ready to walk along the beach than run a high-end gallery. Her appearance was rough around the edges, like her voice, giving her dimension and texture like the glass gave the painting. Even though they stood a few feet apart, Mel had known the woman's hands would be the same. Rough-gentle. Demanding. Giving. The pain of wanting, apparently not as dormant as Mel had believed, had lanced through her, and she'd suddenly felt out of place in her ironed slacks and silk tank. To cover her confusing thoughts, she'd gestured toward the painting. "I like the way the waves are edged with glass, like they're shattering on the beach."

"The endless destruction of the surf," the woman had added, her blue-green eyes locked with Mel's.

"Change, not destruction," Mel had said, surprised at the conviction in her voice. She rarely felt this confident talking about art, especially to an expert, but she knew how the painting spoke to her. "Breaking apart old patterns and habits so something new can form."

"That's a more positive way of looking at it," the woman had said, giving Mel a lopsided smile. "But isn't something always lost when that happens?"

"Sometimes loss is good," Mel had countered, trying to convince herself as much as the gallery owner. "It opens the door for new possibilities."

The proprietor had just shrugged but didn't argue. And Mel had felt a sudden and desperate need to grab hold of the truth of her statement. She was afraid to let go of the glimpse of hope she had just found in the beauty of shattered fragments inspired by the artwork. And in the long-forgotten glimmer of arousal inspired by the gallery owner. Indulging in a rare moment of personal extravagance, Mel had bought the painting.

And as if the single act of doing something for herself had cracked open the box she'd built around her dreams and started a new trend, she'd gone directly from the gallery to the realtor's and bought her painting a new home.

The painting had been mildly extravagant, the house ridiculously so. The thought of her new home, a sprawling and dilapidated old inn, was enough to jar Mel back to the present. She took advantage of a temporary double lane and passed the slow-moving minivan she had been impatiently following for several miles. She couldn't explain her sudden haste to get to Cannon Beach. Her drive was harrowing on the slick and steep mountain road, but she had a premonition that once she saw the inn again, the journey to it would look pleasant in comparison.

Her new home. No matter how many times she repeated the phrase, Mel could barely picture the house in her mind, let alone accept it as a replacement for the elegant rambler she had lived in for the past fifteen years. Every previous trip to the ocean had included a stay in an upscale oceanfront hotel suite. Beds made, bugs removed, freshly baked cookies on the reception desk. This time she would be the one responsible for all those amenities, all the work required to make the long-neglected old inn habitable not only for her, but for a new crop of guests.

The real estate agent had assured her the house only needed the right person and a little effort to return it to its former glory as a B and B, but Mel should have asked how many centuries had passed since the house had been such a success. Unfortunately, she didn't remember asking many questions. She remembered signing her name on the papers, but the decision-making process—what little there had been of one—was still a blur. She had gone directly from the gallery to a real estate office on that beautiful August day, not pausing long enough to think through her half-formed, capricious plan. She asked about a large home she had seen on a bluff, overlooking the ocean, with a weathered for sale sign on its lawn. The agent had talked about low interest rates and cash bonus options while Mel's mind wandered into some vague and distant future. She could hang Whitford's painting on the wall, gaze at the real waves below, decorate each room with charming, color-coordinated furnishings…

The thought of living full time in one of her favorite places had seemed like a dream come true. As she had walked through the small town of Cannon Beach with hordes of tourists and the memory of happy family trips surrounding her—and with the encouragement of her eager realtor—Mel had found it easy to imagine filling a large, empty inn with paying customers.

Now she berated herself for being so hopelessly gullible. She had lived in Salem for years, only a few hours from the coast, and she knew how often it rained in Oregon. Yet in her mind she had pictured year-round sunny days. Given the likelihood that the current weather would be the norm from October to May, she had no idea how she would be able to make a bed-and-breakfast turn enough profit to repay her loans.

For once in a life filled with safe, rational, carefully studied choices, she had acted on a foolish, expensive whim. She had no training in the hotel business, and being an innkeeper hadn't been part of her life's plan. But neither had she planned on being alone at forty. Or being divorced, with all the accompanying baggage, from her eighteen-year marriage to Richard. She'd always imagined she would feel free—relieved—if she ever had the chance to remove the shackles of her conventional life, but instead she felt her throat constrict, her stomach clench in panic. For better or worse, she had tied her fate to a dilapidated house and weedy yard when she signed her name on the loan papers. Unless she declared bankruptcy, Mel saw no way to gracefully back out of the deal.

After a lifetime of clouding herself and her desires with other people's expectations, she longed for truth, for transparency. But she didn't even seem capable of offering it to herself. She tried to picture the house as she navigated the wet highway, but the only images she could call to mind were from her fantasies and daydreams. She had walked through the old house with her realtor and pictured each room fully decorated and fully occupied. She'd imagined a sanctuary for gay and lesbian travelers, a place where they could find the acceptance and freedom to be themselves she had so often longed for.

But now, try as she might, she couldn't recall the actual state of the house, and that scared her. She didn't think her arts and crafts experiences as a Boy Scout den mother qualified her to renovate an inn, especially if the rooms needed more than a simple coat of paint. And she had a nagging suspicion that the problems with her new home would be deeper than simply cosmetic. In fact, she would be surprised if the damned house hadn't collapsed under the first autumn rains. She had a vague recollection of the inspection report, but she hadn't read much beyond "structurally sound" before she'd put the papers in the bottom of one of her moving boxes. And filed the memory of the house's actual condition in the back of her mind.

She only had herself—and the artist Pamela Whitford—to blame for her rash decision. The painting had been the catalyst for Mel's move, but she had been seduced by more than the art. She had fallen for the artist herself, or at least a fantasy version of her. She felt somehow connected to the hand that had drawn those crashing waves, embedded the rough sea glass in the still-wet paint. For the past months, Mel's daydreams had been full of images of Pamela drinking wine and discussing art with her as they watched the sunset from Mel's back porch. A rickety back porch Mel had to learn to repair if she wanted any part of her fantasy to come true.

What had she seen in the house? A chance to erase the nagging regrets she felt after a lifetime of self-denial and safety. To reinvent herself. To start over. But now, two months later, the reality was finally starting to surface. Mel headed toward a new life with the wrapped painting on the seat beside her and her earlier optimism lying in broken pieces in her heart. Desperate to regain some hope for the future, Mel pulled off the road when the shoulder widened. A sign marked it as a scenic-view spot, but all Mel could see beyond the trees were rain and clouds. She dug a business card and her cell phone out of her purse and hoped she had enough signal to make the call.

"Seascape Gallery."

Two simple words, but the seductive sound of the gallery owner's voice slammed Mel right back to that summer day.

"Hello?"

Mel raised her hand to her chest as if she could slow her racing heartbeat with her touch. She forced herself to start talking. "This is Melinda Andrews. I bought a mosaic from you in August. Do you remember me?" *Please say yes,* she added silently.

Pam's grip on the phone tightened. Of course she remembered Melinda Andrews. She could visually recall every person who had bought one of her paintings since she had opened the Seascape Art Gallery eight years ago. Of course, it helped that she had only sold seven of her own pieces amid the hundreds by other artists, but Pam would have remembered Melinda even if she hadn't bought anything. Pam could picture her distinctly from a few months earlier as she'd moved through the gallery wearing the excited glow reserved for tourists to the coastal town of Cannon Beach. Locals only came to Pam's shop to complain about those tourists, and their irritation was usually reflected in their expressions. Pam had just walked out from the back of the shop, called by the chime on her door, when she'd seen Melinda standing by the front window. The sunlight caught something wistful, longing, in her eyes as she stood in front of the mosaic. Her carefully combed hair and too-pressed linen-and-silk outfit—a sure sign of a well-to-do traveler—had faded into the background as Pam had watched her connect with the blue-gold waves Pam had drawn. Pam had known Melinda would buy the painting no matter what price she put on it.

"No," Pam lied. She fought down her desire to sketch the slight curve of Mel's nose, the sharper line of her chin, and instead doodled a series of connected triangles across a piece of paper. "I'm sorry, but I have so many customers it's difficult to keep track of them all."

"Oh. Of course." Melinda's voice didn't mask disappointment well. "It doesn't matter. The painting I bought is by an artist named Pamela Whitford. I'd like to buy a few more of her mosaics for my new inn. I bought an old house and I'll be running it as a bed-and-breakfast. I'm calling it the Sea Glass Inn, so I'd like to have some art using sea glass in each of the rooms. Do you have more of her work in your gallery?"

Her sentences ran together as if she needed to spit them out as quickly as possible. Pam couldn't tell if Mel's haste was due to nervousness or excitement, but she knew for certain it should have been the former. New businesses were as common as seagulls on the coast. She had seen so many people, drawn to what they imagined was some idyllic way of life, attempt to open a little surf shop or inn or restaurant. They expected to wander through town in sandals and cutoffs and make money off tourists without stress. But, over and over, Pam had watched the businesses pick their owners clean and leave their empty carcasses on the sand, like gulls pecking at seashells. The long hours spent catering to the tourists during the high season. The creative effort needed to survive the rest of the year. Pam knew from experience that the schedule was grueling even for someone driven heart and soul to support her ocean-side, reclusive life. She accepted the workload, but she hadn't come to Cannon Beach expecting paradise or an easy life free from pain. So she hadn't been disappointed.

"Congratulations," Pam said, silently adding the words Melinda really needed to hear. *Oh, honey. Back out of the deal while you can. You'll be bankrupt before the next tourist season even starts.* "I don't have any Whitfords in the gallery right now, but I'm sure you'll be able to find something here to decorate your rooms."

"I guess…maybe…but I really wanted…" Her words died away and Pam forced herself to remain silent. "If I could just get in touch with her, maybe she'd take a commission for more paintings."

"She's difficult to reach." Pam hedged, not wanting to admit she was the artist Melinda was trying so desperately to find. Pam couldn't accept a commission for more work when she could barely finish one painting a year. She started them frequently and would lose herself for a brief time until something broke her focus and the deceit of painting would come rushing back to her conscious mind. And make her stop. How could she create something so lasting, so permanent, when she knew too well how transitory beauty and love really were? All she could promise Melinda was a big enough pile of broken canvases to fuel a decent beach fire.

"But I'll try," Pam said.

Pam didn't know why she made the weak promise, but Melinda accepted it with obvious gratitude. Pam hung up after taking down her cell number and sat behind the front desk, her hand stiff from holding the phone so tightly. She looked at the paper on the counter and sighed. She had scrawled Melinda's number and a series of geometric patterns in ink across the consignment form for a group of seal sculptures. She folded the paper and tucked it behind the register. Now she'd have to ask the artist to sign a new form. And find a way to disappoint the beautiful Melinda.

Pam rarely had trouble disappointing people who wanted her paintings, and she was surprised by her reluctance to do so to Melinda. Even more surprising, Pam wanted to see her again, to draw her, maybe in pastels. Pam chose a pale green background to set off Melinda's hazel eyes and the chestnut tones in her dark hair before she could stop herself. She had painted hundreds of portraits, had made a living at it, but there were very few people she had felt this yearning, this *itch* to paint. Not to capture Melinda's beauty—Pam had seen plenty of gorgeous women, but she was usually content to admire and appreciate them in person, in the flesh, in bed. But Melinda offered something more, something Pam couldn't define. Something she didn't *want* to define but that her disloyal hand wanted to grab onto, suffuse with color and texture. Melinda had stood here, determined to look at Pam's painting and not only accept the wave's destructive power but to uncover the hope in it, while Pam—unable even to glance at her own work—had listened to her and almost believed.

A group of three twentysomething women entered the gallery. Pam's part-time assistant, Lisa, sat at a table surrounded by colored pencils. She was chewing on the end of her long blond ponytail and working on a drawing, but she stood up to greet the customers. Pam waved her back to her seat. Lisa more than earned her wages during the busy tourist seasons, and Pam liked to give her time and space to work on her own art when business was slow. Besides, she needed a distraction from Melinda.

She walked over to the women and smiled with more enthusiasm than she felt when the one with long dark hair made eye contact. She was too young for Pam's usual taste, and within a few minutes Pam knew they didn't share any artistic values. The three were immediately drawn to the cheap, mass-produced—but popular—trinkets and prints Pam carried out of necessity. They bypassed the original, quality pieces by talented local artists without even a glance. But the dark-haired woman glanced at Pam again, for a few seconds longer than before. Pam's hands still tingled from the imagined contact as she posed Melinda for her portrait. Shifting Melinda's shoulders so her face caught the light. Unbuttoning the top of her silky blouse and letting her hands linger as they exposed her neck a little more. Pam forced an image of the dark-haired tourist into her fantasy, and she was relieved to feel the too-intense physical arousal caused by Melinda's phone call ease into something safer. Something sufficient for tonight.

"Where are you ladies from?" Pam asked, directing the question only to the woman cruising her.

"Portland," she said. "We had a long weekend off work, so we came here for a few days."

Pam smiled again. Temporary. Exactly what she was looking for.

CHAPTER TWO

M el woke with the sun the following morning. She had arrived at the house the night before, thankfully when it was too dark to see just how bad her present circumstances were. The real estate agent had accepted delivery of her belongings, apparently instructing the movers to dump everything just inside the door. Mel had turned on as few lights as possible and had torn the protective plastic off her mattress and dropped it on the living-room floor so she had someplace to sleep. Now she wanted nothing more than to pull the blanket over her head and pretend she was safely back in her old life, but the relentless and unexpected sunlight streaming through the curtainless windows forced her to get up.

Boxes and furniture spilled out of the foyer and into the living and dining areas of the house. Barely enough to furnish one or two of the guest rooms, but quite enough to be annoyingly in the way. Mel squeezed past a bed frame and two mismatched end tables and found her overnight bag where she had left it next to the front door. She suspected most of the unwanted residents of her new house—the mice and spiders she was certain occupied the abandoned building—would congregate in the downstairs suite that would be her private part of the house, so she decided to use one of the upstairs guest rooms for her shower.

Faded strips of green wallpaper curled off the wall, exposing dingy yellow paper underneath. The fixtures were coated with grime, and hard-water marks stained the sink and tub. But the shower worked and the toilet flushed. She was thankful for the small gift of functional plumbing as she stood under the spray of hot water and tried not to touch the sides of the shower stall. A wave of resentment rose like a fist in her throat, no matter how hard she tried to swallow it down. She hadn't been overly happy in her Salem home, but at least she had had *something* there. A routine, a role that had defined her. Here she had nothing but an endless list of impossible chores. Nothing but a life wiped clean and demanding to be rewritten in every detail, from where she did her grocery shopping, put gas in her car, or got her hair cut to how she organized the rhythm of her days. Here she was alone.

Mel dried off with a towel she had luckily thought to bring. She took a carefully folded and coordinated pastel-colored outfit from her small suitcase and shook out the wrinkles before she put it on. She had packed for an afternoon of shopping and brunch, not a day full of dusty, dirty work. She sighed at the naiveté she had still possessed less than twenty-four hours ago. When she had first walked through the house, she had been full of dreams of the future. Now all she could think of was the past. From where she stood, overwhelmed and unprepared, the loveless but predictable life she had left suddenly looked safe and appealing.

Then she walked out of the bathroom and stopped short, an involuntary gasp escaping her lips as she really noticed her surroundings for the first time. Sunlight, even though autumn weak and diffused by clouds, streamed into the large corner bedroom. The two west-facing windows showed an expanse of ocean beach. Mel stepped closer. Haystack Rock was to her right, buffeted by the spray of waves. A steep staircase of weathered wood led from her backyard to the beach, winding between two small ocean cottages that were low enough so they didn't obstruct her view. A lone woman, bundled in a heavy coat and with her long hair blowing free in the wind, walked along the sand and occasionally stopped to throw a piece of driftwood for her dog. The relentless sound of the surf finally reached past Mel's daydreams and regrets and brought her back to the present with the constancy of a heartbeat.

Mel struggled with the rusty clasp and tugged until the reluctant window opened. Just a few inches, but it was enough. The ocean breeze brushed her skin with a hint of moisture, of salt. The briny smell of seaweed, strewn across the damp sand in lacy patterns, chased away the musty smell of the long-enclosed room. Mel smiled when a seagull took off noisily from the beach, scolding the dog that ran past it in search of its stick. Yes, she had been deluding herself about the state of the house and her ability to restore it. But the ocean of her daydreams, the setting she had chosen for her new life, was real and tangible and perfect. She felt a renewed surge of hope. She would hang Whitford's seascape in this room, across from this magnificent view and over the space where the guest bed would eventually be. One easy job, one step toward recreating her life in this beautiful place. Mel trotted down the steps to hunt through her boxes for a hammer and nail.

Pam drove to the old Lighthouse Inn and parked behind a mud-spattered blue Honda. During an emergency trip to Cannon Beach's tiny—and expensive—grocery store, she had been flagged down by another local gallery owner, the head of the town's art commission. Pam usually shopped at the Safeway in Seaside where she could shop in anonymity, less likely to be forced into conversation with an acquaintance, but she had picked a particularly bad day to run out of cigarettes. She had no polite way to avoid talking to Tia Bell, so she had forced a smile on her face and obediently crossed the quiet street to the art gallery. Instead of asking the usual intrusive questions about Pam's painting, however, Tia had only wanted to chat about the foolish woman who was attempting to start a new B and B in town. The entrepreneurs who descended on the town every year were alternately a joke and a source of irritation to locals. Each year there were a few new ones who came into town and provided entertaining stories of spectacular failures. Pam had done her share of joking and complaining about the fly-by-night ventures, but she was always aware of the undercurrent of concern shared by the local business owners and the nervousness they all felt when empty storefronts and out-of-business signs marred the small town's prosperous and utopian image, intruding on the attempt to shield happy vacationers from the realities and failure.

In a town with good reason to be wary of newcomers, Pam had been accepted as a local right from the beginning. Thanks to Tia. Tia was instrumental in raising Cannon Beach's art scene to a national level, attracting tourists from across the States to the events and shows she planned. She had talked up Pam's reputation when she first opened her gallery, and the rest of the business owners had accepted Tia's endorsement of her as gospel. Pam had made her gallery a success, and no one seemed to mind that she hadn't lived up to her reputation as a productive artist. Except Tia. She regularly scolded and cajoled in her attempts to make Pam paint, seemingly undeterred by the months or years between Pam's works.

Their styles couldn't be more different, Pam mused. As much as she tried to fade into the background, Tia forced her way front and center with her garish clothes and loud comments. Still, as different as Tia was, Pam couldn't help but respect her contribution to local art and feel grateful for her support in the community. Pam wouldn't admit it out loud, but she usually enjoyed small doses of Tia's flamboyant conversation. But today Tia had seemed prepared to discuss Melinda's impending failure for a long time, so Pam had finally lit one of her cigarettes. Tia hated the smoke, and Pam felt only a little guilty using that as a way to escape her company.

Pam stubbed out a second cigarette in her ashtray and stepped out of her car. She had no intention of accepting Melinda's commission for more of her sea glass paintings, and her first inclination had been to call her and decline the offer. After talking to Tia, though, Pam wanted to check out the old house herself. If the needed repairs were as extensive as Tia claimed, maybe Pam could warn Melinda in time to save her some money and useless effort.

The former Lighthouse Inn was one of the landmarks of Pam's childhood, but it had been empty and in disrepair so long she could barely remember how it used to look. She had never seen the inside of the old building, so she decided to make a rare neighborly visit and turn down Melinda's offer face-to-face. Although she had meant to tour the place when it was on the market, she hadn't gotten around to it, and this seemed as good an excuse as any to snoop around the property.

Pam slammed her car door. She had plenty of acceptable excuses for coming here in person, enough of them to let her ignore the one reason she needed to stay away. Her interest in Melinda Andrews was dangerous. She had felt an almost overwhelming urge to step up and defend Melinda against Tia's gleeful predictions of failure. Pam pictured Melinda's beautiful features shrouded with disappointment when her house foreclosed, and she wanted to brush her hands over Melinda's face and wipe away her sadness. Who knew why? All Pam knew was Melinda admired her painting—something they definitely didn't have in common. Her interest in Melinda was simply physical attraction. Or fascination with anyone who would take on such a monumental project as the old inn.

But fascination led to sympathy and caring too much. That led to heartbreak. Pam recognized the early stages of her same old pattern, and she was determined to stop herself before she got any more entangled in Melinda's fate. She had watched enough businesses go under to know not to get personally involved. Just last year she had been disappointed when the new candy shop closed after just two months, but she hadn't imagined personally consoling the owner. True, Melinda was easier on the eyes than old Joe Morrison, but neither of them was Pam's concern. Succeed or fail, Melinda would have to face the consequences of her investment without Pam's help.

Pam went to the side of the house and peered over the fence into the overgrown backyard. The cement patio was barely visible under a mess of decaying furniture and stuffed trash bags. Weeds had taken over the yard, so Pam was hardly able to tell where flower beds had once ended and lawn began. A small raised porch at the back of the house promised a great view of Haystack Rock, but she wasn't convinced the rickety structure could support her weight. Besides, rusty tools and plastic toys, their shapes and protruding edges barely visible where they had fused with the thick undergrowth, littered the path.

Pam couldn't remember the last time she'd had a tetanus shot, so she stayed on the safe side of the fence and gingerly climbed on a haphazard pile of rocks to see the rest of the yard. An old building, tucked under the red limbs of a sheltering madrona, ran along the north side of the fence. Gaping holes lined with lichen-covered wood had once framed large south-facing picture windows. Probably a studio or sunroom before time and gravity had stripped away its door and gave its roof a scalloped effect. Pam let herself imagine the studio fully restored, full of natural light and space, before she turned away from the fence and walked up the cracked sidewalk to the front door. Melinda had better have an army of workers and a sizable fortune at hand to help her. The inn looked months away from being ready to receive guests.

After a few minutes of knocking and ringing the apparently nonfunctioning doorbell, Pam opened the unlocked door and stepped inside. "Hello?" she called, standing on the threshold. She felt like she was walking into someone's home, even though she knew it was meant to be a public place. She finally moved into the hallway and shut the door behind her. She stood in stunned silence as her eyes adjusted to the dark interior. The short walk from her car to the front door had done its best to lower her expectations, but she was still surprised by the cluttered and run-down foyer. The backyard looked like an idyllic meadow compared to the chaos inside the house.

Pam moved slowly around the various pieces of furniture and into the large living room. A mattress, bare except for a single rumpled pillow and blanket, lay on the ratty carpet that might have been green. The incongruously intimate setting and her sudden vision of Melinda sleeping there—alone?—disconcerted Pam. She abruptly turned away and went into the next room. There were open boxes everywhere, with some of their contents and packing materials strewn around as if someone had been searching for particular items and not unpacking in any sort of logical way. The mess distracted Pam's attention momentarily from the dingy walls and stained surfaces. A cracked ceiling and peeling wallpaper decorated what looked like a once-elegant dining room. The walls were scantily clad in the remnants of decades-old fashions, the dark cherry paneling and rose-colored wallpaper a faded testament to how many years the room had been neglected. Pam shook her head as she waved a cobweb out of her way. Melinda shouldn't even bother to unpack. The place didn't look worth the effort.

The sound of something dropping upstairs reminded Pam why she was there in the first place, and she climbed the steps to the second story where a muffled noise guided her to one of the bedrooms. Melinda sat in the center of the room, crying. Had she been this way since she arrived yesterday? Was the pillow downstairs wet with her tears? Pam hesitated in the doorway, unnoticed, as she took in the scene in front of her and tried to see it objectively, tried not to be moved by Melinda's obvious and understandable distress.

Pam's own painting was propped against the wall with a hammer lying next to it. Melinda sat facing the window, her face in profile to Pam. She was wearing cream-colored slacks and an apricot blouse with the sleeves rolled up. She sat surrounded by evidence of work, but her clothes were remarkably clean for all the dust in the house. Because she cared too much about how she looked or because she was a careful person? Either way, her elegant outfit wouldn't last long in this house. But the colors were just right. A hint of sand, of the beach, but neutral enough so they didn't detract from Melinda's face. Her brown hair was neatly styled in a classic bob, shorter than it had been in August and tucked behind her ears, Pam noticed with approval. No longer hiding the line of her jaw or her slender neck, instead exposing them to be admired. Touched. Her features were delicate and aristocratic, but a slightly pointed chin saved her face from being too proportionate. For only a moment Pam acknowledged the desire to paint Melinda's portrait. Just like this, with her eyes staring out but looking inward, like she was seeing a memory. Melinda was all angles and curves, from her too-prominent collarbones to the hair softly framing her small ears. Pam blinked and clenched her fists, and the urge passed.

Pam's presence in the room felt too invasive, the moment too intense and unguarded to share. Pam wasn't sure which one of them she needed to protect, which one was more vulnerable, but she had to be the one to leave. She was about to turn and sneak away unobserved when Melinda turned and saw her standing there. Pam watched her unguarded expression shift from surprise to recognition.

"I knocked," Pam said, mesmerized by the hazel eyes, shining with tears, that were watching her. "I'm Pam. Pamela Whitford. From the gallery." Pam waved toward her painting, cringing inside at her halting speech. She was a sucker for crying women, especially beautiful crying women. She had to get the hell out of the house before she agreed to paint more seascapes, paint the walls, paint the damned garden fence.

"You're my artist?" Melinda asked.

"Yes," Pam said. Her easy acquiescence to the possessive note in Melinda's voice confused her. She rarely accepted the title, let alone the modifier, and she took a step back in an attempt to put more distance between them. "And you're Melinda Andrews, proud new owner of the Lighthouse Inn?"

"Mel," she corrected with a short laugh. "And that probably should be stupid, not proud, new owner of the Sea Glass Inn."

Pam shrugged, wanting to hide the fact that she had thought the same thing when she first walked into the old house. "I remember the Lighthouse from when I was a kid. My grandparents and I spent holidays at Cannon Beach, and I always thought it was the most beautiful place."

"So you used to stay here?"

"No, we rented a cabin just outside of town," Pam said, smiling at the memory of lazy summer days on the beach. "The Lighthouse was much too posh for us."

"Posh," Mel repeated, glancing around the dimly lit room with a wry frown. "That is the first word that comes to mind, isn't it?"

Pam laughed. "Well, at least the *p-o-s* part…" At Mel's confused expression she tried to explain. "Piece of shit? Sorry, that was a bad joke."

Mel shook her head and weakly attempted to laugh along with Pam. "No, you're right. The house is a mess. And I can't even hang a painting let alone fix the rest of the problems."

Her voice trailed off with a sniff, but she slapped her hands to the floor and pushed herself to her feet so she was nearly eye level with Pam. Pam shifted her gaze away from Melinda's still-red eyes and noticed a bent nail stuck in the wall above her painting which was the only bright spot in the room. Blue and tan brushstrokes sketched out a sandy beach and summer sky, but the ocean's waves were crusted with blue and white sea glass. Pam remembered every moment she'd spent at work on it, picturing the relentless waves of time that shattered a person's life into unrecognizable fragments. She turned away from the pain it represented and focused instead on the simple problem of getting the heavy painting securely on the wall. She spent her days hanging other people's artwork. There would be no emotion attached to that act.

"I can help you hang it, but it weighs too much for a nail," she said, deciding now wasn't the time to suggest that the distraught Mel either paint or paper the stained wall before she decorated it with a picture. "We'll just need a…"

"God, don't *tell* me," Mel said as she covered her ears like a child.

"What?"

"I'll figure it out myself," Mel insisted. "I'll get a book or go to a hardware store, but let me do it."

Pam frowned. Mel had moved from tearful to controlled to angry in a matter of seconds. From sensual to downright sexy. "How is that different from having me—"

"It just is," Mel said, facing Pam with a determined look on her face. "Don't ask me why, but it is. This is my inn, and I'll take care of it."

Pam raised her hands in surrender. She had to get off Mel's emotional roller coaster before the next big plunge. Every time Mel's confidence appeared to inch higher, Pam's stomach dropped a little deeper. Tears made her want to help, but confidence made her want to rip off some clothes. "Okay, lady, have it your way. I was just trying to help."

She turned and headed down the stairs. She should feel relieved because she certainly didn't need to get caught up running someone else's business. Step in to help with one small chore, and soon she'd be the inn's handywoman. She should be glad to escape and not unaccountably hurt.

Mel watched Pam leave and ran her hands through her hair, still expecting it to be as long as it had been a week ago. She was angry.

Angry with her tears, her frustration, her inability to do more than make a useless hole in the bedroom wall. But not angry with Pam. She jogged after her and caught up just before Pam could let herself out the front door. "Wait, please," she said, pulling on Pam's arm.

Pam tugged away and crossed her arms over her chest, but she at least stopped long enough for Mel to apologize. "My husband took care of every detail like this," Mel said. She stayed close to Pam, wanting to reach out and reestablish contact. Anchor herself to the soft, worn cotton of Pam's shirtsleeve. But she had no reason to reach for her, no excuse for fondling a relative stranger, except that she had been so long without intimate human contact and she craved even the fleeting warmth of a simple touch. And she wasn't about to explain her lonely desire to Pam.

But the Pamela Whitford of her fantasies—the intellectual artist Mel had conversed with so often in her mind—gradually fused with the real Pam. The Pam who stood right before her, looking strong enough to weather the waves she had painted, strong enough to help Mel. But Mel didn't want help. She wanted, *needed,* to stand on her own. She struggled to control her racing thoughts and find a way to explain why she had rebuffed Pam's attempt to hang the painting, without thrusting all her personal issues into the open where they didn't belong.

She rarely spoke without thinking as she had done, but she had been shocked to find someone in her house, staring at her with such intensity it made her skin shiver. And then to discover her elusive artist and the sexy gallery owner were the same woman—Mel's emotions had been careening around so much lately she had started to react to every new problem or revelation without her usual calm and thoughtful approach. She had changed from a controlled woman to one of pure reflex, and the transformation was disconcerting. Her self-doubt and fledgling steps to make it on her own were bearable when kept inside. They stung when exposed to the air. "I guess I didn't realize just how helpless I'd become until I tried to do the simplest thing like put a picture on the wall. I don't want to feel this way anymore, and if it means I need to embarrass myself by asking a hundred questions in a hardware store, then that's what I'll do. I didn't mean to be rude."

Pam uncrossed her arms as if relenting a little, and Mel relaxed as well. Pam looked the same as she had in August, but with long pants and a University of Oregon sweatshirt instead of her summer clothes. Mel inhaled. The same ocean-clean smell she remembered, but with an overlay of cigarette. A smoker, and in need of a nicotine fix if her fidgeting hands were any indication.

"It's okay. It's cool that you want to do this stuff on your own," Pam said. She looked pointedly around the room. "But by the time you're done with this place, you'll probably know the clerk in the hardware store better than you know your husband."

"Ex-husband," Mel corrected. But Pam was more accurate than she could have realized. Mel had never really known Richard. "And I have a feeling you're right."

"Oh, well, good luck with…everything." Pam took a step backward. "I'm sorry I busted in on you like this. I should get going."

"Wait," Mel said when she finally remembered why she'd been looking for Pam in the first place. "Assuming I ever get this first painting on the wall, I'd like to commission more for the rest of my rooms." Mel followed as Pam edged toward the door. "That'd be four more, plus one for the common room."

"I don't like to paint on commission," Pam said, avoiding direct eye contact. "And it's getting harder to find sea glass. And my prices are kind of high."

"There's no rush, and I'll pay what you ask," Mel said stubbornly. For an artist who owned a gallery, Pam didn't seem intent on actually selling any paintings. Even during yesterday's phone call, Pam had been willing to help Mel decorate her inn, but not with her own work. False modesty? Coy self-deprecation to make Mel offer more money? Mel didn't think so. Neither of those would explain the tight frown lines on Pam's face whenever Mel mentioned her art. "I won't try to tell you what to paint. Whatever you're inspired to do is fine with me."

Pam grimaced. Mel wasn't sure if her expression was one of pain or annoyance at Mel's persistence. "Please," she said, angry at the tearful quaver she heard in her own voice. Her body kept betraying her emotions, no matter how mentally resolute she tried to be. She wouldn't beg again, but she wasn't about to let Pam leave without agreeing to paint.

"Okay, I'll do it," Pam said with obvious reluctance, as if she could read Mel's thoughts. She quoted a price per painting that was a few hundred less than Mel had spent on the seascape. "It might be a month or more between paintings, though."

"That's fine," Mel said, reaching out and shaking Pam's hand to seal the agreement before she could back out. Skin roughened by coastal weather, grip firm and confident. Just as Mel had anticipated. Her own hand must feel soft in comparison. She broke contact at the thought. "I can give you a check for a deposit."

Pam waved her off, hoping to shake off the sensation of Mel's hand in hers as she did so. Mel had struck like a snake, snatching at Pam's promise the moment it had been halfheartedly given and retreating again after a too-brief touch. "You can pay me as I finish each one," she said. She hoped her confident attitude would erase the tormenting vision of five empty canvases. It didn't.

Pam got in her car and drove slowly home, wondering why she had not only agreed to produce more mosaics but to do so at a less-than-market price. Tears, beauty, and stubbornness. A deadly combination. Mel might be coiled and ready to fight for her new life, but Pam wasn't about to join the battle. And she certainly didn't need the stress from an obligation to paint hanging over her. But she had given her word, had calmly shaken Mel's hand when all her instincts were screaming at her to run.

Mel's grip had been unhesitating and sure, at odds with the woman who only minutes before had been sitting in an empty room and crying over a bent nail. Warm and alive, as if she had been soaking up the October sun and could have shared the heat if she had only held on a few seconds longer. Shared her trust in Pam's ability to paint, when Pam herself had no such faith. She had an uneasy feeling Mel was the type who kept her promises and expected others to do the same. She had no idea how she would be able to keep her part of the bargain and deliver five paintings over the next six months when she hadn't been able to complete that many in the past few years.

Mel had said to paint whatever *inspired* her. She couldn't have realized how much that word hurt. Except for a brief glimmer of a vision, a flash of yearning to capture a scene, Pam rarely felt inspired to do more than a brief sketch on a restaurant placemat or on the back of a grocery receipt. Her muse, or whatever, seemed to have abandoned her, and she wasn't even sure she cared. Art had been her connection to life, to the people—whether family or strangers—who caught her attention and wouldn't let go. Now she breathed empty air, untouched and tasteless, except for those few occasions when a scene or landscape managed to get past her lips, into her lungs, and change her somehow. Those breaths were bitter, and she barely remembered the time when painting had been simple and painless. She could only hope Mel would give up on her business and move away before the paintings were due.

Pam fumbled for another cigarette. As much as she wanted to be free from the commission, she was surprised to realize a part of her wanted Mel to succeed. She appreciated Mel's desire to be independent and to take care of herself. Pam had always strived to be the same way. And she grudgingly admired Mel's ability to get what she wanted, no matter how reluctant the other person involved might be. But in Mel's quest for a successful business, something was going to have to give—either the broken-down mess of a house or her vision of a thriving inn. When Pam had first looked around the cluttered yard and time-worn rooms of the old Lighthouse Inn, her money would have been on the house as victor. Now she wasn't so sure.

CHAPTER THREE

A s soon as Pam was out of the driveway, Mel grabbed her purse and drove to Seaside to find a hardware store. For the first time since she'd arrived in Cannon Beach, she felt a glimmer of hope, and she wanted to seize it before it disappeared and left her floundering again in the depressing state of reality. She had managed to convince Pam to supply her with mosaics. Now she just needed to learn how to hang the damned things. She had spent the morning halfheartedly unpacking items and moving them to different rooms in the house while she noted repairs she needed to make. She had finally written *burn down and collect insurance money* on the bottom of her long to-do list and tossed it aside before searching in earnest for the toolbox she had bought for the new house. The box seemed so small and inadequate in the face of her mammoth project, but at least it held a hammer and some small nails. She'd feel better once her painting was hung. Who couldn't do something as simple as hang a picture on the wall?

Apparently she couldn't. She had pounded the nail into the wall and then managed to catch it on the strange hook on the frame. Only her quick reflexes had saved the painting from falling and pulling the nail all the way out of the wall. That had been too much to bear. She had followed the painting back to the ocean. Changed her life—and her son's life—because of what it meant to her. Freedom, independence, self-sufficiency. Hanging the mosaic on the wall of her new home had taken on a sort of symbolic meaning. Nearly dropping it on the floor had suddenly seemed like a very bad sign.

She had spent years keeping her emotions carefully under control, smoothing over her true feelings and rarely letting them be seen in public. The bent nail had been enough to make her wallow in a rare—and private—moment of self-pity and frustration. Not meant to be witnessed, especially by Pamela Whitford. Mel had imagined their first meeting so many times. She'd be relaxed and gracious in her inn, or witty and charming at an art show, or sexy and windblown on the beach. Never in any of her fantasies was she sitting on the floor sobbing.

Mel parked in front of the hardware store and mentally prepared to feel foolish again. The only way to get through this renovation was to start asking stupid questions and not stop until she ran out of them. It might take the rest of her life, but she was determined to do whatever it took to not ever feel so completely helpless again.

Mel walked into the store with what she hoped was a competent air. She had been in hardware stores before, of course, but usually as an observer, not a participant. She wandered up and down the aisles. Hammers, screwdrivers, tool belts, drill bits. She touched everything. Smooth wood and cold metal. Trying to make the objects seem less foreign, to make herself feel more confident in her ability to use them as she turned her piece of shit—as Pam had so accurately called it—into a home. She stopped in front of a display of power tools and picked up a cordless drill. She hefted it, surprised to feel comfortable with its size and weight in her hand. She could use it. For what, she wasn't certain, but a motorized tool at least sounded more fun than anything manual.

Another day. She returned the drill to its shelf and walked down the next aisle. Screws and nails. Exactly what she needed for today's project. Maybe. She peered into the little drawers, unsure what she was looking for. The sheer variety was overwhelming, from thin slivers of metal to screws thicker than her thumb. Silver, gold, black. Galvanized. She picked up one of those because it sounded like it meant business, but it didn't look much different from the nail she had tried at home. She tossed it back and closed the drawer. She didn't think a bigger nail was the solution, and she almost wished she hadn't interrupted Pam when she was about to tell her what to do.

Almost. But Pam seemed so sure of herself, so composed. So damned sexy and comfortable in her skin. She had everything Mel wanted for herself—an independent life at the ocean, a fulfilling career...

A working knowledge of tools and hooks and picture hanging.

Two days ago, she'd been admittedly envious of both Pam-the-gallery-owner and Pamela-the-artist. Mel's own vision of success had been a perfect inn, creatively decorated and full of guests. Now success had been scaled down to this one project. Find out how to hang a picture, and then actually get the job done. On her own. Or, at least, with minimal help from an impartial clerk. Somehow, letting Pam solve the problem would have been as bad as calling her ex-husband and having him drive over from Salem to do it. She couldn't explain why, but she knew it was necessary for her to stand in this store on her own. Uncertain, but ready to learn. She could have handled it better with Pam—and she regretted snapping at her—but this new life was about Mel herself. Not who she was in relation to anyone else. She turned a rotating bin full of bulk nails. God only knew what project loomed in her future that might require her to buy nails by the pound.

"Can I help you?" a man asked from behind her, and Mel turned to see what looked like a garden gnome come to life. He was several inches shorter than she was, with a pointy gray beard and ears that stuck out through his thick hair.

"Yes, please, um...Walter," she said, reading his name tag as she remembered Pam's prediction that she would get to know this guy very well over the next few months. "I need to hang a painting on a wall."

"What size?"

Mel caught herself before she asked whether he wanted the size of the picture or the wall. She held her hands several feet apart to show him the dimensions. "About this size, but it has glass on it so it's pretty heavy. Maybe twenty pounds?"

"What you need is a molly bolt," Walter said with a nod. "I'll show you."

"Okay," Mel said noncommittally as she followed him to a different aisle. She wasn't sure if that was some sort of sexist joke or not, but he handed her a small plastic package with the name across the top. "Oh, it really is called a molly bolt."

"Sure is," he said. He ripped open the package and showed her how to hammer the contraption into the wall and pull it back so it would support her painting. "Do you have a stud finder?"

"No, thank you," Mel said absently as she studied the small metal pieces in her hand. "I mean, do I need one? You said this didn't go into a stud."

"Well, now, you'll need to find where one is to know where one isn't."

Mel laughed for the first time in what felt like weeks. "Walter, that makes perfect sense to me."

❖

Mel gingerly let go of the painting and stepped back. Surprisingly, it stayed put and didn't fall to the floor. She pushed at one corner with her finger, straightening the frame, and sighed with a mix of pleasure and sadness. Something accomplished, but no one to share in her small victory. The project—trivial as it might be to others—seemed worthy of champagne and celebration to her. She considered calling Pam, her only real acquaintance in town so far, but she figured Pam had more important ways to spend her time than chatting on the phone about molly bolts.

Mel frowned as she finally looked past the painting to the wall behind it. The off-white paint was stained and peeling, and the Sheetrock was pockmarked with nail holes. She slipped the seascape off its sturdy hook with a resigned air. Time for another trip to see Walter. And his paint selection.

CHAPTER FOUR

Pam parked behind the dirty Honda and let her car idle for a few minutes. Apparently Mel had been too busy with her home improvement projects over the past three days to have time to wash her car. Or go into town. Pam hated to admit how many times she had caught herself staring out her gallery window at Cannon Beach's main street, watching for Mel's car. She had even changed her route to and from work so she drove past the old house. She hadn't gone far out of her way, though, and she'd managed to justify her detour each time. She'd hoped to see a new for sale sign in the weed-filled front yard because, once Mel packed up and moved out of town, Pam would finally be free of the stress she had felt ever since she had agreed to paint. But she'd seen no indication Mel had abandoned the inn. Instead, day after day, she saw the unchanged scene that was before her now.

She finally got out of her car and picked up the pizza box she had left on the backseat. She certainly wasn't concerned if Mel was eating or trapped under a collapsed ceiling or quietly having a nervous breakdown. Pam had enough to worry about without adding Mel's welfare to the list. She had brought the pizza as a peace offering since she wanted to come clean with Mel and tell her she couldn't fulfill the commission.

She had tried to paint something, anything, the night before. How hard could it be to sling some paint on a canvas and call it good enough? Some blue water, some sand and driftwood. Glue on a few pieces of sea glass and sell the damned thing to Mel. Who cared if she produced crap? She didn't. Her reputation was only a liability now. Pressure, expectations, jealousy. She'd be happy enough just to get through the paintings and go on with her normal life. Or what passed as normal these days.

But she had been paralyzed. Her mind had been empty, and she had been unable to even open a tube of paint. She couldn't create without feeling something first, and she rarely felt anything now.

"Hey!" Pam looked up at the shout and saw Mel leaning out of an open upstairs window. Pam had expected to find her huddled in a room crying tears of despair, and she felt a wave of relief to see Mel smiling.

"Hey," Pam said with an answering smile.

"Is that one of my paintings already?"

Pam sighed, her relief turning immediately to irritation. She couldn't survive under the constant pressure to paint. She wished she could go back in time and get out of this obligation without fuss. Go back three days and tell Mel she had no idea how to contact Pamela Whitford. Or go back to that sunny August day and close the gallery early, so she never would have met Mel in the first place. Some part of her rebelled at the thought, and her reaction only made her angrier. "No. It's pizza."

"Just as good," Mel said. "Come on up."

She disappeared again, and Pam shifted the pizza box to her left hand and opened the front door. She really needed to lecture Mel about leaving her house unlocked. Pam walked up the stairs, fuming about Mel's insistent interference in her life and trying to ignore her own complicity in the situation. She had come here once before to let Mel down, and she had ended up agreeing to paint for her. She couldn't fail again this time. She reached the first floor landing and stopped, her anger momentarily forgotten as her eyes adjusted to the airy brightness so at odds with the dim stairwell. The three bedroom doors were propped open, and weak sunlight reflected off their freshly painted walls and ceilings. All the windows were wide-open as well, and a light breeze wafted into the hall.

"Does it look a little better?" Mel asked as she appeared in the doorway of one of the rooms.

"Much," Pam said, as mesmerized by Mel's appearance as she had been by the décor. She had been transformed along with the rooms, reflecting a light from some source other than the sun. Pam couldn't turn away, and all her excuses disappeared. Had she simply wanted to see Mel? Now she wanted to leave, but Mel gestured for her to come into the room.

Pam walked in and managed to focus on the walls. She had thought the paint was white at first, but now she could see it was a very pale yellow. With a slight gloss, like the inside of the shells Pam used to collect here when she was a child. Lined up on her bookshelf when she returned home, they were reminders of safe and warm summer vacations. Pam was relieved there were no bold patterns or trendy colors in Mel's rooms. Just an organic lightness, like the background wash on a painting, that pushed the attention toward the sea. Guests would love it here.

"Beautiful," she said, looking at Mel again. They were in the same room as a few days ago, but the difference was startling. Before, Mel had been impeccably dressed and the room had been a mess. But now Mel was the mess, in a gray sweatshirt and old jeans, her face as paint splattered as her clothes but with a bright smile instead of tears. Pam would have agreed to add ten paintings to her commission if Mel asked her to. She took a step backward and held out the pizza box.

"Fortuna's Pizza," she said. "If you're going to be a local, you'll get to know them very well. Best pizza in town, and they deliver."

Mel laughed. "Are you moonlighting as their delivery woman?"

"No, but I haven't seen you in town for a few days. I wasn't sure if you were eating."

Mel fought off the pleasure she felt at Pam's concern. And at having any company at all in the big, lonely house. Pam had been thinking about her. The realization felt as tangible as a caress, as comforting as a hug. But Pam was just being polite and welcoming. Typical small-town businesswoman.

"I like the color," Pam said, gesturing at the walls.

"Thanks. I wanted to keep it light. Neutral," Mel said, keeping her voice casual as if the project had been as simple as choosing the right paint. For the first time in her life, Mel was responsible for every decision, every aspect of a mammoth project, with no input except for Walter's occasional suggestions. Pam's obvious approval of her color scheme wiped away some of the self-doubt Mel had been battling. But, despite her uncertainty, Mel was proud of the work she had done. Even if Pam didn't necessarily understand all that had gone on beneath the layers of paint, Mel certainly did. She had spent hours on the rooms. Washing the walls and ceiling, priming them, painting. Moving from molly bolts to spackle and roller brushes and painter's tape. The rest of the house might look dingy in comparison, and she had only done a tiny percentage of the needed renovations, but Mel felt a thrill of accomplishment and pride in her newfound self-reliance. Though she had a long way to go, she was beginning to trust her ability to get there. But the road was sometimes lonely, and she was happy to share even the surface of her success with Pam.

To share *something* with *anyone*. Mel couldn't rely on Pam forever, expect her to put her own life on hold just because Mel missed the companionship of sharing her life with someone. Mel had never spent so much time on her own. At night, while working, while eating.

Eating. The house had consumed so much of Mel's time and attention that she had barely bothered to do more for herself than take an occasional shower or eat a simple meal. Her stomach rumbled as the smells of yeast and basil and tomatoes finally overcame the paint fumes and caught her attention, driving the question of what it would be like to have Pam keep her company at night away from the forefront of her mind. Having Pam there to talk about her renovations was a pleasant enough change. And to share a meal? What had once been an everyday occurrence was now a cause for celebration. "I have a bottle of wine downstairs," Mel said. "Why don't we eat outside?"

Pam followed her down the stairs and out the back door. Mel had cut an uneven, choppy path through the backyard with an ancient lawnmower she had found in the shed, but the dull blades on the push mower had been woefully inadequate for the job at hand. After an hour of rolling over sections two or three times before they were cut and stopping every few feet to pry rusted crap out of her path, Mel had been sweaty and cranky. She would have thrown the mower in the ocean if she'd had enough energy to carry it down the stairs to the beach.

None of the tools or appliances in the old house seemed sufficient for anything beyond basic survival, if that. Except for a relatively new microwave and a fancy wine refrigerator—and Mel had brought both with her—the kitchen looked like a relic from pioneer days. Those two appliances, along with the coffeemaker Mel had bought on her first day, at least covered her personal needs, but they wouldn't be enough when she had an inn full of guests. Still, she'd make it work until she could focus beyond the essential renovations.

Mel led the way along her messy trail. She could have done a neater job if she had used a pair of scissors to cut the grass, but at least the destination made up for the untidy journey. Mel sat on the top step of the staircase leading to the beach and uncorked the wine while Pam set the pizza and napkins between them. The weathered roofs of neighboring cabins flanked them, and the stairs led steeply down to the sandy beach.

"I've been lucky with the weather," Mel said, cringing inside at her inane choice of conversation topic. She had spent her time alone belatedly adding up the money and time she would need to make the inn ready for guests. The phrase "home equity line of credit" had seemed so innocuous and benign when she had signed the loan papers. Now it had turned into a monster devouring her profits before she even made them. She was afraid to bring up anything more serious than the weather in case her worries about finances and her ability to actually carry out this project leaked out. She didn't want to spill out her private stresses, but she felt them so close to the surface she could barely keep them contained. "I haven't had to wait long between washing and priming because everything dries so quickly with the windows open."

"Don't get used to it," Pam said around a mouthful of pepperoni. "We'll probably have a storm this weekend."

Mel took a gulp of her wine. "How can you tell?"

Pam gestured at some innocent-looking clouds on the horizon. "You can see where two systems are colliding. It's called a mackerel sky." Pam leaned back on one hand and looked at the scene before her. The term fit. The tapestry of the sky was filled with wispy clouds, like scales on a fish, echoing the pattern of foam on the choppy ocean. A bluff in the distance provided a good focal point. Its dark outline and straight fir trees contrasted nicely with the frilly clouds. She'd center the painting…

Pam caught herself, focused on the words, not the images. The habit had become automatic, but never effortless. "Cirrocumulus. There's a warm front coming in," she explained. She sat up and held her hands out in front of her, sliding the right one over the left. "Warm air rises, so it flows over the pressure system we have in place. Droplets freeze in the upper atmosphere and form those clouds."

Mel squinted at the bright sky. "They don't look very threatening."

"They're not," Pam said with a shrug. "But they signal change. Sometimes nothing more than a shift in temperature or some light rain. Sometimes a big storm. You'll recognize the signs after you've been here a few seasons." Pam was surprised to find she believed Mel might be able to stick it out. She certainly was putting in the work required by her demanding old house.

Pam was impressed as hell because she understood exactly what Mel had gone through just to get her rooms looking so fresh and bright. Pam's gallery had been neglected by its former tenant. Water stains, sloppy patching of holes, layers of garish paint. It had taken her hours of steady work to get just that small space back to a presentable condition. Exhausting work. Now that they were out in the natural light, she could see Mel's bright smile was a little too forced. And her slumped shoulders and the dark circles under her eyes showed how tired she must be.

The urge to touch Mel caught Pam by surprise. To rub the aches out of her shoulders, to stroke her hair until the worried lines on her face relaxed. Pam reminded herself Mel was straight. Unmarried, but uninterested.

"How long have you been divorced?" she asked. Pam decided to keep their conversation on safe subjects. Weather, ex-husbands, anything to make her lose interest in Mel as a woman. And just see her as a client who needed to be politely turned away.

"We filed six months ago. We had been married eighteen years, but I'm a lesbian," Mel said. Pam heard a slight hesitation in her voice, as if she wasn't yet accustomed to openly defining herself. "I've known for years, but we stayed together anyway for Danny. My son."

Pam didn't interrupt. So much for a safe subject. She busied herself by serving them each another piece of pizza, refusing to meet Mel's eyes while she talked. Pam pulled some stringy mozzarella off her slice and put it in her mouth, licking sauce off her fingers. She had eaten almost half the pie, but her sudden feeling of hunger wouldn't be eased by more pizza.

"I thought we had a deal, to remain married so we could give Danny a conventional home and family. I kept my part of the bargain and didn't tell anyone I was gay. I thought what we had was enough."

"But your husband didn't?" Pam guessed as Mel's voice faded to a stop.

"No. He asked for the divorce. He's getting remarried."

Pam picked at the crust of her pizza slice. *Let it go. Change the subject. Go home.* "Will Danny come live with you?"

"No. He's in his senior year, and I wouldn't pull him away from his friends and his school. We have plans for him to spend weekends here, and holidays." Mel balled up her napkin and half-eaten slice. "Do you...most people think I'm a bad mother for doing this. They don't understand."

Pam reached for the wadded napkin and briefly let her fingers brush against Mel's. A son. A woman determined to be a permanent fixture in town. Complicated. Pam didn't do complicated. She needed to leave, but she couldn't stop asking questions, drawing out Mel's story. "What don't they understand?"

Mel stared out at the ocean, and Pam watched the emotions play over her features. She could read Mel's expression as easily as if she had words written across her face. Love for her son, guilt, determination. Whatever decisions she had reached, Pam knew they hadn't come lightly. Pam had originally thought Mel was crazy to come here, delusional if she thought she could rebuild this inn. But she hadn't realized how much Mel had at stake. Her identity, her family. Pam might feel a physical pull to Mel—aggravated by Mel's admission that she was a lesbian—but there was too much emotion in play. Pam wanted simple and easy and transitory. Mel was pouring her heart into creating exactly the opposite.

"He'll be in college soon," Mel said, her voice stilted. "And when he comes back to visit, Richard will have a new house, a new family. I would have been the displaced one. On my own. With nothing to offer."

Pam glanced back at the house when Mel did. It was barely visible from their seated position. "I thought if I could make a home of my own, someplace I had helped to create, he might be proud to come here. Proud of me. Not sorry for me. I wanted to have something to offer."

"A legacy," Pam said.

Mel gave a half shrug, half nod. Pam gave in to the urge to reach over and give Mel's hand a brief squeeze before she let go and hugged her knees to her chest. Mel seemed to have locked herself away in her memories and worries, and Pam was relieved to sit in silence, struggling to ignore her sudden craving for a cigarette. She understood what it meant to love a son so much you would do anything for him. Mel had gone from hiding her identity to stepping out on her own, all for her son. At a time in her son's life when most parents were resisting change, trying to hold on to the past, Mel was looking forward. And daring to *move* forward, leaving behind everything she knew in the process. Pam believed that a mother who was proud and independent was a much greater gift than one who was hiding her sexuality and her potential. She only hoped Danny would be able to appreciate what Mel was doing. Pam sighed. There was no way she could back out of the commission now. She had no choice but to help Mel in the only way she could. By painting for her.

Chapter Five

P am stared at the painfully white canvas and tried to summon the nerve to make the first brushstroke. The initial touch of color was the hardest. It stained the perfectly blank linen, started a process while her mind screamed that it was all meaningless and not worth the effort. She looked around for something to distract her, to give her an excuse to abandon the image simmering in her head, but nothing offered itself. The small A-frame was clean, the laundry done, the bed made. Even her springer spaniel, Piper, wouldn't oblige her by begging to play or go for a walk. The brown-and-white dog dozed in the weak autumn sunlight, oblivious to her owner's inner turmoil.

If it hadn't been for the memory of Mel's handshake when she accepted the commission for more paintings, Pam would have shrugged off the rare urge to capture the scene she noticed that morning. She and Piper had gone for a walk at low tide, just after sunrise, to a large basalt formation about a half mile down the beach. One of Pam's favorite spots, the tide pools created by the cluster of rocks captured such interesting sea life. Usually she brought a nature guide with her to force her mind to concentrate on identifying one thing at a time. This morning, however, she had forgotten her book at home. Instead of looking at each piece of the little ecosystem— naming and breaking down the characteristics of each creature in the shallow water—she had started to notice the interplay of elements, of light and shadow, in the microcosm in front of her.

Before she knew it, she was framing sections of the scene that could work as paintings. She'd walked around the formation until she found the right perspective, where the rising sun caught the seven-foot-tall hunk of basalt with a deep pool at its base. A cluster of starfish clung to the edge of the pool, illuminated as if by a spotlight as they seemed to reach for a wave that receded into the shadows and left them stranded. Pam's hands had clenched as she'd tried to ignore her rush of desire to paint, but then she'd remembered Mel's hand firmly gripping her own. She had returned home to take care of some suddenly pressing chores before she finally gave in and hauled out a canvas and her paints.

Pam had labored under the unexpected weight of the easel and the lightweight frame of her canvas. She'd had to move them three times before she was satisfied with the way the light hit the rough cloth. She'd pulled the kitchen table close so she had a place to set her brushes and paints. The effort of moving everything into place had been exhausting, and she hadn't even started to paint. She'd wanted to scrap the project and sit down with a drink, but she had come too far to stop. The image of the rock had pounded too insistently in her head, trying to get out.

Resigned, she dropped her box of brushes on the table with a bang loud enough to make Piper raise her head. She settled down again as Pam quieted her movements, opening the box and taking her brushes out one by one. She feathered each against her hand, the bristles pliable and soft on her palm. She must have cleaned them thoroughly after her last bout of painting—the seascape Mel bought—but the act was so ingrained, so automatic, she couldn't remember doing it. She took her time arranging the brushes in rows, their ends perfectly even, before she started to unpack her paints.

She opened the first tube and closed her eyes as the viscous, smudgy smell of the oils hit her nose. No turning back now. Even stronger than any visual cue, the scent of her art connected her to the first drawings she had made as a child. Waxy crayons, chalky pastels, cheap sets of watercolors. Sometimes she could ignore the landscapes, the faces, the images that inspired her. But once snared by the smell of the paint, she couldn't stop the rest of the painting from pouring out.

Pam took a deep breath and smeared a line of black paint on the canvas, outlining the jagged silhouette of the back side of the large rock. She was surprised her hand didn't shake as she sketched the dark outline since her willingness to return to painting for this woman was so frightening.

Of course she found Mel beautiful—there was nothing unusual about that. She could admire beautiful women. Sleep with them. Even take care of chores or projects for them, often against her better judgment. But draw for them? Not even a sketch on a bar napkin. Agreeing to paint for Mel, opening herself to friendship and connection, was dangerous. For years, she had survived by avoiding close relationships, ignoring any attraction that might lead to something deeper than a one-night stand. Tourists and itinerant visitors to her small seaside town were fine, offering sex with no strings or commitment, but Mel seemed determined to stay.

Even though Pam would normally bet her life savings that a new entrepreneur hoping to open and run a successful bed-and-breakfast would fail as so many had before, there was something about Mel that made her hesitate. If anyone had a chance to fulfill her dream and build an inn that would be a haven to tourists, it would be Mel. She seemed to represent family and permanence, sanctuary and home—myths that Pam had foolishly fallen for long ago.

The memory of what she had lost, the very things Mel was fighting to create, hit her with such force. In the belly, in the heart, in her mind, everywhere she was most vulnerable and most susceptible to the pain. She wanted to smash her canvas, snap the brushes in half, throw her tubes of paint against the wall. Destroy, not create. She had trusted in forever only to have it torn away. She couldn't allow it to happen again, regardless of how tempting Mel could be. All Pam had to do was deliver her promised paintings—no matter how painful it was to finish them—and get Mel out of her life.

The colors Pam slashed across the canvas were dark and shadowy. Black for the basalt, with a hint of red flame from its volcanic past. Deep purples, blues, and greens for the anemones that remained in place and mocked the starfish as they strove to save themselves. Stark blue-black mussels and white barnacles that clung to the rock. The textures were thick as she layered coats of paint on the canvas. But when she moved to the ocean's waves, her colors softened, her paint lightened into teal and aqua, with a whitish foam that marked the edge of the surf. She added a glint of sunlight on the water and allowed it to illuminate several tiny fish in the tide pool, some fronds of seaweed that softened the harsh edges of the rocks, and a tiny waterfall where the ocean's waves still drained into the pool.

Once she started to paint, her brain and hands seemed to move automatically, translating the image in her mind into a series of strokes and hues until the first stage of the painting was finished. She didn't even stop to consult the hastily made sketch she had drawn when she returned from her walk—on her kitchen counter since no paper had been available. It seemed as if she blinked three hours after that first brushstroke, waking out of a trance, and stepped back from the almost-complete picture. She had captured the scene, caught the starfish in their dying moment. Nothing left to do but add the fractured, polished mosaic of sea glass. Her first thought was that she had somehow painted more optimism into the image than she had expected. Where she had seen only hopeless, helpless starfish, there was somehow a sense of reaching, striving for a salvation that seemed possible.

But as the hypnotic effect of creation gradually evaporated, the image that was never far from her mind returned full force. She somehow transposed a vision of the child she had loved—the boy her partner had taken from her—onto the painting. She suddenly could see her son, who had been lost to her for so many years, kneeling next to the pool and reaching toward the starfish. The brief respite from despair was over, the glorious amnesia brought on by concentration and immersion was gone. Finishing a painting was even more painful than beginning as Pam's mind returned to the present, and a rush of grief, held at bay for a brief time, returned in force.

Piper had left her bed to sit by the back door, and she whined softly, asking to be let outside. Pam grabbed a box off the kitchen table and followed her dog into the small backyard. She sat in a weathered Adirondack chair and sifted through the box's contents while Piper wandered around the tiny patch of lawn. She hadn't been lying when she'd told Mel that sea glass was getting harder to find, but she hadn't let on how much she had collected over the years since she had started coming to the ocean with her grandparents. She sorted through the glass until she had a good-sized pile of red tones, from pale pinks to rich burgundies, to use on the starfish bodies. She added some lavender-colored glass as an accent and then called Piper inside for dinner. She poured some kibble in a bowl for her dog and a few fingers of tequila in a glass for herself. She hesitated and then poured a little more. Pam sat on the couch with her drink and turned on the television, ignoring the painting she had turned to face the wall so she wouldn't have to see it.

Pam called Mel a few days later to tell her the starfish painting, the first of her commissioned pieces, was completed. She felt a stab of disappointment when the call went to voice mail. She hung up without leaving a message. Even though the process had been difficult, now that her mosaic was finished she wanted to share it with Mel. Because she was relieved to be finished with a painting. Exhausted and relieved and ready to have it out of her house. And maybe because she wanted to see the painting through Mel's eyes, to replay the August afternoon when she had found Mel in her gallery, standing in front of the seascape. To use Mel as a buffer between her and her art, a filter so she could maybe bear to look at it.

She picked up the phone and dialed again, waiting through Mel's businesslike message.

"Hey, Mel, this is Pam. From the gallery." Brilliant. Like Mel knew at least six different Pams in Cannon Beach. Be cool. "I finished one of your mosaics."

Was Mel on a date? Not an unreasonable explanation for her absence on a Friday night. And it wasn't like Mel would have trouble finding someone…Pam's silence had stretched a little too long. "So, um, give me a call when you want me to bring it over. Or you can come get it. Whatever."

Pam gave her address and mercifully put the call out of its misery. Yes, very cool. She had no reason to be so tongue-tied. Or to care what—or whom—Mel was doing on her weekend. Mel's social life was none of her concern, and the only reason she called again a few hours later was because she wanted to get the painting off her hands and Mel's check into her account. And that was the same reason she drove by Mel's inn the next day, only to find the big house dark and empty, no blue Honda in the driveway.

Pam slowly drove home along the winding road that edged the ocean and collected Piper for a walk on the beach. The brief glimmer of satisfaction she had felt when she'd finished the starfish painting disappeared as she realized Mel might have given up on her business and left town. She had expected it to happen, but her disappointment caught her by surprise. No matter, she decided. Tia would be glad to have the painting in her upcoming art walk, and life in Cannon Beach would go on as usual, minus yet another hopeful entrepreneur. Pam pulled her jacket tighter as the wind increased. It was blowing from the south, pushing dark clouds across the sky. Pam whistled for Piper and turned back toward her house, hoping to get home before the approaching storm.

Chapter Six

Mel jumped to her feet with the rest of the crowd as Danny rushed eight yards for a touchdown. She hadn't seen him since she'd moved to Cannon Beach. She had initially been upset that she didn't have a chance to talk to him the moment she got back to Salem, but now she was relieved to have the extra time to get herself together. Even the sight of him in his helmet and uniform, barely recognizable as her son among his teammates, triggered an unanticipated range of emotions. Happiness, guilt, doubt. She had expected to feel them, just not all at once, clamoring for her attention and threatening to steal her self-control. Mel settled back onto the bleachers when Danny left the field with the offense. She moved as one with the other fans, blending in with the sea of green on the home team's side of the stadium, but she felt like an outsider. At the game, in her former city, as she brushed against her old life. She felt out of sync, different, in the very place she had called home for so many years.

Although she hadn't spoken to Danny yet, she had managed to run into Richard and his fiancée, Lesley, earlier at the concession stand. All very polite, very grown-up. Mel had walked away after the few minutes of casual chitchat with an irrational feeling of anger. And regret.

Regret. She hated the word. It implied poor choices, no second chances, sadness. In some ways, she regretted not leaving her marriage sooner. Starting over when Danny was a child, when she was younger. When she might have had the chance to build a new family like Richard had done.

But as she sat in the stands—an island of turmoil and second-guessing amidst the cheering fans—she rejected each of the negative implications of her regret one by one. She hadn't made poor choices. She had considered what was best for Danny at every crossroads in her adult life. Yes, she might have missed her second chance at romance and true love, but she had a new opportunity, a new life waiting for her in Cannon Beach. And of course she had moments of sadness and loneliness and doubt when she was alone in her decrepit inn, but she also had pride and accomplishment and the happiness that came with freedom. She'd reveled in the first tastes of those emotions, and they'd whetted her appetite for more.

No, Mel didn't want to return to her old life. Not a chance. But she envied the ease with which Lesley had taken her place. Mel's own transition hadn't been simple. She had been thrust into her new life with all the pain and agony she remembered from childbirth. But she was surviving. Growing stronger. Mel filed out of the stands with the rest of the crowd and went in search of Danny. Circumstances had changed, but now she'd be able to be a role model for the kind of life she wanted him to have from the start, one of honesty and hard work and self-determination.

She found Danny on the sidelines, surrounded by his friends, and she waved with what she hoped was a casual smile when he looked up and noticed her. She had communicated with him every day since she'd left, either by phone or e-mail, but seeing him in person overwhelmed her. As a teenager, he was so easily embarrassed by any show of parental affection, so she was determined to keep her cool. But Danny detached himself from the crowd of players and pushed his way through the stream of spectators, grabbing her in a big hug as soon as he was close.

"I missed you," she whispered as she gave him a squeeze before they stepped apart.

"Me, too, Mom," he said, not looking directly at her as he leaned against the bleachers, his helmet tucked under an arm.

"Great game," she said, changing to a less personal subject. She was surprised to see her own emotions echoed on Danny's face. She brushed her hand over her eyes. Just a few tears, but she didn't mind. She'd earned them. "Over a hundred yards rushing was pretty impressive."

"Thanks," he said. He shrugged and gave the shy grin he usually wore when his accomplishments were the topic of conversation. "Their team sucks, but the stats still look good on my record. Are you ready to go to dinner? I'm starving."

Mel laughed as he ran off to get his gym bag. At least some things never changed. The normalcy of picking up her son after his game, taking him to dinner, just being his mother seemed magnified somehow, turned into something precious because it was the one constant in her sea of change. The one truth that had always been with her, that she would fight to protect.

"How's the old house?" Danny asked when he returned and they started walking toward the parking lot. Mel had texted him with regular updates and—responding to his enthusiastic answers and excited to get him involved in the project—had started asking his opinion about color swatches and wood stains. He had sent back encouragement, endless questions, and suggestions for paint colors. Mel was grateful for the technology because she felt closer to him than she had when they'd lived in the same house.

She had been a stranger there, and he had been a typical teenager, in his room wearing headphones, at practice or school, off with his friends. They had long since given up on family meals, and Mel had strict rules against texting at the table, but since she'd moved they had fallen into the habit of having dinner together over the phone. Mel would describe her day of renovations, and Danny actually talked about school, his friends, his goals. Somehow communicating through those shorthand messages opened up a new relationship for them. Indirect and brief, but real. Mel knew more about what was going on in Danny's life and in his mind than she had when he'd been sitting in the next room.

"Coming along," Mel said, dredging up the most enthusiastic response she could find. "I finished laying the laminate flooring in the bedrooms yesterday."

"You did that by yourself?" Danny asked, sounding surprised. Mel nodded. She was surprised, too, but she had successfully completed the intimidating project with only minor setbacks, thanks to three trips to visit Walter. And thanks to the personal motto, inspired by two very costly mistakes, "Measure ten times, cut once."

"Cool," Danny said. "Wish I could have helped. What'll we be doing when I come see you next weekend?"

"I'm planning to paint downstairs this week, so there'll be plenty more flooring to keep us busy over the weekend," Mel said, keeping her voice casual. She saw the pride in Danny's eyes. Usually, he spent most of his free time off with friends or playing sports, and she couldn't remember the last time he had voluntarily offered to spend time with her. She had expected him to either bring a friend when he came to visit or hang out at the Cannon Beach rec center with the local teens. The thought of working side by side with her son made the massive job of renovating the inn suddenly seem a little less like labor and more like fun.

"Great, just show me what to do and I'll help all I can," Danny said, surprising Mel first by his eagerness and then by giving her a quick kiss on the cheek.

"I will." Mel opened her trunk so Danny could toss his bag in. She sent a silent thank you to the old house, to her aching back and knees, to her mountain of debt. Whether or not she managed to turn the inn into a thriving business, she had succeeded in something even more important. She had moved to the ocean to build a home and a new life for herself and her son. The thought of sharing the process with him gave her a sense of optimism she hadn't felt since she had forced a reluctant Pam to paint for her. She had spent her life acquiescing to everyone else's choices and needs. Now she was finally making her own path and discovering other people were willing to join her. For a brief moment she didn't feel so alone.

"Golden Moon for dinner?" she asked as they climbed in the salt-stained Honda. "There isn't a single good Chinese restaurant in Cannon Beach."

Mel finally pulled into her driveway and grabbed her overnight bag off the backseat. She ran to the front door and slammed herself inside with a sigh of relief. Her shoulders ached from the effort of driving through the storm on poorly lit roads, and her heart ached after saying good-bye to Danny again. She had felt certain about her decisions while talking to Danny, confident as she explained her work on the house. But driving through the dark night and returning to the dark house made her question this move yet again. Was it worth all the effort for this lonely life?

Mel dropped her bag in the foyer, a habit she was going to need to break before guests arrived. She moved through the house, reacquainting herself with rooms that were slowly growing familiar and flipping on every switch so she could at least fill the inn with light. A snack might help, so she went into the kitchen to microwave whatever happened to be in the freezer but stopped when she saw the light blinking on her answering machine. She pressed the button, and Pam's voice filled the room, dispelling the shadows better than the lights had done. She was calling about the painting, nothing more personal, but the growing sadness Mel had been feeling since leaving Salem tonight was eased by the sound of a friend's voice—her only real connection to her new town. And a new painting. Another splash of color to help chase away the dinginess of the old house. She should have been disappointed because the call wasn't from a potential guest, someone to help chase away some of Mel's debt, a check to deposit rather than one to write for the painting. But Mel needed the contact, the friendship—no matter how casual—more than she needed the money.

She was listening to the message for a second time, focused more on the husky timbre of Pam's voice than on her words, when the power went out. Mel gave a squeak of surprise as Pam's voice cut off and the inn was plunged into darkness and silence. Silence, except for the wind gusting against the windows, the scrape of tree branches against the side of the house, and a flapping sound overhead that must be coming from a loose shingle.

At least she hoped it was a loose shingle. Her masochistic mind started replaying every horror movie she had ever seen as she went in search of a flashlight. Deranged dolls with chain saws and bloody ax murderers might be dancing around on her roof. She had been in the house alone all week, but never without the weak glow of the streetlights and the lamp or two she always left on in case she needed to get up during the night. Now the utter, isolating blackness made her feel cut off from even the glimmer of connection she had felt while listening to Pam's message. She focused on practical matters. Of course she should have anticipated rough coastal weather. Pam had even warned her about an approaching storm. She should have flashlights in every room, candles, matches, extra blankets. Her list of supplies to help her weather the next storm grew, but even the promise that she would be more prepared for emergencies in the future couldn't save her from two bruised shins and a string of swear words.

She pawed through four still-unpacked boxes before she found the flashlight, and she followed its weak beam back into the storm and to the detached garage. She managed to make her way through the clutter and over to the generator with only one undignified shriek as she walked through a cobweb. She played the light over the dusty machine, searching for some indication of how it worked, and found a small power switch. She flicked it to the on position and stepped back, giving in to the fantasy that the generator would magically rumble to life and light up the house, even though she figured the heavy cords draped over it needed to be attached to something. She didn't relish the idea of fumbling in the dark with electrical circuits, so she struggled against the wind and back into the house.

Helpless again. And unprepared to look after herself, let alone an inn full of guests. Her frustration at least helped distract her from the odd noises coming from every corner of the inn. Okay, somewhat. She was drenched after the brief step outside, but a hot shower was as elusive as light. She changed into dry clothes and crawled under several blankets, moving *learn how to operate generator* to the top of her mental to-do list.

❖

Pam startled awake when the electricity went out, and she sat up in her bed in the A-frame's loft. Piper's small snores were reassuring in the dark, and she settled back again and listened to the wind whistling between the closely spaced beach houses. Only a moment later a loud cracking sound made her sit up again. Piper woke with a snort at what sounded like one of the neighbor's pine trees slamming into Pam's house. She grabbed a powerful flashlight from her bedside table and trotted down the circular staircase.

"Damn," she muttered as she shone her light on the branches that had ripped through a section of her roof. Rain dripped onto her living-room floor, splashing onto broken glass from the south-facing window, and the wind slashed loudly through the hole. It would be small consolation to say *I told you so* to her neighbors when she called to tell them about the damage. She had mentioned the unhealthy tree several times, suggesting they take care of it before leaving to winter in Arizona. Their homeowner's insurance would cover the cost of repairs, but Pam knew the process would be long and slow.

She thought she might be able to pull the pine off her house, but it was actually providing some shelter for her floor. So, instead, she climbed on a chair and struggled against the wind to tuck one of her canvas drop cloths between the branches and the jagged edges of her roof. Another cloth covered the broken glass, so Piper wouldn't accidentally cut her paws on it. Then she pulled stacks of soggy books from the broken bookshelf and laid them out on the linoleum floor in the laundry room. There wasn't much more she could do in the darkness. She briefly considered trying to find a hotel for the rest of the night, but she hated the thought of leaving her broken house. After one last resigned look with the flashlight, Pam climbed the stairs again and changed into a dry T-shirt. In a rare moment of weakness, Piper left her cushion and huddled on the bed. Pam burrowed under the covers with her dog curled in a tight ball at her side and finally fell into a fitful sleep to the sound of flapping canvas.

Chapter Seven

P am answered the door with her cell phone held to her ear and the tinny sound of Muzak grating on her already frayed nerves. Mel. Great. She had almost forgotten the message she had left on Mel's machine the night before, giving her address and an invitation for Mel to come by anytime to pick up her painting. Naturally she had come at the worst possible time, as if to remind Pam why she rarely let anyone know where she lived.

"I'm on hold with a contractor," she explained as she waved Mel inside. "A tree fell…Yes, I need to speak with someone about repairing my roof."

Pam gave a detailed description of the damage to her house for the fourth time that morning. The first storm of the season always seemed to bring a rash of downed trees as the weak and dying ones, unnoticed over the summer, succumbed to the winds and rain-soaked ground. The earliest estimate she had so far was two weeks away, and she was torn between toughing it out in her dripping house and cramming an air mattress in her tiny office at the gallery.

"Careful, there might still be glass on the floor," she called to Mel before returning to her conversation with the contractor. Mel nodded and stopped a few feet away from the standing water on the floor while she inspected the tarp-covered hole. Pam, with the help of a neighbor and his chain saw, had gotten the pine off her house early that morning only to find the damage was more extensive than she had thought. If she could have covered the hole with plywood, the house would have been habitable, but the tree had managed to fall on a corner and take out large sections of two walls and the roof.

"Yes, I'll hold," Pam said with a sigh. She watched Mel turn away from the damaged area and look around the rest of the downstairs. It didn't take long for her to scan the entire living room, and Pam knew her bare walls and uncluttered surfaces were more revealing than a room full of personal items would have been. Mel was bringing vibrancy and light to her run-down old inn, transforming it into something beautiful, but Pam brought nothing of herself to this house, hadn't enhanced it in any way. Anyone could see how unproductive and uninspired she was.

She spent her days at the gallery surrounded by other people's art, by reminders of her own emptiness. She found it soothing to come home and be free of the taunting creations, the explosions of color and inspiration. The few times she had invited women to her house, she had heard comments about how they had expected her to have paintings covering her walls and had expected an artist's loft to be messy, as if she was constantly in the throes of creative passion. Well, Pam had had expectations of her own once upon a time. And she had realized they were never going to come true.

She had stopped bringing anyone to her home once she discovered how much of her soul was reflected in the barren environment, and seeing Mel walk through her space—and guessing at the judgments forming in her mind—made Pam feel as cracked open as the side of her house.

The contractor came back on the line and promised to be out by the end of the week to check the house and give her an estimate. Pam gave him the address. She would believe it when she actually saw him arrive on her doorstep.

"How did your house weather the storm?" she asked Mel after she turned off the phone.

"Aside from being cold and dark, there was no damage," Mel said, putting the nature guide she had been leafing through back on the kitchen table. "I found the generator, but I didn't have any idea how to run it. I'll figure it out before the next blackout."

Pam just nodded. No doubt Mel would learn how to use the generator before the week was out. Pam would commiserate as she, too, struggled with the aftermath of the storm. But she wasn't obligated or expected to help. In fact, Mel wouldn't want an offer of help. Usually women wanted something from Pam, not caring if she had problems of her own, but this new relationship was different. Pam felt an easing in the tension she had experienced when Mel first walked into her house.

"How long will it take to fix that?" Mel gestured toward the dripping tarp.

"I have a couple of appointments set up," Pam said. "We'll see who gets here first. It'll be at least a week, but more likely three."

"Oh. I've finished the upstairs bedrooms, if you need a place to stay. Two of them even have beds."

Pam heard the hesitation in Mel's voice and she hurried to turn down the offer. Of course Mel would offer her place. She had a huge inn and an even bigger heart. Pam hoped she hadn't sounded as if she'd been fishing for an invitation. It was tempting, especially when Pam remembered sitting on the steps leading to the beach talking with Mel, and the feel of Mel's hand when Pam had brushed against it with her own. Even now she felt the tickle of the light touch, vibrating into her belly. She had to say no. Not because she couldn't control her physical reaction to Mel—of course she could. But because she felt bad enough having Mel look around her empty house and make assumptions about how little she painted. She didn't need to give her proof day after day. "Thanks, I appreciate the offer. But I'll stay at a hotel. I know how busy you are without having a guest underfoot before you're ready to open the inn."

Mel was surprised by how disappointed she felt at Pam's refusal. She hadn't realized just how lonely she was in the big house until she had extended the invitation. And this wouldn't be just a stranger, someone passing through town briefly. This would be Pam—a woman Mel wanted to know better, a woman who could help Mel transition to life as a local. A woman she was attracted to…Mel hurried past that thought. She was attracted to Pam's talent and her standing in the community. And she hadn't quite shaken the residual fantasies of sipping wine on the porch with Pam and discussing art. Nothing more intimate than that.

"A hotel will be expensive, especially if it takes longer than you expect to get the work done," Mel said, suddenly determined to convince Pam. "You won't be in my way, and I'm sure you don't mind a little paint smell." She stopped talking, confused by Pam's frown, and then continued. "I'd really love some company."

"I have a dog," Pam said, going over to the sliding glass door and opening it to let a small dog inside. "Her name is Piper."

Mel knelt down and rubbed behind the animal's soft ears. She was out of the habit of touching, of tactile contact with another being. She felt hypersensitive to every brief contact, whether it was the rough and gentle feel of Pam's hand or Piper's silky coat. Texture, warmth, the feeling of blood and vitality flowing through another creature and into her. "She's very polite," she said as the dog sat quietly, accepting the attention without fuss. She and Richard had argued about having a dog in the house for several years before Mel had finally given up. His complaints about dogs being destructive and intrusive couldn't possibly have applied to this animal. A dog would keep her grounded, engaged. Not so lonely. Once the major repairs on her inn were complete, Mel would find a dog of her own. For now, she'd try to share Piper for a short time. "You must have trained her well."

"She came that way," Pam said. "I found her at the Clam Shack in Seaside. She was outside looking for handouts, and the waitress said she had been there for almost a week. I brought her home and tried to find her owner, but no one claimed her. She's always been very quiet."

"I love dogs. I figured I'd get one once I'm settled in the inn. I have a big backyard, and I'm sure Piper won't mind how overgrown it is. You can't make her stay in a hotel room." Mel stood up. "Any more excuses?"

"I smoke," Pam said, but Mel could see her mouth starting to curve in a smile.

"In the backyard," Mel said. "So you'll stay with me?"

"Maybe. Don't you want to see your painting?"

"Oh, of course," Mel said with a laugh. "I forgot why I came."

Pam led the way to her small laundry room. She had given in to an irrational need to protect the painting from the remote possibility of water damage. Mel claimed to have forgotten about it, but Pam was certain she'd be more demanding about the mosaics once she had Pam under her roof.

She was only considering the offer of a place to stay because Piper would be happier in a house with a yard. She had tried to use Piper as a reason not to stay with Mel, but the plan had backfired. Pam had watched Mel's gentle fingers scratching the dog's ears, and she saw her eager expression when she talked about getting a dog of her own. Pam wondered if having a pet was yet another sacrifice Mel had made during her marriage. But she absolutely was not considering Mel's offer because Mel's voice had revealed too much loneliness when she admitted she wanted company.

Pam stood back as Mel followed her into the laundry room and silently stood in front of the painting. She'd be stupid to accept. She had a feeling Mel's driving need to do everything in the inn on her own would be wearing off soon. She must be exhausted by the work she had done already, and soon she would be only too willing to enlist the help of her reluctant houseguest. In between nagging her for the rest of the paintings.

"It's beautiful," Mel finally said. Pam exhaled in relief. She had wanted just to paint anything in order to get Mel off her back, but she felt strangely happy to hear the truth in Mel's voice. This wasn't someone trying to impress her, flatter her, seduce her, like so many of the women who visited Pam's gallery. She had seen Mel's pride in her inn, and she believed Mel would only allow beauty in it. She wouldn't display something she disliked on the walls she had worked so hard to transform. Pam had wanted Mel to like the painting, had trusted her to tell the truth when Pam was unable to judge it objectively. Neither the desire for approval nor the willingness to trust was normal for Pam. She wasn't sure which surprised her more.

"The black rock. It's so powerful," Mel continued. "And the starfish. I love how the tide is coming in to rescue them."

Pam bit back the need to correct Mel and tell her the tide was flowing away from the starfish, not toward them. They were dying, cut off from the nourishment and protection of the sea. Starving in the same way Pam was when she tried to paint and nothing was there, or when she felt the familiar urge but desperately had to fight it off. But, of course, Mel would see the more hopeful version of the painting, just like she persevered in seeing Pam as someone talented, creative, productive.

Pam was accustomed to having other people see her paintings in different ways. Part of being an artist was letting go of her work and turning it over to be interpreted by the public, and she had experienced a similar disparity in viewpoint when Mel had bought her seascape. But this time was different because for a brief moment she'd seen Mel's optimistic perspective superimposed over the actual painting. Then Pam's focus had shifted, and she saw what was really there.

"Thank you, Pam," Mel said. "I love it. It'll be perfect in the front bedroom since I painted the walls a light lavender. You can stay in that room, too."

Pam struggled to find words to explain why she couldn't possibly live in one of those airy bedrooms and face the painting every day, but Mel brushed by her on the way out of the room with Piper right at her heels.

"Come on," Mel said. "Let's get you packed."

Chapter Eight

Mel added more water to her scone batter, accidentally tipping the measuring cup too far and making a sticky mess. She sighed and added another handful of flour. Crazy. She had been baking for years, but today she was making breakfast for Pam as if she were a completely inexperienced cook. On their first morning together in the old inn.

Mel turned the dough out onto the counter and tried to knead it into submission, stopping now and again to scrape the gooey mess off her fingers. She hadn't slept well, and she had finally given up the pretense and headed to her kitchen to make a trial run at a large breakfast. Already she was surrounded by the scents of cinnamon and cloves, the aromas reaching far back in her memory, back to weekend breakfasts when Danny was a child. She patted the overworked dough into a large circle and then cut it into wedges. She put the scones in the oven, set the timer, and checked them off her list. She didn't have much faith in the ancient appliances, but maybe the oven would explode and destroy all evidence of her miserable scones. Her microwave was reliable, so if all else failed, she could just serve nuked breakfast burritos every morning.

At least she had cleaned the kitchen so it was sanitary enough for cooking. Any major renovations would have to wait until the public areas of the house were finished. Mel tucked a loose strand of hair behind her ear and washed flakes of dough off her hands before starting on the fruit salad. Appliances aside, she loved the old kitchen with its intricate tile backsplash in jewel tones of blues and greens, the old-fashioned enamel sink, and the large window with its view of the backyard and a glimpse of the ocean beyond it. Right now she could just see Pam's head where she sat at the top of the stairs leading to the beach. She was bundled against the cool morning breeze and, judging by the haze surrounding her, smoking a cigarette. Waving grass was the only sign of Piper's exploration of the yard.

After all her insistence on dragging Pam back to her house yesterday, Mel had felt strangely shy once they had moved Pam's suitcases upstairs. She had been proud to have Pam walk through the room and see the improvements she'd made. But having Pam live there? Oddly disquieting. How much more intrusive would it be when strangers came to stay? Mel was going to have guests living in her home—plenty of them, she hoped, for her bank account's sake—and she needed to get comfortable with the idea. At least Pam was an acquaintance. A friend.

Or was her discomfort worse *because* Pam was a friend? One she was admittedly attracted to? Mel sliced the skin off an orange, narrowly missing her thumb, and cut segments of the fruit into her bowl. Mel had decorated the room, cleaned the bathroom, and made the bed. Her personal touch was everywhere. Pam would sleep between the sheets Mel had chosen, shower behind the see-through curtain with its pattern of lilac and green seashells. Dry off with the fluffy purple towels Mel had picked after running her hands over every option in the store. The intimacy of Pam's presence was overwhelming. She'd infused the room with the scent of the ocean more indelibly than opening a window would do.

Mel licked the sweet orange juice off her palm before washing her hands again and starting on a melon. She had lived without any intimacy for years, coexisting in a house with Danny and Richard, and she had been unprepared for the experience of having someone outside of her family living under her roof. The sensation of being pulled to a woman was so unexpected. How much more unfamiliar to have her close—so very close—at night, in the darkness, when the only sound was the steady pounding of the surf. But Mel could either ask Pam to leave or give herself time to adjust to the reawakening feelings inside her. To enjoy the stirrings as she came back to life.

Mel caught herself staring out the back window instead of cutting up cantaloupe. She turned toward the stove and away from the sight of Pam walking slowly back to the house. She had to admit, she liked having someone else in the creaky old house. She liked having *Pam* there. For all her inscrutable silences and changing moods, she was easy company, and Mel sensed an honesty in her that she appreciated. Pam's features flowed between tension and release with no in-betweens, like a seesaw moving from one extreme to the other, unable to rest on its fulcrum. Pam had a tightness around her eyes and mouth when she looked at her paintings or even, sometimes, at Mel. And a relaxed and easy smile when she was playing with Piper, or in sight of the ocean, or alone and seemingly unaware she was being observed. Mel might not be able to decipher Pam's emotions yet, but they were clearly displayed on her face as if she didn't have many barriers between herself and the outside world. Given time, Mel was sure she'd be able to read Pam's thoughts, maybe even help her find the balance that seemed to be missing in her life…

Mel shook her head as she stirred the simmering oatmeal. She didn't have time. Pam's visit was only temporary. She would stay until her house was repaired, and then she would leave, just like all of Mel's future guests. If things had been different, if Mel had made better decisions along the way, she might be living with someone like Pam as her partner. But she had chosen her path, and she had to be satisfied to have transient relationships, to merely observe love from the outside.

Pam stood in the doorway and watched Mel by the stove. She had stopped stirring whatever was in the pot and had the faraway look Pam had come to recognize in the short amount of time she had known her. Pam wasn't sure what Mel saw when the rest of the world faded away. All she knew was that Mel's regrets or hopes or visions were none of her business. She cleared her throat, and Mel turned toward her, dropping a glob of oatmeal off her spoon.

"Sorry to startle you," Pam said, reaching for a dishcloth and wiping the mess off the floor.

"Thanks," Mel said. "I was just…thinking. Are you ready for breakfast?"

Pam looked around the small kitchen. There was enough food for an entire inn full of guests. Blue-and-white stoneware platters, perfectly matched to the kitchen's tile work, sat on the counter. A meal served family style. Pam looked past the food in the bowls to the breakfasts that would be served in the inn. Laughter, talking, physical contact as elbows bumped and plates were passed from hand to hand. Community. Companionship. Things Mel would inspire in her guests. Things Pam avoided whenever possible. "You really don't need to go to all this trouble for me. I usually just have some cereal…"

"I need the practice," Mel said. She waved toward a card table she had set up in the corner. "Do you mind eating in here? I haven't even touched the dining room yet."

Pam had been through the dining room with all of its cobwebs and greasy paint. The cheery little kitchen was definitely preferable. She sat at the table, and Mel put several platters of food in front of her.

"You can eat whatever you want, but just promise you'll be truthful about what you like," Mel said as she stood back and leaned against the counter. "Remember, I'm going to be feeding guests. I don't want them demanding a refund."

Pam used her foot to push the second chair away from the table before she started dishing up her breakfast. "Then you have to join me," she said, waving toward the chair. "I can't eat while you're standing there and staring at me. Your guests won't like it, either."

Mel brought a plate and sat down. She started chatting about different seasonal recipes she wanted to try, and Pam tried to follow her conversation. All she could think, however, was what a mistake it had been to ask Mel to join her. A cozy breakfast at a cozy kitchen table suddenly was almost too stifling to bear. Pam reached for her pack of cigarettes before she remembered where she was and pulled her empty hand out of her pocket. She flashed back to family breakfasts with her ex. Diane would talk about her lesson plans for the day or her students and their struggles with her art assignments. Even then, the topic of Pam's painting had hung unspoken in the air between them, just as it did now with Mel. But then Pam had been prolific, successful. And as her portrait business had grown, so had Diane's jealousy of her talent. Diane would have preferred the new

Pam. The Pam who couldn't pick up a paintbrush and complete a few strokes without shaking so badly she needed to stop.

Pam realized Mel had stopped talking and was looking at her. "What?"

"Nothing," Mel said with a shrug. "I was just talking about plastering the chips in the downstairs molding. Boring. Don't you like that?"

Mel pointed at the oatmeal Pam had been eating, and Pam wanted to assure her that the conversation hadn't been boring at all. She had just been too far away to hear it. She took another bite of the oatmeal, with its apple bits and cinnamon and a healthy dose of cream poured over the top. The oats were cooked well enough to please Goldilocks, smooth and tender, with enough bite to keep them from turning to mush. But each time Pam lifted her spoon, it was the smell that transported her to her grandmother's kitchen when she was baking oatmeal-raisin cookies. To Tia's annual Christmas party—one of the few social events Pam anticipated with something other than dread—when Tia served her lethal spiced wine. Yes, Mel would serve her guests more than simple meals. More than just food. "It's delicious."

"Good. Now try one of these blueberry scones."

Pam took a taste and coughed. "Um, did the recipe actually call for plaster, or did you accidentally mix up your two projects?" She ducked, laughing, to avoid the chunk of scone Mel threw at her head.

CHAPTER NINE

Three mornings later, Pam opened her bedroom door at the insistent knocking to find Mel standing in front of her, wearing only a thick terry cloth robe, her hair wet and uncombed.

"Are you serving breakfast in bed this morning?" Pam asked, trying to cover up her discomfort with a joke. The contrast between the rough-textured robe and Mel's soft-looking skin was mesmerizing. The decidedly unsexy robe only highlighted Mel's sexiness, but Pam was already quite aware of her attraction to Mel. She didn't need the emphasis. Living in the same house with Mel was already too intimate when all they did was sit at a breakfast table together. Having her walk around upstairs half-naked every morning would be unbearable.

"What? Oh, no. There's quiche downstairs. I just wanted to find out if your shower was hot this morning," Mel said. She seemed completely unaware of the suggestive nature of everything she was doing and saying. Her naiveté only made her hotter. Pam managed to stop staring at the swell of her breasts, just visible where the front of the robe gaped open slightly. The scent Pam had come to associate with Mel, the merest hint of rose petals, was magnified and intensified by her recent shower. Pam breathed her in.

"Yes. Plenty hot," she said. She leaned against the door frame and crossed her arms. The collar of Mel's robe was turned over on one side, as if she had hastily thrown on the first thing in sight to cover her naked body. Her naked body, flushed and warm from her shower. Pam crossed her arms more tightly. She wouldn't reach out and straighten Mel's collar, wouldn't slide her hand under the robe and…Mel needed to leave. Or Pam needed to shut her door. "And you might be taking the concept of catering to your guest's every need a little too far."

"Wonderful," Mel said with a broad smile. "I was taking a shower at the same time. And doing a load of laundry."

Pam tried to pull her focus off Mel's body and onto her words. Her imagination still had her hand under Mel's robe as she slowly worked on straightening that damned collar. "Why didn't you flush the toilet while you were at it?"

"Good idea. I'll try that tomorrow." Mel turned and headed toward the yellow bedroom.

"Wait," Pam said. "I thought you slept downstairs."

"I do, but I still have work to do down there, and the bathrooms up here are much cleaner."

Pam knew the guest rooms on this floor all had en suite bathrooms, so she and Mel had been separated by several walls at all times. But her showers wouldn't be the same, knowing Mel was sopping wet, only two doors away. Apparently trying to either scald or freeze her.

"Why were you trying to ruin my shower?"

Mel laughed. "I wasn't trying to freeze you out of the shower. I was testing the new hot-water tank I installed yesterday."

"You. Installed a hot-water tank," Pam repeated in disbelief. The woman who couldn't even hang a painting a week ago was now a plumber?

Mel shrugged, but Pam could read the pride in her smile. "The only hard part was moving the tanks."

"Next time call me and I'll help," Pam said without thinking. Hell, she didn't know how to install a hot-water tank. But at the moment, she wanted to do something to help Mel. Anything at all, especially if it was somehow connected to hot and water and showers. "I mean…not that I don't think you can…"

"I'll let you do the heavy lifting next time," Mel said over her shoulder as she walked away. Her ass shouldn't have looked so good in the bulky robe, but it did. Mostly because Pam assumed it was bare under the robe. And as flushed pink from Mel's shower as the rest of her skin. Pam, distracted by Mel's robe-covered backside, didn't move quickly enough to grab Piper as she squeezed past her and into the hallway. The dog slipped into the yellow bedroom just before Mel shut the door. Pam considered following them, if only to retrieve her dog, but she turned away instead and closed herself in her own room.

❖

Mel wiped condensation off the mirror and looked at her reflection with a sigh. Hair sticking in all directions. Nothing on but a robe. Her skin still flushed after taking the hottest shower she could stand. She had gone to Pam's room without thinking, too excited about the new tank that doubled the available hot water for her guests to care about her appearance. Until she'd noticed Pam's expression and realized how little of her was covered by the terry cloth. Mel plugged in her dryer and started to dry her hair. Maybe not all of her redness could be attributed to the shower.

Mel's response to having Pam in the house confused her, but she knew for certain she needed to be careful. For the first time in years she was living on her own and was free to pursue a relationship with a woman. She had to guard against imagining feelings for Pam simply because she was *there*. And she had to protect her newfound autonomy and independence. It was natural for her to want to share her small but satisfying adventures in home improvement, but her dependence on Pam couldn't go further than simple companionship.

She pulled on a pair of paint-splattered jeans and a navy T-shirt. She would eventually adjust to being alone, and then the foolish desire to attach herself to Pam, to another person, would fade. She had lost part of herself because she had trusted in Richard, in their marriage. Pam didn't even offer the pretense of permanence, and Mel would not subordinate her dreams and her feelings ever again. Maybe someday she'd have enough to offer a woman, to be an equal in a relationship, but until then, she was fine alone.

Mel opened the bedroom door and followed Piper down the stairs. She briefly pictured how easy it would have been to drop the robe, the only barrier between her and Pam. She imagined Pam in the shower with her, felt Pam's hands everywhere the hard spray hit her body. Running through her hair, over her breasts, up her thighs. She shook off the vision. During her marriage her desires and attractions had been so long denied and resisted, they had practically disappeared. Now they were returning in force—because of Pam's proximity—and Mel would need to change her battle tactics. A long day of scrubbing and painting walls ought to tire her enough so she'd be able to defeat her interest in Pam.

Pam had been fooling herself to think she could stay here with Mel, live alone with her. The inn wasn't big enough. If she were simply battling a physical attraction, she'd be able to handle it without any problem. She was accustomed to denying her desires when they were impractical, dangerous. But Mel was attractive in too many ways. Independent, brave, warm. Something had been turned off inside Mel, and she seemed completely unaware of how sexy she was. Pam desperately wanted to be the one to turn her back on. But Mel—and her son—were planning to stick around long-term. Pam wasn't getting enmeshed in another family, so she had to fight her feelings for Mel. She couldn't come up with a good excuse to leave the inn until her house was finished, but she could manage to avoid the enforced intimacy of mealtimes. She needed to get to the gallery early, she couldn't stop and eat breakfast, sorry. Pam rehearsed her speech as she walked down the stairs, but she forgot the words for a brief moment when she and Mel met in the kitchen doorway. Mel started to speak first.

"I have to run to the hardware store for another brush, and then I'll be painting all day so Danny and I can lay the flooring in the living room this weekend," Mel said in a rush as she sidled past Pam. "Did I tell you my son will be here this weekend? There's leftover fruit salad in the fridge and quiche on the stove. Let me know how you like it."

"Okay," Pam said, but Mel had already let herself out the front door. Apparently, Pam's excuse for leaving had been unnecessary, and she helped herself to some food and sat at the kitchen table. She should feel relieved to have the place to herself, without having to lie or skip breakfast. She took a bite of quiche. The filling was good, but Mel had overworked the dough again, so the crust was a little tough.

Piper came and sat beside her, resting her chin on Pam's knee with a forlorn look. Damn. How many breakfasts and dinners had Pam eaten alone, content with just her dog for company? And how determined had she been to avoid sharing this meal with Mel? So why the hell couldn't she think of anything but Mel? Mel chatting about spackle or plaster. Passing plates and asking for honest feedback about her cooking. Looking out the window with a soft expression before squaring her shoulders and facing whatever the inn was about to throw at her. Pam fed Piper some of her crust. "I know," she said. "I kinda miss her, too."

Mel pulled her car onto the shoulder and rolled down her window so she could take a picture of a herd of elk grazing in a field right alongside the road. She sent the photo to Danny and merged back onto the highway. He would be coming tomorrow for his first weekend at the old house, and she felt a nervous energy creeping through her. She was overwhelmed by all the changes in her life and she desperately wanted to make Danny feel at home in her new world. She had a car full of groceries—favorite foods, familiar brands—to make him feel comfortable with her fridge, at least.

He had handled the news of his parents' divorce with concern, but when the three of them sat down to discuss the details of visitation and holidays, they had all been surprised by how far apart their worlds had grown. The logistics had been simple to negotiate, especially since Danny was old enough to share in the discussion and not be bandied about like a small child. After his initial search for answers and reassurance, he had adapted with the enviable resilience of youth. The unacknowledged tension that had filled their home had dissipated, leaving them all shell-shocked but ready to move forward.

Danny had been awkwardly accepting when she'd told him she was gay, but she didn't think either of them was ready to see her in a relationship. Not yet, when there were so many changes in both their lives. Or was she using him to avoid taking any risks of her own? He had accepted Lesley without a problem. Had wholeheartedly supported Mel's new venture. He had even tentatively started to share some details of his own dating life during their dinnertime conversations. She had been worried he would jump to the conclusion she and Pam were living together, but maybe her own attraction to her houseguest was making her imagine sexual tension and energy when nothing was there. But, whatever the reason, whatever her excuse, Mel wasn't ready to push herself into the dating world, to risk disappointment and pain. To take a chance she would sublimate her own needs and desires to someone else's. To require any more adjustments from herself or Danny until the dust had settled from the major upheaval they'd already faced.

She was too fragile. Too drawn to Pam. And too unaccustomed to living under the same roof with someone she found so sexy. But she'd better get used to it fast. She'd have guests at the inn. Women. Lesbians. She couldn't make a habit of developing crushes on every one of them simply because they were there.

Mel slowed as she drove through town. She saw Pam, of course. Her house and her new town were too small for there to be any real distance between two people. Only a silly crush. No reason to feel jealous because the woman Pam was talking to was standing so close to her. She waved and forced a smile. She'd better start avoiding the street in front of Pam's gallery, just like she'd been avoiding any part of the house where Pam might be.

Pam raised her hand and waved as Mel's Honda drove past. She had gotten used to scanning the quiet streets for the blue car whenever she was in town. She was supposed to be coming to the gallery to get away from Mel, away from her persistent attraction. Instead, she was aware of Mel's movements all day. So she knew when Mel went to buy groceries or to the hardware store. When Mel stayed home and worked.

"Are you paying for your room at the inn, or are you working off your board with your pretty new landlady?"

Pam whipped her head around. She had been staring after Mel's car and had nearly forgotten Tia was leaning against the building next to her. She had come outside for a cigarette and had been accosted before she could light up.

"Mel and I are friends, that's all," Pam said fiercely. "Don't you dare start spreading rumors about us. She's new in town and doesn't need to have everyone talking about her behind her back."

Tia laughed and grabbed the packet of cigarettes Pam had taken out. "You are not going to chase me away with these nasty things," she said, tucking them in the pocket of her voluminous silk pants. She winked at Pam in her usual flirtatious way. "You want them, you'll have to go in after them."

Pam sighed. She normally laughed off Tia's habitual flirting. Neither of them took it seriously, but Pam really wanted to smoke. Almost enough to break the unspoken rules of their friendship and go in after her pack.

"Now first of all," Tia said, taking a step back as if she could read Pam's intentions, "I meant helping her *with renovations* in exchange for your room and board. You apparently had another form of currency in mind. You're turning red."

"Because you made me mad," Pam said, longing for an out-of-reach cigarette.

"Second, I don't need to bother spreading the rumor that you're staying with her because everybody already knows. Your house was damaged, and suddenly your car's in her driveway every day and all night. The whole town has been able to piece together that particular puzzle."

"There's nothing going on. We're just—"

"And third, she's the topic of most dinner conversations anyway," Tia continued. "She buys the Lighthouse after it's been on the market for absolute ages, and she plans to open a gay and lesbian B and B. Write the sexy local hermit into the story, and most people around here would rather talk about her than turn on the television."

"I'm not a hermit. Or sexy. Just do me a favor and please don't add any of your personal speculation to the rumor mill."

"Okay. Then do *me* a favor and paint something for the charity art show."

Pam sagged against the wall. Every conversation with Tia came to this. "I'll donate something from the gallery, of course. But don't expect me to paint anything else. I have enough on my mind with…"

Pam stopped midsentence, but Tia had heard enough to jump on the unfinished thought. "With…what? You're painting for her, aren't you!"

Damn. Five minutes of nicotine withdrawal and Pam couldn't control her tongue. She battled with the improbable hope that she could keep Mel's commission private. She sighed. Tia would find out eventually, anyway. And Pam had never told Mel the mosaics were a secret, so she had no reason not to tell people she was supplying artwork for Mel's inn.

"Yes. She asked me to do a few sea glass paintings for her rooms. I don't know how many I'll get to, though."

Tia nodded her head. "Very shrewd of you," she said as she fished out Pam's cigarettes and returned them. "Get in good with the innkeeper before she starts drawing every lesbian in the state here for vacation. If she's successful with her inn, you'll have plenty of short-term lovers rolling through town."

Tia walked away laughing, and Pam lit a cigarette with a sense of relief. And confusion. What Tia said was true. She wondered why the thought hadn't occurred to her before.

CHAPTER TEN

Saturday morning, Pam hesitated on the bottom of the stairs. She had heard Danny arrive the night before, the house suddenly and palpably energized by the teenaged boy's presence, but she had stayed in her room. When the sounds of Mel and Danny having dinner and touring the inn subsided, she had snuck down the stairs to let Piper out in the backyard. She had been tempted to join them, pulled by the changed timbre of Mel's voice, clear and carefree—and punctuated by laughter—in a way Pam had heard only on the rare occasions when Mel told funny stories about her attempts to fix something or other, or when she described one of her numerous visits with Walter. But Mel was with her son this weekend. Pam told herself she didn't want to intrude on their brief time together, but deep inside she knew the truth. Living in a house with a mother and son was too painful, too reminiscent of her former life. She couldn't avoid Danny all weekend, but she didn't feel ready to sit at a family table just yet.

Mel had apparently finished cleaning the bathroom downstairs after her robe-clad visit to Pam's room. Pam hadn't even seen her upstairs, clothed or not, since then. Mel left food in the kitchen for her and chatted briefly about the various dishes, but Mel had become too busy with her work on the house to have time for them to eat together. Pam should have been happy with the arrangement since she had been trying to find a way to minimize their interactions, but instead, she perversely attempted to prolong their conversations. Until Danny came.

Piper didn't share Pam's reticence, and she trotted into the kitchen and directly to Danny.

"Hey, a dog! You didn't tell me you got a dog."

The sound of childlike delight in the tall, nearly adult boy's voice threw Pam. She had expected him to be old enough not to trigger her memories of Diane's son, the boy she had loved like a mother until their breakup. But, as she watched Danny kneel to play with an ecstatic Piper, all she could imagine was a vision of what the eleven-year-old Kevin would look like today.

"Danny, this is Piper. And her owner, Pam," Mel said. Pam noticed Mel's odd inversion as she introduced the pet first and the owner second. Either she considered Piper the star of the show, or she was trying to downplay Pam's presence in her house. Maybe a little of both.

"Pam is staying here while her house is fixed," Mel continued. "It was damaged in the storm. She's the artist who painted the mosaics in the rooms, although you've only seen one since she's sleeping in the room with the other..."

Mel's voice faltered to a stop. Danny reached one hand for Pam to shake while he kept scratching Piper with the other. Pam hesitated a moment, still confused by her jumbled thoughts of Kevin and Danny, the past and the present.

"Hi," she said, finally stepping toward him. Danny's handshake was firm. Mel must be so proud as she watched the boy growing into a man. How proud Pam would have been to watch Kevin go through this awkward transition from childhood to adulthood. How painful to be reminded of what she had lost—not just her past with Kevin, but also the future they had been denied.

"Nice to meet you," he said. "You told me about her last night, Mom, so I kind of figured out who she was when she walked in the kitchen. But you didn't say she had a dog."

"Didn't I? I thought I did." Mel turned back to the counter. She looked and sounded a little flustered. Was she embarrassed to have another woman in the house? Worried about what conclusions Danny might reach about their relationship? She had no reason to be, since the only indiscretions had taken place in Pam's mind. Of course, Mel *had* shown up at her bedroom door wearing nothing but a robe, but that didn't count since Mel had seemed to have no clue how sexy she had looked.

"Will you join us for breakfast?" Mel asked Pam without looking at her. "I made pumpkin muffins."

"They're pretty good," Danny said. He sat in his chair again, and Piper planted herself under the table at his feet.

"I'd like that," Pam lied. "But I really need to head to my house this morning. The contractor is coming today."

He wasn't scheduled to arrive until eleven, but Pam had to get out of Mel's house. She called Piper, but her dog had apparently decided she would rather stay with Danny, and she refused to budge.

Mel handed Pam a bag of muffins to take with her. "Piper will be fine with us today," she said. Pam looked concerned, and Mel wanted to reassure her even though she had a feeling the animal wasn't the cause of Pam's deep frown. She had seemed upset since she'd walked in the kitchen. Mel was used to Pam's nervous energy when they were together, as if Pam was long unaccustomed to being in close quarters with another person. But this was different. Pam looked at Danny with the same expression of pain she had whenever she saw one of her own paintings or whenever Mel talked about Pam's art.

"Okay, I guess," Pam said. "I'll be back a little after five."

"See ya," Danny said.

"Yeah. 'Bye," Pam said. She bumped into Mel as she backed out of the kitchen. "Sorry."

Mel reached out a hand to steady Pam, but she edged away and left the room without another word.

Mel had put out her hand as a reflex. To help Pam rebalance. To try and absorb some of Pam's tension. To reassure her Piper would be okay with them, even though she really didn't think Pam was worried about leaving her dog for the day, unless she'd be lonely without her. Mel felt a mix of hurt and relief at Pam's avoidance of her touch, but she was too focused on her own emotions to be able to decipher Pam's. She had felt unaccountably awkward introducing Danny to her, even though Pam was simply a friend staying in the house. Not a lover. Occasionally in Mel's mind, perhaps, but not in reality.

"Let's get started on the flooring, Danny," Mel said, employing her regular answer to the confusing feelings Pam roused in her. Work. Mel didn't know what she'd do when work on the inn was finally complete, and she'd have to face some of her tumultuous reactions to Pam. Maybe by then she'd have a steady stream of guests, and she'd be too busy keeping up with their laundry and demands to acknowledge her ever-increasing arousal in Pam's presence. Or her interest would be transferred to one of her guests, and her attraction to Pam would be proved temporary and meaningless. And easier to forget. Or ignore.

But work on the inn was mercifully far from complete. Mel knelt next to Danny in the living room and explained how to cut the laminate flooring, how to snap it in place, how to seal the edges. She occasionally repeated one of Walter's expressions, making Danny snicker when her voice slipped into an imitation of Walter's nasal tone.

They laughed and chatted as they worked, and Mel's mind was at least somewhat occupied and off Pam. How different this was from her first day, when she had sat on the floor in despair, refusing to let Pam help her. She had moved from observer to participant to teacher. With Danny's help, and her own improving skill, she laid the laminate floor in half the time it had taken her to do the smaller bedroom she had started with the week before. The job looked neat and professional, and she and Danny celebrated by taking a picnic lunch to the beach. Mel watched Danny throw pieces of driftwood for Piper to fetch, and she finally allowed herself to dwell on Pam's changing moods.

She had been avoiding Pam the past few days, but she had noticed Pam seemed to be staying out of her way, as well. Mel hadn't seen her painting at all since she had come to the house, and she had been so concerned about her own loneliness and attraction to Pam that she hadn't really considered how difficult it might be for Pam to be away from her own home. Away from her routine and privacy. Mel had seen the starfish painting in the small laundry room. Maybe Pam painted in there, alone and quiet, without Mel and her projects and now her active teenaged son surrounding her.

An idea started to form in Mel's imagination, a way to give Pam a studio space while also creating a useful extra room for her inn.

And a way to selfishly have a chance to stay in touch with Pam after she moved back to her own home and completed the commissioned paintings. With her vision in mind, Mel began mentally listing the supplies she'd need to buy and the steps she'd have to take to complete the project. Her first step was to share her idea with Pam as soon as she got home.

❖

Mel drove Danny into town to pick up a pizza for dinner, and she left him in the living room hunting for a movie for them to watch while she took Piper back to Pam. She had noticed a now-familiar cloud of smoke in the backyard when she'd gone into the kitchen for pop and ice. The dog raced over to Pam for a brief reunion before she set off to explore the backyard. Mel followed more slowly, enjoying the sight of Pam leaning against the weathered madrona. The old tree had watched over countless guests at the old house, and Mel hoped it would see many more when she finally opened the Sea Glass Inn for business. She felt a kinship with the tree. Aged and battle scarred, observing life quietly from a distance. She could so easily picture Pam painting in the refinished studio while she and the madrona watched from the sidelines.

"Thanks for keeping Piper today," Pam said once Mel was near.

"She's easy company, and Danny loves dogs," Mel said. "I hope you don't mind we took her in the car."

"Not at all. She likes to go for rides." Pam exhaled a deep puff of smoke.

"How did it go with the contractor?" Mel asked. After her efforts to avoid Pam over the past few days, Mel was surprised to feel disappointment at the thought of Pam moving back home so soon.

Pam shrugged. "He's starting work next week. Typical though, he won't make any promises about how long it will take. Hopefully I won't be in your hair too much longer."

"I like having you here," Mel admitted. "That's something I wanted to talk to you about. I got a call this morning from a couple who are planning a wedding in Cannon Beach. Their venue canceled at the last minute because of some water damage from the storm, and they want to have the ceremony here in a couple of weeks."

"Oh, and you need me out of here by then," Pam said, pushing off the tree and stubbing out her cigarette in the ashtray she kept by the staircase to the beach.

"No." Mel hastened to assure her. "They only need a couple of rooms for the weekend, so there's plenty of space. But I need to fix up the backyard for the ceremony. And I wanted to get the windows and roof replaced on this old studio so we can have the reception here."

Mel gestured at the sagging building next to them. She had walked through it after the phone call, and the framework seemed sound. New glass, some scrubbing of floors and walls, a fresh coat of paint. Nothing she couldn't handle. When she had first arrived here, the project would have seemed impossible. Now she not only could visualize the necessary steps, but she had faith in her ability to actually do them. Even though she hadn't done the work yet, her newfound self-confidence felt damned good.

Pam went over to the building and leaned against one of the empty window frames. "I can see that," she said with a slow nod. "It's a good size for a reception room, and it'll get lots of natural light. Sounds like a good investment if you want to draw more wedding parties here."

"Exactly what I was thinking," Mel said, excited to have Pam sharing her vision. "And when I'm not using it for guests, I thought it would make a nice studio for you."

"What?" Pam turned to face her.

"I just thought…with the light and space…even when you move back home, you could use this place for painting." Mel's confidence in her plan rapidly disappeared as Pam's entire demeanor seemed to shut down before her eyes. Pam crossed her arms over her chest, and her closed expression mirrored her body language. Pam got tense whenever her art was discussed, but there was always some sign of emotion visible behind her tight expression. Pain or reluctance or embarrassment, Mel wasn't sure. But now Pam had shut off all connection. A brick wall wouldn't have been more impenetrable. Mel didn't want to admit she was reluctant to lose Pam's company, and now she was afraid of losing even their still-young friendship, so she tried to use logic to convince Pam her idea wasn't crazy.

"You don't seem to have much room at your house to work. It wouldn't cost you anything, of course, since it'd be nice for me... well, for my guests to walk by on the way to the beach and know you're painting in here."

Pam couldn't believe what Mel was suggesting. "You want to put me on *display*?" Mel had already exposed too much of Pam's private pain by forcing the commission on her and highlighting the infrequency of Pam's inspired moments. Now she wanted a parade of guests to watch her stare at a blank canvas? Mel was creative and industrious and talented, and she was under the impression Pam was the same. Once she had been, but not now. But like Mel's insistence on seeing the starfish painting in a hopeful, life-affirming way, she continued to believe Pam was capable of creating at will. Affirming her gift. Embracing it. Pam might be able to keep up her charade if she could get the commissioned work done and get out of Mel's life, but working here every day—or, rather, sitting around not working every day—would expose her as the fraud she knew she was.

"No one would disturb you. It'd be a unique experience for people to watch a real artist at work, especially since your artwork is hanging in the rooms. Something to draw people to my inn, and a great advertisement for your gallery. And I'm sure you'd sell plenty of paintings. Guests will want to bring a piece of the ocean home with them, like I did when I bought your seascape."

Pam leaned her hand on the madrona's trunk for support. She felt as revealed and unprotected as the blood-red, barkless wood under her palm. Mel had changed the rules. A simple business deal had become an unacceptable obligation. Pam had to refuse the offer. Admit she couldn't possibly be an artist in residence because she was no longer a true artist. Mel would see firsthand how Pam had failed her art, her talent. She couldn't let Mel's guests witness her disgrace, as well.

"I'll make it a nice place for you. We can add lighting, and a heater so the temperature is good for your—"

"Listen, I don't care if you add a hot tub and a steady supply of nude models. I am not going to entertain your guests for you."

"I'm not asking you to draw caricatures of them riding surfboards." Mel's voice rose to match the angry tones Pam heard in her own. "I'll have this big room sitting here empty most of the time, so why not let you use it?"

"Don't do me any favors. I promised you the mosaics, and you'll get them. But I don't owe you anything beyond that."

Pam whistled for Piper and stomped into the house. She paused at the bottom of the stairs. Danny was most likely in the living room, judging by the smell of pizza and the sound of television coming from that direction. Through the small windows by the back door, Pam could see Mel still standing by the madrona, looking out toward the ocean. Pam shook her head and trudged up the stairs with Piper at her heels. She didn't belong here. She needed to finish her paintings and move back into her own home. Back to the solitude she had built around herself.

Chapter Eleven

After Danny left on Sunday afternoon, Mel spent a self-indulgent evening in front of the television to help drive away the sudden quiet in the house. But on Monday morning she got back to work. She pulled a pile of new purple towels out of the dryer and started to fold them. Once she had hung Pam's starfish painting on the lavender wall in the front bedroom, the rest of the décor had been easy for her to envision. She wanted to keep the rooms simple and uncluttered, with Pam's mosaics as the main focus, and she had to be patient and wait for each new piece before she could finish the room around it. For some reason, Pam refused to be encouraged in her painting. Mel tried to be respectful of her talent and methods, but she still felt hurt by Pam's indignant reaction to her offer of the studio. She didn't want to put Pam on display and charge admission, and she couldn't understand why Pam was so opposed to letting anyone watch her paint. Mel had seen plenty of artists working in galleries or on boardwalks along the coast, and they didn't seem to mind having an audience.

She carried the neat stack of towels upstairs and came to an abrupt halt on the landing. Pam stood in the oceanfront bedroom, her back to her seascape painting, actually holding a paintbrush and palette for the first time since she had come to stay in the inn. Mel held her breath, not wanting to disturb Pam even though the concentration on her face looked impossible to shake. Mel had a feeling she could march through the room playing a tuba and Pam wouldn't even glance her way, but she didn't move as she watched Pam swirl a brush across the canvas. Mel could only see the easel and the back of the canvas. She was surprised to realize she wasn't even curious about the subject of the painting, even though she had been anxiously waiting for Pam to get back to work. Somehow this moment was only about Pam and the act of creating. Not about the work of art.

Mel hugged the towels to her chest. She had recognized the strength in Pam's other paintings, and she had expected the creative process to be one of passion, a bright red fury of action. But this was childlike and vulnerable, as if Pam were crying the paint onto the canvas. Mel backed up a couple of steps before she turned and crept down the stairs. Walking in on Pam naked would have been less a violation, and Mel suddenly understood why she couldn't possibly be exposed while she worked. She wondered how Pam managed to return to normal after being so raw and open. Mel had thought her own chaotic emotions and personal upheaval had colored her interpretation of Pam's paintings and made her find such intensity in them. Now she knew the power had come from Pam herself.

Pam caught a flash of color at the edge of her line of vision, and the thought of Mel hovered at the edge of her mind, but she pushed both aside and focused on the unfolding painting in front of her. She arced her brush across the canvas, outlining a curved trail of sea foam across the sand with a confusing sense of confidence. She had awoken with an image in her mind of a stormy sea, a world in turmoil, and she had unsuccessfully tried to ignore the insistent desire to paint. She thought she needed to reproduce the storm that had broken her house and sent her to Mel's, but instead, when she finally gave in and brought out her paints and drop cloth, she had immediately started sketching a debris-covered beach. Driftwood and shells, kelp and dirty foam. Sandpipers and gulls searching for food. Waves receding from the shattered beach. The aftermath of a storm. The meaningless destruction of a once beautiful and serene place.

Even though Mel had given her permission to paint anything she chose, Pam had nearly managed to convince herself that a raging storm wouldn't be appropriate for the peaceful sanctuary Mel wanted to create. The logic of subject matter hadn't been enough to stop the compelling need to put brush to canvas. Pam stepped back from the picture, the constant and tense movements of the past two hours replaced by a sudden sag of exhaustion. Looking at the completed painting, she decided the active fury of the storm itself would have been better than the impotent, passive anger left in its wake.

She had painted her own rage and hurt into the littered seascape, but maybe she would be the only one to notice. She was growing accustomed to the way Mel interpreted her work, so she might see a lovely place for a picnic where Pam saw nothing but her own pain. Pain she felt because Mel had exposed her inability to paint by forcing the studio on her and because, simultaneously, Mel was breaking down the shields Pam had erected to keep herself from painting. Pain when she looked at Danny and instead saw only a reminder of her lost son and an image of the unfinished portrait she had of him. Pain when she sat at breakfast with Mel or passed her on the stairs with all the intimacy of a married couple. Pam set her palette and brushes aside and rubbed her arms. Her skin felt raw to the touch, and she knew she wouldn't be able to step back into the world this way.

Pam took her box of sea glass and quietly headed down the stairs. Maybe she could steal past Mel, hide out behind the old house for an hour or so with only the sound of waves and circling seagulls for company. She was accustomed to being alone the few times she'd managed to paint over the past eight years. Before, when she had lived with Diane, she had learned to hide away from her company as well. Pam would be unprotected and vulnerable, still caught in the emotion of her art, while Diane would be moody and angry. Pam didn't believe Mel would have the same issues of jealousy as Diane had, but Pam couldn't trust Mel to understand how she felt, and she silently cursed when she came around the corner at the bottom of the stairwell and nearly ran into her.

"Oh, hi," Mel said. "There's soup on the stove if you're hungry. I'll be working in the dining room and could use some help when you're done. I guess I got used to company after having Danny here this weekend. And I...well, I thought you might not mind helping out today. Unless you'd rather be alone, go for a walk."

Pam watched Mel disappear into the dining room without another word. The relief of not having to respond immediately left Pam a little more relaxed, and she realized she was hungry. She went into the kitchen and lifted the lid off the heavy enamel pot, taking a tentative sniff of its simmering contents. Not clam chowder, thank God. Seafood would have reminded her too much of her painting. Tomato, but not the kind from a can like she usually made herself. She dished up a bowl before settling at the kitchen table. She had noticed a basket of heirloom tomatoes on the counter this morning. Mel must have magically transformed them into this velvety deep-red soup. Sweet and creamy and comforting. Soothing enough to help Pam relax and move on to the next stage of her mosaic.

In between bites, she dug through the box of sea glass, looking for inspiration. She considered using whites and grays for the sea birds, or brown and black for the cliff face. Eventually she found herself pulling out an assortment of browns and greens, deep and murky colors. She would scatter them over the sandy beach on her painting, representing nothing but broken bits of sea glass left behind by the storm.

She finished her soup and left the pile of sea glass on the table. She thought about slipping out the back door and taking Piper to the beach, but her curiosity and improving mood brought her to the dining room instead. This was the first time Mel had asked for help with any of her home-improvement projects, and Pam wondered what she'd be asked to do. Hopefully nothing requiring deep thought or decision making. The morning of painting had exhausted her, and even the simple task of choosing pieces of sea glass had depleted what little mental and emotional energy she had left.

She stopped in the doorway of the dining room, captured by the sight of Mel on a stepladder. She was carefully applying painter's tape to the ceiling, leaning precariously to one side so her sweatshirt rode up and revealed a few inches of her small waist and smooth back. Pam stuck her hands in the back pockets of her jeans to keep them still. Not because she felt an urge to paint Mel, but because she wanted to touch her. The yearning to feel Mel's skin under her palms surprised her. She was about to sneak out of the room when Mel turned her head.

"Hi," said Pam. "You needed help?"

Mel pointed at a pile of painting supplies with her free hand. "I'm going to be painting the trim around the floorboards next, so it'd help if you could sand off the old paint."

"Oh, okay," Pam said, surprised. She had expected to be asked to do a chore requiring more strength or challenge, not one of the routine and simple tasks Mel always seemed to want to do on her own. She picked up a piece of sandpaper and settled on the floor with Piper beside her.

"I'm sorry I snapped at you about the studio," Pam said after a few minutes. "It was a nice offer."

"No problem," Mel said as she moved the stepladder and climbed it again. She didn't look at Pam. "I understand."

Pam wasn't sure what exactly Mel thought she understood, but she didn't question her. She scrubbed at the carved molding, removing the faded and cracking paint. She settled into the silence and rhythm of her task, shifting position after each section was finished, and felt the tension of painting gradually ease out of her shoulders and mind. The work was mindless and repetitive as she slowly erased the ugly surface of the molding. Maybe she should worry about being caught up in Mel's renovations, in her dream. Maybe she should be concerned that she'd be called on to complete more chores after this one. But she let it go. The room was quiet except for the occasional scrape of Mel's stepladder or a snore from Piper. Companionship with no expectations. Pam focused on the steady sweep of her sandpaper as it gradually exposed the smooth grain of the wood beneath the old paint.

CHAPTER TWELVE

Pam sat cross-legged in the studio the next weekend, a sketch pad on her lap. Gaping holes, long since emptied of their windowpanes, let a light mist into the studio, but the roof still provided protection from the worst of the weather. Pam nibbled on the tip of a graphite pencil as she stared out at the overgrown backyard and listened to Mel and Danny chatting about his football game from the night before. She didn't know why she was there. Well, she was there because Mel had asked her for a favor. What she didn't know was why she had said yes. Guilt? She couldn't accept Mel's offer to use the studio for painting, but she could at least sit in it and sketch. She was giving Mel something. All she was capable of giving.

Mel hadn't mentioned the studio since last weekend, but Pam thought about it every time she walked into the backyard. Of course it would be a perfect place for an artist to work when it was completed. She had admitted as much the first time she saw it. Light and airy, it afforded a view of the ocean and would have the ever-changing panorama of a yard full of vacationers, once the inn was open for business. Couples strolling toward the beach, locked in their private worlds even as the whole horizon opened up before them. Children running through the yard, pulling kites or toys or their parents' hands as they rushed headlong toward the ocean. A constant supply of subjects and inspiration. But not for Pam. Today Mel only wanted a rough draft, a general plan for her garden, and Pam wasn't sure she could do even that small job. But the rubbery taste of her eraser, the dusky smell of graphite, took over. She slid her pencil across the pad, noticing every tiny bump in the lightly textured paper.

Pam drew an outline of the yard. She wasn't a landscaper or a wedding planner. And who spent a rainy weekend in October gardening? She penciled in a stone walkway leading from the house to the beach access, then an offshoot path to the far corner of the yard. Pam sketched a small fountain in the corner. She could see the wedding taking place there, and a couple of wooden benches would make it an ideal place for guests to read or sit at other times of the year. Not that Pam planned to be around to see them. Once her house was fixed, the commission completed, Pam would be free to return to her quiet and comfortable life. Far away from the happy tourists who would eventually fill Mel's inn.

The voices behind Pam faded away as she added a grassy area big enough for a game of croquet or a family barbecue. She feathered in fronds of hardy grasses and switched to a sharper pencil to draw the leaves of some rosebushes and ornamental plants. A few dwarf apple and maple trees would add height and texture, but they would be easy to maintain and would withstand coastal storms. And they wouldn't block the light streaming into the studio. She didn't draw the studio itself. Instead, she sketched a line to mark the edge of the yard.

When Pam finally set her pencil down, she realized Mel and Danny had stopped talking and were watching her.

"Awesome," Danny said. "You drew so much detail, I bet I could find those plants at a nursery just from your sketch."

"It is beautiful, Pam," Mel added. She leaned over Pam's shoulder and pointed at the fountain. "I love this private area. It'll be perfect for the ceremony."

Pam inhaled and caught the smell of roses, suddenly transported back to the morning when Mel had shown up at her bedroom door wearing only a robe. Wet hair, flushed skin, the curve of Mel's breasts where the robe dipped open. Pam felt the tingle of Mel's breath against her neck, calling her back to the present, and she wanted her own breath, her hands, her lips on Mel's skin. Pam cleared her throat and looked out into the rainy yard. She had been focused on the vision in her head and hadn't stopped to consider all the labor standing between reality and her finished sketch.

"Maybe I should make something simpler since you only have a week to get this done," she said, flipping to a fresh page in her sketch pad.

"No," Mel said as she snatched the pad from Pam's hands. She turned back to the drawing. "We'll need to start by mowing the grass and cleaning out the old brush. Then we'll cut out the path. I'll measure and go buy the paving stones…"

She turned to a blank page and slipped the charcoal pencil from Pam's unresisting fingers. Danny poked Pam in the ribs as Mel continued to list chores.

"See what you did?" he whispered. "We'll be slaving away all afternoon."

Pam still felt uncomfortable around Danny, but his easy familiarity softened her a little. He spoke like a put-out teenager, but he had driven to Cannon Beach that morning just so he could help Mel prep her inn for the upcoming wedding party. Even Pam could see how much he enjoyed being part of Mel's new life. Pam stood apart, determined to keep her distance from Mel and Danny, but she was able to watch them interact. She was an outsider, allowed temporarily inside the family's private world. They had experienced so many changes in the past months, and she could see how they anchored each other. Stability and trust. An unwavering faith that no matter what happened, they would always be mother and son.

Danny obviously loved his mother, but at times Pam saw him looking at Mel as if seeing her for the first time. And he was, in a way. Seeing her not just as a parent but as a woman who was capable of following her dreams, working hard to make a better life. And while Mel never stepped out of her natural role as his mother, she also never hesitated to show her vulnerability, to admit when she didn't know something or to ask his opinion, to let him share as they rebuilt their lives and renovated the inn. Pam was happy the two of them had found this common project to draw them closer. But she didn't want to be involved. Their bond was strong, permanent. Their connection to Pam was circumstantial, transitory. Nice while it lasted, but not to be trusted. She'd made that mistake before.

"I probably should get back to the gallery since I left Lisa there alone," she said, standing up and stretching her lower back.

Mel looked up from her list. "Lisa? You said she works for you every holiday season. And that your gallery doesn't get really busy until Thanksgiving weekend."

"Busted," Danny said quietly.

Pam gave him a mock glare before turning back to Mel. "I really shouldn't do manual labor. You wouldn't want me to risk hurting my hands before I finish your paintings."

Mel waved away her excuses. "I'm sure the next mosaics will have more depth of character after you've done some honest hard work."

"'Depth of character' means you aren't going to like what you're about to do," Danny said.

"Yeah, I kind of figured that out myself," Pam said. She was starting to enjoy the banter, especially since each interchange between her and Danny brought out a smile Mel couldn't quite hide. "Okay, I give up. What do you want us to do?"

"Danny, you can run the lawnmower. I found a gas-powered one in the back of the garage, so no complaints. When I mowed last, I had to use the push mower. Start with these areas, where the path will go. Pam can mark the boundaries of it, and I'll measure and go buy the stones."

Pam walked side by side with Danny out to the garage. She searched for something to say to break the silence, but she had no idea what a teenaged boy would want to talk about. He seemed comfortable with the silence as they cleared a path and pushed the lawnmower into the backyard.

"Hey, someone's flying a kite in the rain," he said, pointing toward the beach. A rainbow-colored box kite was barely visible at their height before it dipped out of sight.

"As long as there's a breeze and it's not pouring, you'll see kites on the beach. Cannon Beach has a kite festival in April, and you'll have a great view from up here."

"I don't want to watch, I want to fly one. Do you know how?"

Pam shrugged. "Sure. I usually make a few to sell in the gallery during the festival. There are always a few tourists who get caught up in the excitement, and they'll pay a fortune for something unique."

Danny checked the mower's gas tank. "Maybe you can design one for me. A duck. A big green-and-yellow duck."

Pam laughed. "I would have expected you to pick something fierce like a dragon or a tiger."

"My school mascot and colors," Danny explained. "Think you could make one?"

"Huh. I made an eagle kite last year. Just a variation of a delta, so it was easy to fly. No reason we couldn't adapt the pattern and turn it into a duck."

The moment the words were out of her mouth, Pam wanted to retract them. She wasn't getting involved with this kid or his mom. She was here for a few weeks, and then she'd be out of their lives. She tried to ease the panicky concern that she had made a commitment she had no intention of keeping by assuring herself Mel would be out of business and gone by then. Unfortunately, as the days passed she was having more and more trouble selling herself that lie. She hadn't really believed it since Mel had painted her first bedrooms. Contrary to what Pam had expected, the work wasn't breaking Mel down. It was building her up.

Danny appeared unaware of the internal chaos she felt simply because they had talked about possibly making a duck kite together. He just said, "Cool," and continued tightening bolts on the mower. He stood up and pulled the starter cord.

"You need to pull harder than that," Pam suggested, ready for the noise of the mower so they could stop talking. Before she offered to do anything else with the kid.

"If I do, the cord'll probably snap in two."

"Well, if you don't, it isn't going to start," Pam said, mimicking his smart tone.

He looked at her, his hands on his hips. Pam could see laughter in his eyes—so like Mel's—but he seemed stubbornly prepared to refuse to move if she continued to tell him how to do his job. He got more than his eyes from his mother. "Then why don't *you* take care of the mowing since you're such an expert."

Pam raised her hands in mock surrender. "Hey, your mom said you mow, I mark the path. I'm not going to disobey."

Mel set the sketch pad on a dusty bench and watched her two laborers having a laughing argument over the ancient mower in the rain. Pam had seemed so reluctant to be around Danny, but he was slowly breaking down her barriers without even trying. Mel saw Pam's body language soften and relax, mirroring the change in her speech patterns as she started to talk more normally, without the hesitation and reticence she had shown at first.

Mel brought some string and small stakes over to the patio. She had been determined to prove she could do everything on her own when she started to renovate the inn, but there was something so much more satisfying about today's project. She watched the odd parade move through her backyard—Pam in the lead as she showed where the meandering path should go, Danny behind with the old lawnmower, and Piper following them both with occasional yips as if she was concerned they might damage her yard. There was no way Mel could get all the yard work done in time for the wedding by herself, but her easy acceptance of this assistance made her nervous. Having Danny there to help was wonderful, but learning to rely on Pam's presence, to think of her as part of this new little family, was dangerous.

Pam was only there temporarily, and Mel would be foolish to expect more than a few weeks of her companionship. And Mel hadn't even had a full week of living here alone before she had invited Pam to move in. How could she get back in touch with who she was when she couldn't even live on her own? She had spent too many years with someone she let change the way she thought and acted and lived. Mel wouldn't allow Pam, as strong and confident as she was, to dictate who she would become.

And now Pam's influence would permeate the backyard. Every time Mel walked along the garden path or hosted a party in the studio, she would see Pam. In fact, every room in the house would have part of her on the walls.

"You don't like kids, do you?" Mel asked when Pam came over and picked up a handful of stakes. Danny was still mowing the resisting yard, stopping occasionally to uproot a tough weed or shrub by hand.

Pam looked surprised by the question. "Well, I wouldn't say… it's not that I don't like them, I just…"

Her voice faltered to a halt. Mel shrugged. What was she doing? Picking a fight in order to push Pam away? She wasn't sure if she was trying to keep Danny from being hurt by Pam's reticence or if she was afraid of her attraction to Pam, her fleeting desire to see Pam as part of their family. As a mother, she'd always try to protect her son. But she would protect her individuality by being strong, not by pushing weakly at anyone who got close. Anyone she was *tempted* to let close. She needed to have more faith in herself and in her newfound, hard-won independence. She changed the subject back to the work at hand. "Why don't you mark one side of the path. I'll measure and mark the other side so the width stays the same."

"Okay," Pam said, bending over to push the first stake into the ground. "Danny's a great kid," she said as she walked forward a few steps and bent again to mark a curve in the path.

"I know," Mel said shortly. She held the measuring tape in place with her foot and used both hands to force a stake into the hard soil. Pam might be able to say the right things a mom would want to hear, but she couldn't hide her desire to avoid interacting with Danny. Mel didn't understand why Pam seemed to reel between stiffness and an easy joking manner with Danny. Why she struggled so hard against her art, but produced such exquisitely beautiful paintings. Pam was complex, hard to read. But one thing was simple for Mel. Danny. Yes, he was getting older and would be on his own soon, but she was building a home for them as a family, a place where he'd always belong. Mel wouldn't settle for any relationship, friendship or otherwise, in which Danny wasn't welcome.

"He's smart and funny and easy to talk to," Pam said. Her back was to Mel as she created the left border of the path. Mel followed more slowly, measuring to accurately delineate the right side. She had to strain to hear Pam's quiet words over the mower.

"I know," Mel said again when Pam paused.

"You must feel proud about how you raised him," Pam continued, apparently undeterred by Mel's brief responses. "To see how well he does in school and in sports. And how much he wants to spend time with you and help out here."

Mel thought she detected a wistful edge to Pam's voice, but she didn't respond to her comment. She didn't want to know more. Didn't want to find out whether Pam's reaction to Danny had been caused by discomfort or sadness, rather than simple dislike of young people. She shoved the last stake in the ground and stood to join Pam by the back gate. She looked at the outline of the path leading back to her patio. If she had designed it on her own, she would have made a direct line from the inn to the staircase leading to the beach. But Pam had given the walkway a free-form route. The gentle curves would still be easy to maneuver, but they fit more naturally into the rest of the planned garden than a straight line would have done.

"I like it," Mel said as she walked back to the house along the grassy path with Pam right behind her. She had to admit Pam's artistic eye was already improving the garden. And she'd be foolish to turn away a much-needed laborer. She'd control her growing interest in Pam and her unease with whatever had happened in Pam's past to give her what seemed to be a conflicting longing and reluctance to be close to Mel and Danny.

"I appreciate your help," she said as she handed Pam an edger. "Danny and I couldn't do all this without you, and the design you made for the garden is lovely."

Pam looked at the garden tool and then back at Mel. "I do much better work with a pencil than with an edger."

"I'm sure you do," Mel said as she jotted down the measurements from the garden path. "But we'll take what we can get."

On Thursday morning, Piper trotted halfway down the staircase before she leapt off it to explore the hillside leading to the beach. Pam rested her back against the gatepost as she lit a cigarette. She kept an eye on Piper's progress through the brush, but her attention wandered occasionally to Mel's newly renovated backyard. There was still a long way to go before the yard was complete and perfected, but Mel had made a good start. Pam had been surprised by Mel's ability to make her vision come to life. She had merely sketched some ideas on a piece of paper, but Mel had turned the pencil drawings into a living garden.

The fountain and benches were missing, and the yard had a patchy, weedy look that would only be fixed by months of fertilizing or a complete re-sodding. Still, the gardens were outlined neatly and filled with shrubs and wild grasses. They were sparse and too symmetrical for Pam's taste, but time would soften them. The path was completely finished in a geometric pattern that Mel and Walter had designed. It had taken Mel hours to finish, but Pam loved the stark mathematical precision and how it contrasted with the wavy outline she had created.

Most of all, though, she had enjoyed the feeling of hard work. She and Danny had hauled wheelbarrows full of old brush and carved-out sod out of the yard while Mel painstakingly laid her paving stones and bricks in the loose sand. Pam had complained about the labor involved, but as long as she was sweating and working in the chilly drizzle, she didn't have to worry about painting or creating. She just followed orders. And once she had gotten over her initial reluctance to be around Danny—something Mel had noticed and commented on—Pam had enjoyed working with the teenager. He had a typical young person's aversion to work combined with seemingly boundless energy, and Pam found the combination energizing. They groused every time Mel assigned them a new task, but they met each one with a whirlwind of activity and determination. They were like balls of energy orbiting around the stable sun of Mel, and Pam found she enjoyed the release of constant activity.

Still, she avoided any sense of family Mel and Danny tried to offer. They'd invited her to eat dinner with them, watch a movie and relax in the comfortable new living room, but Pam had gone up to her room alone instead. Piper had chosen to remain with Danny, but Pam ignored the urge to join her dog and give in to the temptation—

and illusion—of happy family life. The habit of avoiding people and closeness was familiar, an ingrained habit by now. What she hadn't expected was the pull she felt toward Mel and Danny. Usually she could shut her door on any relationship that threatened to get too intimate. Why had she stood with her hand on the doorknob last night, so close to opening it?

Pam saw Mel step out of the back door and walk along the path. She wished they didn't have these barriers between them. Every time she saw Mel, whether she was wearing a robe or paint-splattered jeans or today's neat slacks and peasant blouse, Pam had the uncomfortable urge to get closer, to touch her. If Mel didn't seem so hell-bent on making this inn work, so determined to make a life for herself at the ocean, Pam would give in to her desire to seduce her. But Pam couldn't sleep with Mel and walk away. Run into her in town or at the store and pretend nothing had happened. Mel seemed to be building forever here. Pam couldn't offer that.

"Good morning," Mel called as she got closer. "How do you think it looks out here?"

Pam straightened and stubbed out her cigarette in her ashtray. "It's great. Once you get the chairs and some flower arrangements set up, it'll be a perfect place for a wedding."

Mel smiled her thanks as she sat down. She handed Pam a plate covered with a napkin. "Ham and Tillamook cheese omelet," she said. "I thought I'd serve something local and hearty for a winter breakfast."

Piper lost interest in her exploring and came to sit by Pam as she bit into the omelet. Mel picked a chunk of ham off Pam's plate and fed it to the dog.

"This is great," Pam said around a mouthful of eggs. "And it's no wonder she always wants to be around you and Danny. You both keep feeding her scraps."

"I saw the picture," Mel said, instead of responding to Pam's joking accusation.

Pam fed Piper a piece of melted cheese. "I thought it'd look good in the dining room," she said casually. The moment she had seen the finished room, with its eggshell-blue paint and the Wedgewood dishes Mel had placed on the sideboard, she had known the exact picture that would complement Mel's vision. She had gone home yesterday, pretending to be concerned about the contractor's work, and had dug through the old paintings she had tucked in the closet in her loft. She had exchanged frames to match the warm wood tones of the sideboard and table Mel had sanded and stained. And she had hung the painting after she knew Mel was in bed. "Think of it as a housewarming present. And a thank you for letting me stay here for a few weeks."

"Thank you," Mel said, just brushing Pam's shoulder with her hand before she clasped her arms around her knees. "It's exactly right."

Pam knew it was. She had seen the subject of the painting years ago when she and her partner had brought little Kevin to the beach for the first time. He had slept, snuggled tight against her in his backpack, while she'd sketched the young girl at the edge of the ocean. Diane had been angry because Pam had spent so much of their time at the beach capturing various scenes that caught her attention, so she had been forced to quickly get the outline of each image onto paper. She'd finished the paintings weeks later, in the privacy of her studio at home. She remembered the layers of the painting—the actual girl standing on the beach, the first strokes of color on the virgin canvas, the resolution when she packed all her paintings into boxes and shoved them deep into the closets and nooks of her new, small home.

The girl had worn a blue sundress, makeshift and knotted at the shoulder. She'd stood with her back to Pam, holding the dress up and out of reach of the ankle-deep water that covered her bare feet. The juxtaposition of her innocent frailty against the powerful, relentless waves of the ocean had grabbed Pam's attention. And once she saw the room Mel had worked so hard to perfect, she had immediately wanted the girl's portrait on the wall.

"I'm glad you like it," she said as she broke off a piece of cinnamon scone and ate it. Mel had definitely learned how to work with dough, and the pastry was tender and flavorful.

"I do, and it makes me feel guilty for asking a favor," Mel said, looking toward the ocean and avoiding eye contact with Pam.

"A favor?" Pam repeated. She set her fork down. "I am *not* digging up any more sod. My hands are callused enough from last weekend."

"Not a working favor," Mel assured her. "I just got a call from one of the grooms. His mother has decided to come to the wedding. It's great for him, but it means I need one more room…"

"Of course," Pam assured her. "I'll move back to—"

"I thought you could stay in Danny's room," Mel said in a rush. "Just for a couple of nights."

Pam had been planning to go back to her own house, even though the contractor and his workers would be finishing up their work over the weekend. She could handle their noise and dust for a short time. She should avoid spending time with Mel in her private part of the house.

"It's my first weekend with real guests," Mel said in a confiding tone. "I'd feel better if I had some company with me. Someone I know."

"Danny's room," Pam repeated. "That sounds fine. I'll be here."

CHAPTER THIRTEEN

On the morning of the wedding, Mel rearranged the chairs in the studio for the fourth time. She shifted the punch bowl a little to the left and fussed with the napkins for a few moments before she picked up her glass of scotch and went over to the window. Walter's nephew had replaced the windows, and she had spent the past three days scouring moss and cobwebs and dead leaves out of the room. She needed another few months, not a few hours, in order to really prepare the studio for company. But once she had put the string of colored lights along the ceiling and set out the rented tables and chairs, she'd stopped noticing all the chores she should have done and saw a reception room.

She felt the same about the guest rooms and the garden. Once they were filled with people and their luggage and voices and laughter, the inn seemed to absorb their energy and take on a new life. The house's faults were somehow less noticeable. It wasn't perfect, but it was ready for guests. She remembered the confusing ambivalence she had experienced as Danny had grown up, letting go with a mix of pride and sadness. Like Danny, the inn would always need her—to take care of repairs and upgrades, to finish the basic renovations she'd started such a short time ago. But she had learned most of the tasks required, and she was confident she could conquer whatever new ones were on the horizon. She had accumulated an impressive collection of tools, and she knew how to use every one of them. The initial phase was finished.

Her inn had grown up. She wanted to feel excited about having her first real guests and proud of how much work it had taken to get from ready for a wrecking ball to ready for a wedding. But, perversely, she felt sad as she faced yet another transition in a year crammed full of them and as she helped plan a wedding, a new start, while memories of her own broken marriage hovered in the background. She had grown steadily more downhearted as more people arrived. Her grooms had come first, the night before, with friends and family to fill the three finished rooms. A stream of wedding guests had been descending on the inn since breakfast. Mel had lain awake for hours last night, too aware of Pam in the room right across the hall, and had faced a new and unexpected kind of loneliness.

She had finished decorating. She had organized the wedding and served breakfast and cleaned the inn as much as she could. All she had left to do was step back and watch the wedding as an outsider. She braced her hand on the wall next to the window and watched a couple of guests wander through her yard. She had planned to run the inn on her own, to be an observer of other people's holidays and special events. She had expected it to be enough, but the more she watched the wedding preparations and listened to the joy and laughter in the voices around her, the more she filled with regret and longed to be part of life and not merely a bystander. She sighed and took a sip of her drink. One night with guests and she was already having second thoughts about running the inn. Not a good start to her new career.

At times over the past weeks, Mel had been lonely, scared, unsure, but she had pushed through as she'd discovered the strength and determination to do what had seemed impossible at first. With Pam's help, as she brought the warmth of another human and a dog into the empty house, and Danny's, as he worked alongside her or sent support through texts and calls. But now, work on the inn didn't have to be all-consuming. It didn't have to keep her away from people, from her new community. She couldn't use it as an excuse to avoid new relationships any longer. The intense loneliness she felt while surrounded by happy people, by people in love, was threatening to drown her. She could either give in and live miserable and alone—

with only her imagination to keep her company—or she could get to work and rebuild her personal life. Just like she had rebuilt the inn.

"Hey." Mel turned away from the window at the sound of Pam's voice. She walked to the center of the studio and turned slowly. "You've done a great job in here. It's beautiful."

"Thank you," Mel said. She was only happy to see Pam because she was feeling lonely and ambivalent about her role as innkeeper. And because Pam was the only familiar face around. Her response to Pam was in no way related to the sleepless night Mel had spent listening for the sound of Pam moving around in the room next to hers. Or to her fantasies about Pam touching her, soothing her anxiety about the day ahead, calming her mingled hope and fear as she shifted focus from renovating the inn to creating the life she really wanted. She had imagined Pam's hands on her, refusing to let her slip into darkness, forcing her to move through her emotions until they burst forth into something new and hopeful.

"Sorry I left so early this morning, but I needed to spend a couple of hours in the gallery today. Inventory."

"That's okay," Mel said. She was sure Pam had left to avoid eating breakfast with a table full of strangers. She still didn't understand the reasons behind Pam's emotions, but she was learning to read them. Her intensity, her need for beauty and quiet. The way her breath grew shallow when there was too much noise or chaos around her, and her long exhale when she was at peace again. "Can you stay for the ceremony?"

"Yes, and I had an idea for decorating the area where it'll take place. You know that old wooden boat in the garage? I thought we could put it in the small garden where the fountain will eventually go. It'll look interesting with the nets and floats you've put out there, sort of like they're getting married on a desert island." Pam pointed at the glass Mel held. "What's that?"

"Punch."

Mel tightened her grip as Pam slipped the glass from her hand and took a drink. "Jesus," Pam said with a cough. "This is the punch?"

"Well, it also has some scotch in it," Mel said, taking her glass back. "And no actual punch."

Pam laughed. "You keep managing to surprise me. But, seriously, you don't have anything to worry about. Today will be great. They'll be happy and they'll tell all their friends. Your inn will be *the* place for commitment ceremonies in the Northwest."

Mel gave Pam a smile, but she could feel its weakness without needing a mirror to check it. She didn't want to admit that she was more worried about today being a success than a failure. Her guests understood the rough state of her inn, and they seemed pleased with their rooms and the yard. Judging by the short time it had taken for breakfast to be consumed, Mel's experiments with Pam and Danny as guinea pigs had been successful. She had planned the ceremony and reception down to the last detail, and she was confident the day would go well. But she wasn't convinced she could face an inn full of guests every day for years to come unless she made the effort to fill her own life with the kind of love she wanted. She wouldn't have Walter's advice or a box full of expensive tools to help her through this project. She'd have to do it on her own. Set a goal and learn how to master each step along the way. Make mistakes and try again. And again.

"Now come on," Pam said, pulling on Mel's arm. "Let's go move that boat."

Pam kept her fingers wrapped around Mel's biceps as she tugged her toward the garage, to keep her from running off and leaving Pam to drag the boat out on her own. The feel of Mel's muscles under her hand was just a bonus. Tight and strong, contrasting so enticingly with her silky shirt and the soft, pensive expression she'd worn all day. Pam could picture how well-defined and sexy Mel's arms would be, braced on either side of Pam's head before Mel leaned down and…Pam let go of her vision and let go of Mel's arm when the cluttered garage forced them to walk single file. She was on edge because of all the strangers milling around the inn. She had to distract her mind from wondering why she felt like the strangers had invaded her home. Mel's place was not her home. She climbed over an old, rusted bicycle and stopped to brush a cobweb out of her hair. "See?" she asked, pointing at the boat that was barely visible under the plastic flowerpots piled on it. "It's perfect."

"For what? Kindling?" Mel stepped gingerly over the bike and stood next to Pam.

Pam ignored the sarcasm in Mel's voice. She stacked the flowerpots on the floor of the garage and picked up one end of the boat to check its weight. "Get the other end," she said. "It isn't very heavy."

Mel moved the bicycle out of the way first, and then she went to her end of the boat. Pam counted to three and lifted. The boat was bulky and awkward to carry through the cluttered garage, but Pam kept her voice cheerful as she called out directions and encouragement as they maneuvered their way into the backyard. She wasn't about to give up on the vision she had of the boat in the garden. Plus, she wanted to keep Mel occupied.

The last thing Pam wanted to do was sit through a ceremony and watch two people making the kind of commitment she had longed for with Diane. But last night, when the first guests had arrived and transformed the quiet house into a noisy inn filled with strangers, Pam had seen a look of desperation and regret pass over Mel's face. She knew what Mel was going through, what Pam herself had experienced when she sold her first paintings—the vulnerability and protectiveness as the object she had nursed along in private was suddenly exposed and public. Pam guessed Mel might be feeling as if strangers were rummaging through her underwear drawer.

Pam wanted to focus on getting Mel through her first weekend with guests and avoid examining why she cared so much about Mel's feelings. Naturally, she and Mel had developed a sort of friendship since they had lived together over the past couple of weeks, even though they rarely socialized and spent most of their time in separate sections of the big house. And just because she found Mel attractive enough that she had spent the night before tossing on Danny's bed, uncomfortably aware that Mel was right across the hall instead of two floors away, didn't mean she was getting attached to her. She could walk away from her without a second thought if she wanted to. She had chosen to come back and support Mel today. As a friend and nothing more.

"Careful through here," Pam said, skirting a pile of gas cans as she stepped out of the garage and onto the driveway.

"Ouch. Can we take a break?" Mel asked as she tripped over a garden hose.

"We've only gone a few feet," Pam complained, but she eased the boat onto the pavement and stretched her back. The boat was heavier than she had expected. When she had imagined the desert island scene, she hadn't factored in the mechanics of moving the damned thing to its new place. She leaned against the boat and lit a cigarette, nodding toward the gas cans. "Are you planning to burn down the inn for the insurance money?"

"The gas is for the generator," Mel said as she propped her hip on the boat next to Pam. She wasn't really telling a lie. She hadn't thought about dousing the house with gasoline for at least a week now. Not counting this morning. She watched Pam exhale a puff of smoke. She'd been smoking more than usual over the past few days, lighting up every time Mel mentioned the wedding. "Have you ever wanted to get married?"

"What's the use?" Pam asked. "You can promise whatever you want on the day, but how many people actually keep those promises? The whole commitment thing just isn't for me."

Mel heard the bitterness in Pam's voice, saw it in the way she flung her cigarette down and crushed it out with her shoe. She should have guessed Pam wouldn't be the type to settle down. She probably had plenty of women trying to get her to commit to a relationship when all she wanted was to date whomever she chose. Pam hadn't seemed to go out while she had been living at the inn, but on the few occasions Mel had run into her in town, she had been obviously flirting with someone. Always a different someone, and never anyone Mel recognized as local.

Pam sighed and picked up the cigarette butt she had ground out. She tossed it in one of the ashtrays she had stashed around the inn. "I can't imagine you'd want to get married again, after what your husband did. And now that you finally have a chance to play the field."

"Of course not," Mel said. Of course she didn't want to get married again. Commit to someone and give up her identity to be part of a couple. Allow another person to lead her on and give her the illusion of forever. Mel couldn't figure out why Pam's vehemence about marriage left her so sad or why she felt even worse when she claimed she felt the same.

Pam nudged her with an elbow. "You have so much to experience, so many women to date, you won't have time to settle down."

"You're right," Mel agreed with a weak laugh. Her anxiety was to be expected. She was used to her quiet life in the inn with Pam, but she'd need to start meeting women, dating, if she wanted to find companionship and love. She was being pushed out of her comfort zone, or what barely qualified as one. But after all the effort she'd put into the inn, it might be able to repay her in more ways than the financial. Most of her clientele would be people with similar interests as hers—a love of the ocean and travel and being outdoors. She wouldn't have to go out and meet women when she'd hopefully have plenty of them knocking on her front door. At least one of them should be able to push Pam out of her dreams. "And if the inn is successful, I'll have a steady stream of women to meet."

"Yes, you will," Pam said, her voice quiet. She paused and then stepped away from Mel. "The ceremony will be starting soon. Let's get this boat in place."

Chapter Fourteen

Mel sat next to Pam in the back row of chairs as the grooms recited vows under the trellis she had made and decorated. She hadn't been convinced of Pam's vision for what she had seen as an ugly, spider-covered piece of junk until she saw the boat in place. Pam had draped it with netting and glass floats that matched those on Mel's trellis. Suddenly the garden had been transformed into a grotto by the sea, with a magical quality that added to the otherworldly feel of the ceremony. As she watched the two men exchange the vows they had written, Mel really did feel as if she had been transported out of everyday life—where not everyone would approve of or accept the love she was witnessing—and into a world where only love mattered.

The differences between this ceremony and her own wedding were enormous. Hers had been formal, traditional, officially sanctioned. She had loved the planning involved. Her days had been filled with lists and meetings, decisions and structure. Yes, she had dated women and experimented with lesbian life while in college. But she had loved Richard in some ways and had been convinced she could make a conventional marriage work. Her friends had done it. One of her sisters had done it. Give up the experiments and youthful flings and settle into the life everyone expected of her. And for a few years Mel had been able to keep pretending she was satisfied and fulfilled. Especially after Danny was born. Until she had a meeting with his second-grade teacher. And she had been hit hard with the realization that what she had seen as a choice was really a matter of a nature she couldn't deny.

Mel watched the two grooms kiss and then turn to accept the congratulations from their guests in an informal receiving line. She had been irritated to have guests in the inn. Scared, intimidated, full of doubts. But the truth was, she was jealous. Strangers had come into her home. They had arranged to have this most intimate of ceremonies in her backyard, had eagerly insisted she attend, had been so excited to share their happiness. And all she could feel was envy because she wished she had been married, body and soul, to someone she really loved.

But she had given up her chance when she married Richard, and again when she told him about her crush on Danny's teacher. They had decided to remain married for their families, for Danny. She might have declared to Pam that she didn't want to get married again, but she wanted...*something*. A lover, a friend. She wanted to make up for lost time. To finally get it right, without giving up the self-sufficiency and strength she had found on her own. She had been raised to believe in the expected route from dating to love to marriage, but she wasn't sure what love would look like this time around. She'd have to invent a new paradigm, forge her own way. The thought was exciting. And scary as hell.

And not something Mel needed to deal with tonight. Tonight she was on the outskirts, hosting the celebration and not really a part of it. She hovered around the edges as her guests moved to the studio. She emptied a bag of ice into a bucket on the self-serve bar and cleared the used cups and napkins off the table. She'd enjoy the evening from the outside, allow herself to feel proud of the atmosphere she had created.

The reception was as unconventional and personalized as the ceremony had been. Guests mingled around the buffet of pastas and salads, the tiramisu instead of traditional wedding cake, and the makeshift bar complete with a drink-mixing guidebook. Mel replaced an empty tray of fettuccini with a full one and looked around for something else to do. She had been pleased to find that what she saw as the studio's shortcomings actually added to the charm and casualness of the event. There was no power or heat in the room, but the strings of small lights powered by an extension cord gave the room a nice soft glow. The guests wore coats and moved freely between the room and the backyard. A light rain, luckily delayed until after the ceremony, beat a comforting rhythm against the newly installed windows.

Mel moved around the room, picking up empty plates as soon as they were set down and returning to the house at every opportunity. She could feel Pam watching her from her post on the edge of the room. Her determination to be a good host drew her over to Pam occasionally, and she chatted about the food or the weather before she would find some excuse to move away again. Observing the wedding had made Mel start to think about how she would have planned hers differently if she had been completely unconcerned about conventions and what her family and friends expected. Imagining the food and music and outfit she would have chosen was entertaining. Imagining herself at the altar, not as a young bride but at her present age, seemed daring somehow. But hopeful. But imagining Pam standing next to her, reciting vows, kissing her, would only get her hurt. Pam had come right out and said she would never be interested in any sort of formal commitment. And Mel didn't really want one, either. In her experience, marriage meant compromise. She had almost forgotten who she was. She wouldn't make the same mistake twice.

Pam sat on a folding chair along the back wall of the studio. She watched Mel return to the house yet again, merely to throw away a couple of paper plates even though there was a garbage can in the room. Pam wanted to leave, needed to get far away from the happy couple and their friendly guests. She had felt claustrophobic during the ceremony even though it was outside, and now she was out of place. At a normal party, she would have been able to mingle with the strangers, but adding a commitment ceremony to the event made it too uncomfortable for her to even consider joining the conversations around her. Her reasons for staying sounded weak even in her own mind. Mel might need help cleaning up after the party ended. A guest might get drunk and cause trouble. Mel might need to talk. Pam was staying because she wanted to explain herself to Mel, to rephrase what she had said when they were moving the boat.

She had been caught off guard by Mel asking whether she had ever wanted to get married. Of course she had. She had proposed, had wanted to start the adoption process so Kevin would be her son legally as well as emotionally. Diane had rejected both ideas, refusing to make any legal or public commitment. Looking back, Pam could see her own urgency in the matter was due to her insecurity in the partnership, her sense that Diane's jealousy of her talent would eventually drive them apart. She had been trying to secure her relationship with Diane and to protect her ties to Kevin. She was his mother in every sense but the one recognized by law. And Diane had used their lack of legal bonds to keep Kevin from her. Pam couldn't forgive her for it. She had fought all her life against a society that kept her from having equal rights. To have her own partner use that prejudice against her was unbearable.

"Want some tiramisu?" Mel asked. Pam looked up to see Mel standing by her chair. She nodded and accepted the plate from Mel's hands.

"Thanks," she said. She grabbed Mel's wrist as she was about to walk away again. "Sit with me for a few minutes."

"I really should…"

"You should help me eat this," Pam said.

Mel hesitated and then sat down with a sigh. "I could use a break. I'm glad I'll only have to worry about breakfasts for the guests most days. If I have to organize a party every weekend I'll go crazy."

"This is a big event for your inaugural weekend. Once you've done it a few times, it won't be as stressful." Pam took a bite of the tiramisu. "Mm, this is wonderful. Try some." She handed her fork to Mel and watched her sample the creamy dessert. Mel licked some mascarpone from the corner of her mouth, and Pam looked away.

"The grooms seem happy," Pam said, eager to get her mind off Mel's tongue and to return to their earlier topic of conversation.

Mel shrugged and took another bite of dessert. "I looked happy on my wedding day, too. In fact I *was* happy. Blindly so."

"Would you go back and change it if you could?"

"No," Mel said, giving the fork back to Pam. "I have Danny because of my marriage, and I'd never want to give him up. But I won't make the same mistake again."

"You mean getting married? Committing to just one person?"

Mel hesitated. "Exactly."

"Life's too short for monogamy." Pam raised a forkful of tiramisu in a mock toast then put the fork with its uneaten bite back on her plate. Mel was just like Diane, keeping the option to walk out the door at any time. Pam could understand it since Mel had been betrayed, had lived too many years in self-denial. But for some reason understanding didn't stop her from being disappointed to hear Mel's admission.

Mel stood and took the plate with its half-eaten dessert from Pam's unresisting hands. She collected a few more empty cups and plates as she walked through the studio. The party was starting to break up, and Mel headed back to the house with a few of the wedding guests who were staying at a hotel in town. They asked for business cards, and Mel gave them a couple from the dwindling pile she had carried in her pocket. She shut the front door behind them and added *design brochures* to the lengthy list in her mind. She had been so consumed with the physical building, she had barely thought about advertising the business. But she had made contacts tonight and had even booked a group of four for the weekend before Christmas.

She tried to dredge up some excitement about the successful launch of her business, but she kept returning, instead, to her declaration to Pam. No, she wasn't interested in a relationship that stifled her, changed her into someone unrecognizable as an individual. But could she find some way to share a commitment, love, and support with another woman without losing herself in the process? Or could she be satisfied with casual dating? Casual sex, the kind Pam seemed to prefer? Maybe, if their physical attraction was too strong to deny. Or if neither of them was willing to offer more. Why not?

She returned to the studio in time to say good night to the last of the guests. Pam wasn't there, but Mel could see the shadowy figures of a person and a dog, and the glowing tip of a cigarette, in the back of the yard near the beach access. She quickly cleaned up the remnants of the party. Thanks to her constant trips back to the house with bits of garbage, she had very little left to do. Piper joined her and trotted at her heels, looking for handouts as Mel stacked the trays of leftover food and stowed them in her fridge. Finally she carried a box of liquor bottles back to the house and set them on the kitchen counter. Piper lost interest and slipped into the darkness of the backyard, presumably going back to Pam. Mel considered following her to explain to Pam that she had only agreed with her dismissal of marriage because it was too late to start over again, too exhausting to think of learning the ropes of a completely new kind of relationship. As a lesbian. As a woman who made her own choices and didn't passively rely on her partner. Mel could barely remain strong and independent while on her own. How could she stay that way if she was partnered with someone confident and self-assured?

Someone like Pam. Pam, who had no interest in an exclusive, committed relationship. Mel moved away from the back door. She turned off the lights, leaving the back porch lit up for Pam, and went downstairs.

CHAPTER FIFTEEN

Pam came into the kitchen, damp and chilly even in her heavy coat. She poked through the fridge and dished up a plate of rigatoni with sausage, heating it in the microwave and settling at the kitchen table with an eager Piper at her feet. She had spent the past hour sitting in the cold October rain, relieved to be away from the celebrating guests and on her own. She had told herself she was hanging around at the reception to help Mel clean up, but instead she had hidden in the shadows waiting for everyone to go into the inn or back to their hotels. Waiting for the lights in the house and studio to go out and signal that Mel had gone to bed.

She'd left the reception but hadn't gone far. She could have ducked into Danny's room and locked away the crowd. Or driven into town for a drink. But she had sat close to the studio, her coat wrapped around her like a cocoon, and listened to the voices and laughter from the party. Mel had brought laughter here, color and dimension permeating the inn and even seeping into Pam's life. Pam was very aware of the effort Mel had put into this evening, from her renovations on the inn to her backbreaking work on the garden to her realized vision of the studio. What Pam hadn't expected was to see so much of her own input throughout the day. Her garden design, her arrangement of the ceremony space, some suggestions she'd made for decorating the studio. She had created art—not on canvas, but art nonetheless.

She alternated between eating and feeding bits of sausage to her dog while her mind recreated the scenes she had made. Trying to paint, needing to paint, always filled her with pain, but her contributions to this day had been emotionally effortless from concept to creation, without the usual angst and self-doubt and hurt. Why? Because of Mel. Because Mel was so hopeful, so willing to take risks and work hard as she brought her dreams to life. Without fear. No, in spite of her fear. Pam put down her fork and rested her head in her hands. She still struggled every time she picked up a brush, every time she looked at the world and was tempted to capture what she saw, how she interpreted it, on canvas. But Mel had given her this gift, this way to take what her mind created and express it somehow. To let go of the constant filtering, censoring, of her inborn need to create. Pam had no faith it would last, doubted it would transfer to her art, but she was grateful for this brief chance to remember how easy art used to be.

Why, then, had she spent the whole evening lurking around Mel only to disappear the moment they would be alone with each other? Why not share how thankful she was for what Mel had given her? Pam knew exactly how she wanted to thank Mel. Her mind had imagined plenty of scenarios with Mel as the focal point. With Pam's hands, her mouth, her tongue painting Mel's expression into one of arousal, ecstasy, release. Pam had no doubt she could bring *this* vision to life. And she suspected Mel was interested, too, if only in a temporary affair. Mel's adamant dismissal of marriage bothered her more than it should. But Mel wasn't Diane. She had paid her dues, and now she should be free to date, to experience life without being chained to someone else. Instead of being disappointed, Pam should be happy for her.

She rinsed her plate and put it in the dishwasher. More than being happy, she should be relieved to find out how Mel felt. Pam sorted through the box of liquor bottles Mel had left on the kitchen counter and pulled one out. Pam didn't want any attachments, but she couldn't deny her attraction to Mel. And even if she couldn't express her gratitude in words, she could thank Mel with her touch, with shared passion, because now she knew they shared the same dating philosophy. She had tried to hide her physical interest in Mel because she had seen Mel as someone who wouldn't settle for less than forever. Now she knew better.

Pam hesitated outside of Mel's bedroom door. She didn't hear any movement coming from within the room, but she juggled the paraphernalia she held and freed one hand to tap on the door. She was about to give up and go back to her own room when Mel opened the door.

"Hey," Pam said. "I'm sorry I didn't stick around and help clean up. I had to let Piper out."

"It was easy," Mel said with a shrug. "And I don't expect you to work around here. You're a guest."

Pam stared at the opening of Mel's silky bathrobe as her shrug widened it slightly. She obviously wasn't wearing anything underneath. The faint hint of roses brought Pam back to a different doorway, to Mel standing outside her room wearing a bulky old robe, oblivious to how sexy she looked. Judging by the deep red silk barely covering Mel's body tonight, doing little to hide her nipples as it slid over her breasts, she had figured out a thing or two since then. Pam desperately needed this encounter to end differently than the first, with them both on the same side of Mel's door. She dragged her eyes back to Mel's face. "A guest? Well, that explains the hours I spent digging sod out of your backyard."

"Oh, well, that was—"

"That was a friend helping a friend." Pam smiled at Mel's obvious discomfiture. She held up the tequila bottle. "I thought you might want to celebrate after your triumph. Today couldn't have gone better."

Mel hesitated. A relationship with no commitment, no ties. Pam had said she wanted nothing more. If she invited Pam into her room, so late and when she was wearing nothing but a short robe, she would be sending a clear message. It had been a long day, after a long month, after a difficult year. She didn't want to be alone, even if Pam was only offering her company for a night. A friend helping a friend. She stepped aside and gestured for Pam to come in. She had made her decision already, when she had showered and shaved and put on her new robe. Hell, she had made it the day she bought the robe. But now she had all the facts. If she wanted Pam, she'd have to accept her terms. And she really wanted Pam.

"I haven't bothered decorating down here," Mel said as Pam walked by her into the sparsely furnished room. She had bought new bedding and a couple of throw rugs and blankets, but she didn't have the time or money to sink into her private rooms. "There's no place to sit…"

Except on the bed. Mel didn't say it out loud.

Pam sat on the shag rug in front of Mel's bookcase. "This is fine," she said. She set out the tequila bottle, a couple of shot glasses, and a salt shaker. "I like the color scheme you've chosen. Very early Italian Renaissance."

Mel joined Pam on the purple rug, tugging on the robe as she tried to cover as much of her thighs as she could. She had bought it the day after Pam had agreed to sleep in the downstairs room while the wedding party was at the inn, just in case they ran into each other in the hall. Only because it looked so perfect on the hanger. Sexy, but mature. Exactly the type of robe a confident, self-assured woman would wear. But now she suspected Pam would see right through the fabric to the awkward, long-dormant part of Mel with no idea how to begin a seduction scene. She looked around the room, anywhere but at Pam. She had chosen the colors because she liked the way the shades of red, blue, mauve, and gold blended together. She had picked the dark-red robe because it blended with the bedroom's color palette. "I was trying for light, bright, and airy upstairs. I wanted something warmer and richer down here. What are those?"

Pam held up a baggie. "I found limes in your fridge. Can't have tequila shots without limes."

"They're key limes. I was going to make a pie."

"The tequila won't know the difference," Pam said with a shrug. She poured two shots and handed one to Mel with a lime wedge.

"I haven't done this since college," Mel said. She followed Pam's lead and licked the inside of her wrist before shaking some salt on it. She tossed a few grains over her left shoulder. She might not make it through the rest of the night without looking inexperienced, but tequila shots she could do. "As I recall, these lead directly to impaired judgment."

"That's the plan," Pam said. She winked and raised her glass. "To you. For a successful opening weekend."

Mel downed her shot, trying to keep from making a face at the unaccustomed taste. The salt and lime didn't help much. She imagined a much sweeter taste on her tongue as she watched Pam drink her tequila. Pam's short hair was windblown from sitting outside, and Mel wanted to run her fingers through it. To lean close and smell the ocean breeze on Pam's skin. Taste the salt air where it had touched her cheek, her neck.

Pam winced when she bit into her lime. "Ugh, they're bitter," she said.

"That's why the pie recipe calls for two cans of condensed milk." Mel tossed her rind in a nearby wastebasket. She needed something to do with her hands since she was still too nervous to initiate any physical contact. Even sitting across from Pam, she felt an energy, an intimate closeness. As if the unspoken certainty of where the night would lead was something palpable. Pam handed her another lime wedge and refilled her glass.

"Truth or dare?" Pam said as she poured herself a shot.

Mel laughed. Her imagined trysts with Pam had sometimes started with deep conversations, sometimes with no words at all but just a headlong rush into a passionate kiss. Usually the latter. But they'd never started with silly games. She felt a little of her tension ease as she played along. "You're trotting out all the old favorites tonight. What's next, Candy Land?"

"Post office. But we'll get to that later."

Mel hesitated. She was too nervous to do more than sit across the rug from Pam and anticipate the night she had imagined so many times since their first meeting in August. She hadn't yet mustered the courage to touch Pam's hair, or her arm, or her calf as it rested only inches from her own. Whatever the dare might be, she wasn't quite ready for it. "Truth," she said, choosing what seemed like the safer of the two.

Pam took her shot first. She felt a slight softening of lines and edges, and the lime didn't taste quite as bitter this time. She had just come up with the idea of hiding her serious questions within a childhood game. The amused smile on Mel's face indicated she had made the right decision. Keep the mood light, but still get the information she needed. Keep the evening playful and not serious, and she and Mel would both get what they wanted without being trapped by any expectations or obligations. It was all a game.

"Have you ever had sex with a woman?"

Mel coughed as she swallowed her tequila. "You don't mess around, do you?" she asked when she could speak again. "Yes, I have. I had girlfriends in high school and college. But I was attracted to some guys, too, so I thought I was bi. I figured I could just switch it off and pick the more conventional option." Mel shrugged. She paused, trying to find a way to explain her decisions to Pam. A way to justify them to herself, since she'd never fully understood how she had missed something so significant. She had berated herself for years for being too blind, too unaware to figure out her own sexuality. But tonight, sitting across the rug from Pam—anticipating the night ahead before they'd kissed or even touched—she suddenly understood why. If one of those girlfriends had been Pam? No way would Mel have gotten married. No way would she have had any doubt about who she was. She'd never been attracted to anyone the way she was to Pam.

"You have to understand, I come from a big conservative family," Mel said, stumbling over familiar excuses as her mind reeled with a new understanding. She needed to explain her past in a way Pam might find plausible because she didn't want to share her epiphany. If Mel spoke her thoughts out loud, Pam might worry about Mel getting too attached. But this insight wasn't about Pam, not really. Yes, Pam was the one drawing these feelings out of Mel, but this was about Mel herself. And the relief of finally being able to understand and forgive herself for the choices she'd made. For the time she had taken to get to this place.

"Five kids and fifteen grandkids," she continued. "I broke with tradition by only having Danny, and I hear about it every time I'm around my parents. One of my sisters dated women in college, too. I talked to her about it, right after Richard proposed, because I was having so many doubts. She told me how happy she was she'd made the choice to get married and how much happier I'd be with him than with a woman. Looking back, I think she might have had regrets of her own."

"And she was hoping to convince herself she had done the right thing?"

"Maybe," Mel said before she downed the shot Pam had poured for her. The sudden and quiet acceptance of her past was the real reason she felt so much more at ease, although the alcohol—how many shots now?—was helping her relax. She should have been keeping her lime peels to keep track, instead of throwing them away. She crawled over and peered in the garbage. "Three," she said as she sat down on the rug again. "What was I saying? Oh, yes. It took me a couple years to figure out I had made a big mistake. By then I had Danny, so I tried to make things work. Marriage counselors, weekends away, you name it. And then I had a conference with Danny's second-grade teacher. She was lovely."

Pam almost lost track of Mel's story as she watched her crawl on her hands and knees over to the garbage can, the curve of her ass just visible below the robe's hem. Her long thighs, tight and firm, begged Pam to grip them and pull Mel against her. But an unexpected and biting jealousy drew her attention back to what Mel was saying. A lovely teacher. One who made Mel aware of an undeniable attraction to women. One who had taken Mel right there on her desk during their conference? Pam had wanted to make sure Mel wasn't completely inexperienced, that she wouldn't overreact to their night together and think the physical satisfaction meant more than it should. She had her wish. She wasn't Mel's first. So why did the information make her want to go smash the lovely teacher's car windows?

"You had an affair?" Pam prompted. She tried to keep jealousy out of her voice, not wanting Mel to misinterpret it as judgment. She had a feeling Mel had explained why she had married, why she had stayed married, to herself and others far too many times. Pam didn't care what road Mel had taken to get here, to this room on this night. She was here, and nothing else mattered.

"No. But I told Richard about my feelings for her. We were comfortable together by then, so we decided to stay together for Danny. No dating outside the marriage. No pressure within it. I trusted him and gave up so many years, so much of what I wanted for myself. Never again."

Pam swallowed. With relief. With renewed arousal as Mel stretched her legs out, so close to Pam's. So smooth and bare and close. Mel had drawn inward while she talked, pulling her knees to her chest, but now she seemed to relax. Pam mirrored her more open body language, ready to leave the past behind and get back to the promise of the night ahead.

"Your turn," she said. *Dare me. Dare me to kiss you because I need to. Soon.*

"Truth," Mel said instead. "Now you have to answer a question, too."

"I don't get to choose dare?" Pam asked. Mel shook her head. Pam wanted to move forward, shrug off the nagging images of Mel with her college girlfriends and flirting with Danny's teacher. Get to the sex so she didn't have to wonder why she felt sad when she heard Mel admit once again that she'd never commit to someone, would never allow anyone to take her freedom away and make her live with compromise. The whole conversation should have made Pam relieved. Mel had made the ideal confession. Pam wasn't sure why she felt disappointed.

"Why sea glass?" Mel asked, breaking into Pam's thoughts.

Art? Why hadn't Mel asked about sex, Pam's past flings, her first time? Something less personal, less revealing. But Mel had shared too much tonight for Pam to ignore her question. She owed Mel some sort of answer. "My grandparents took me on vacation to the ocean every summer when I was a kid. My grandfather would spend hours hunting for glass on the beach, and he got me hooked." She answered as if Mel wanted to know why she collected it, not why she used it in her art. "I loved the colors and the feel of the smooth glass in my hands. The best part was imagining it whole again. What shape it was, who used it and for what."

"Sounds like you were very close to your grandfather. What about your parents?"

"We had a good relationship while I was growing up." Pam straightened her legs and crossed her ankles before she topped off her glass again. Family questions she could handle. The answers weren't always pleasant, but Pam could face them. She drank the shot and was chewing on her lime when she realized she had forgotten the salt. "I was a real tomboy and Dad loved it. He was my softball coach and drove me to all my basketball games. We'd go rock climbing together. Fun stuff. He didn't care at all that I wasn't girly, so I thought he'd be okay when I came out to him in high school. He blew up. Couldn't even stay in the room with me so we could talk."

"And your mom?" Mel shifted her legs so they were barely touching Pam's.

Pam tried to focus on her story and not on the physical contact of Mel's bare legs. Even through the denim of her jeans, the light touch made her skin feel electric. "I think Mom would have been okay eventually. We were never really close. She tried to get us to reconcile a few times, but she wouldn't go against my dad's decision to cut me out of his life. By then, my grandmother had died, but Grandpa took me in, and I lived with him through high school and college. He and my dad never spoke after that. Because of me."

Mel put her hand on Pam's ankle and squeezed gently. "That wasn't your fault. Your grandfather made a difficult decision, but it was the right one. He must have loved seeing you use the sea glass on your paintings."

Pam hesitated. Full circle back to her art. Didn't the game only require her to answer one question truthfully, not a whole slew of them? She blamed the tequila for making her follow Mel's change in subject. And she blamed Mel's hand, still resting on her ankle. Warm. Safe. Touching her, touching her pain, in a way that was intimate but not sexy. Pam wanted to get back to sexy. "He had passed away before I came here and started making mosaics. He left everything to me, including the beach house. I had just gone through a bad breakup, so I moved here. I don't know why I started putting the glass on my paintings like that. I haven't done many of them."

"How long ago was this?"

"Eight years. I was a graduate student when I met Diane. She was my advisor. We started an affair while I was working on my degree, and we moved in together right after I graduated. She had a son, just a baby then. Kevin." Pam shook her head and the room tilted slightly. Why was she talking about Kevin? She looked at the four lime peels lined up by the salt shaker. Too many. "Anyway, I painted portraits as a career. Made a good living at it, too. Diane asked me to leave when Kevin was three, and I came here."

Mel reached for the tequila bottle. "You do portraits? Maybe you could—"

"No, Mel," Pam said sharply. She'd do the mosaics. No portraits of her or Danny or whomever else Mel had been about to name. No matter how sexy Mel was or how persuasive she could be. Pam could barely piece together her fractured visions. Scratch paint onto a canvas. Stick on some glass. But portraits meant staring a subject in the eyes, letting them into her soul, where they could reach her most vulnerable places and do the most damage.

She used to be open, used to enjoy the connection she'd form even with strangers when she felt some inexplicable urge to paint them. It had been her calling, her way of pulling the essence out of a person and freezing it in time. Permanence. A fallacy Pam no longer trusted. She cared about Mel, was proud of her, admired her. She wanted to know Mel's story, to know her body, to know every fantasy and desire she kept so carefully hidden inside. Trace her outline. Not use brushes and oils to reach any deeper than friendship and sex. "Don't ask me that. I don't paint portraits any more. In fact, I rarely paint at all. Until your commission, I'd only done about one mosaic a year."

"Oh. I'm sorry. I had no idea."

Pam rubbed her eyes wearily. She should leave. Her brilliant plan to use tequila to help her seduce Mel had backfired. The only thing the alcohol had lubricated was her willingness to talk. Like being in a damned confessional.

"Lie down," Mel said.

"I really should…I need to…" Pam wasn't sure what she needed. To get out of this warm room. Get away from the sadness she had seen in Mel's eyes when she talked about her marriage and again when Pam blurted out the story of her own messed-up past. This was nothing like the silly, playful foreplay she had been hoping for.

"Lie down," Mel insisted. She moved so she was kneeling next to Pam.

Pam leaned back on her elbows and then finally rested back on the rug. She closed her eyes. She had to stop this, go back to her room. Or better yet, go back to her own home. The gaping hole in her house seemed preferable to the chaotic emotions she felt as Mel put a little wedge of lime in her mouth and bent over to lick the side of Pam's neck. The bitter citrus stung Pam's lips where they were chapped from the sea air. Even the sprinkle of salt assaulted Pam's nerve endings, and she arched her neck in an involuntary reaction to the sensation. Her skin felt too fragile, too paper-thin to protect her from the abrasive touch of the world, of her memories.

She kept her eyes shut, sinking into herself, but she could feel Mel leaning over her. Pam slid her hands under the sleeves of Mel's robe and anchored them on Mel's bare upper arms, strong and alive and protecting, braced on either side of Pam's head just as she'd imagined that afternoon. She could smell the intoxicating combination of roses and tequila when Mel licked the salt off her neck. The light stroke of Mel's tongue pulled Pam back to the surface, back to all the places where her skin was in contact with Mel's. Her thoughts were jumbled with family, loss, pain, but all of the pieces coalesced and then drifted away when Mel's mouth met hers. A brief kiss as Mel sucked the lime from between Pam's lips. Pam felt all of her awareness hone in on the momentary connection. Mel's lips burned, but in a good way. Pam was wet in an instant, her arousal more intense because she had been so raw only seconds before. She was soothed now. Coming alive again.

Chapter Sixteen

M el sat back on her heels. She chewed the lime and then flicked the peel into the trash can while she watched Pam. Mel had almost lost her to the deep place she went when life or her past was too much to bear. She still didn't understand Pam completely, but she was learning more about her. About the way she experienced the world—as if it had different dimensions, more intensity, than it did for other people. Mel's shyness, her worry about seeming like an inept virgin, disappeared.

The contact and the kiss had been for Pam, but now Mel wanted more. One quick taste of Pam's skin wasn't enough. She needed Pam back in the room, back in the present, because she wanted to kiss her again. Not to rescue Pam this time, but to stir up the passion Mel felt building deep in her belly. Pam was lying so still Mel might have worried she had passed out if it wasn't for the smile twitching at the corner of her lips. Without warning, Pam sat up so she was face-to-face with Mel. Mel caught herself before she moved away in surprise at the sudden movement. She licked her lips, anticipating a kiss, but Pam only brushed her nose gently against Mel's.

"Your turn," Pam said. "Lie down."

Mel hesitated. She was comfortable leaning over Pam and touching her. But to lie back and be touched was a different matter altogether. She hadn't been put in this position for a long time. Not just sex, but letting another person take control, take care of her. Wife, mother, scout leader, PTA member. And now plumber, interior decorator, innkeeper. Never passive, never nurtured or cherished. Even in her fantasies, she had always been the active one, making love to Pam, deriving pleasure by satisfying Pam's needs. But the dark look in Pam's eyes, the smile that promised such wonderful things, gave Mel the strength to let go just a little bit. Pam wanted her, wanted to take care of her.

Mel slowly lowered herself onto her back. They had shared such small touches so far, featherlight and fleeting, but her body felt as aroused as she would have expected after an hour of heavy petting. She had been without any sexual contact for so long she worried she would overreact just to Pam's nearness, let alone her touch. She tightened her throat, holding back a whimper as Pam licked the swell of her breast where it was revealed by the open neck of her robe. Pam's breath on the damp spot where her tongue had been and the barely perceptible sprinkle of salt on her chest made Mel's nipples hard. Pam teasingly dipped her index finger in Mel's mouth before inserting the lime wedge.

Too much. Mel felt too much to simply lie there. Accepting and responding as Pam's tongue trailed over the rasping grains of salt. She raised her head slightly, wanting Pam's kiss, wanting to set the pace. But Pam's mouth barely touched hers as she captured the lime. How much more teasing could her body take before it shattered into a million pieces? Pam moved away, but not far, and she used her teeth to squeeze juice across Mel's throat and between her breasts before she dropped her head to lap it up.

The shift from skimming contact to the determined pressure from Pam's tongue and mouth as she sucked on Mel's neck jolted her senses to full arousal. The relief of action, the promised roughness of Pam's palm against her cheek, tore away the last of Mel's anxiety, her struggle for control. Her fingers gripped Pam's hair, tugging her closer still, and her body arched toward Pam's mouth. Pam licked an errant drop from under Mel's ear before she finally, after what seemed to Mel like an eternity of waiting, raised her head and kissed Mel fully on the lips. Mel opened her mouth to Pam's insistent tongue, and the tastes of fruit and tequila and Pam filled her. She felt Pam shift her weight so her hips pressed into Mel's. One of Pam's knees slid between her legs, pressing against her, and the rasp of denim across her bare, wet lips nearly made Mel come.

Pam eased the pressure of her leg, wanting to prolong the feeling of having Mel squirming underneath her. She moved lower, impatiently yanking the belt of Mel's robe so the knot loosened and she could move the silky material aside and expose Mel's breasts. Mel had been fighting without moving a muscle. Holding back. But when Pam sucked a tight nipple into her mouth, she finally felt Mel release her breath and completely let go. Mel's moans and the audible catch in her breath turned Pam on even more, and she switched to lavish attention on Mel's other breast. She bit her nipple lightly and felt Mel arch toward her. Pam's belly rested between Mel's legs, and she could feel Mel's warmth burning into her skin, Mel's wetness soaking through the thin layer of T-shirt between them.

Pam kissed Mel's stomach and skimmed her hands along Mel's sides. Her fingers roamed over the satiny robe, using the material to caress Mel's torso and breasts before she pushed the robe away and let her bare hands repeat the movements. Mel was alive under her hands. Mel's rib cage rose and fell with her gasping breath, her muscles contracted, and the tiny hairs on her skin shivered at Pam's touch.

Pam pushed back onto her knees and met Mel's eyes. Without needing words, she asked for permission and received it before she pressed Mel's thighs wider apart and dropped her head to taste her. Long strokes of her tongue, and Mel's hands were back on her head, anchoring her in place. Rapid flicks, and Mel's legs wrapped around her in a tight hug. A firm pressure as her lips closed around Mel's clit and sucked, and Mel's hips rose as her orgasm took her. The tequila, only the tequila, made the room spin and tilt for Pam as Mel shuddered under her mouth with a wordless cry, her grip on Pam's hair slackening to a gentle caress. Pam was about to slide up and take Mel in her arms, but Mel stood up instead. She looked a little wobbly on her feet, but she dropped her robe and held out her hand to Pam.

Mel wasn't even tempted to succumb to either the alcohol or her orgasm and take a break, rest on the floor with Pam. Now it was her turn. Finally. She could smell Pam—her arousal, the scent of the ocean she brought into this room. Mel needed to taste her. She led

Pam across the room, aiming in the general direction of her bed, until she bumped into it. She helped Pam pull her T-shirt off and then kissed her. The flavors of tequila and lime had been completely replaced by sex, by the taste of Mel herself, and she reluctantly stopped kissing Pam long enough to unzip her jeans and slide them down her legs. She pushed Pam into a seated position on the edge of the bed and braced a hand on either side of Pam's hips so she could bend down and kiss her again.

No more hesitating or teasing. Mel felt transformed, as if she had emerged from a storm. Energized. Why had she been so worried about getting her mouth on Pam? Any concern about what to do, how to do it, slipped away. She knew only Pam's desire, her arousal. Her need to find some sort of physical and emotional release. Mel dropped to her knees and roughly pushed Pam's legs apart. She took Pam in her mouth—the most natural thing in the world—and felt her own arousal resurface as Pam's clit hardened under her tongue. She felt powerful as she heard Pam gasp and whimper, and when she sensed Pam had leaned back on the bed. And she felt triumphant when Pam called her name and surged against her.

She climbed onto the bed and kissed Pam, somehow managing to pull the covers back and get them between the sheets without breaking contact. Mel finally eased away with a sigh and lay back on her pillow with Pam nestled at her side. Pam slowly kissed her way along Mel's collarbone.

"Mm, that was nice," Mel said, her eyes closed. *Nice?* Fucking incredible. Worth the wait. Definitely worth the wait. Mel kept those thoughts inside, not wanting to frighten Pam off with any melodrama. "You wore me out."

"Wore you out? Are you kidding?" Pam asked between kisses. She licked Mel's neck where the stickiness of lime remained. "We're just warming up."

Pam woke with Mel in her arms, sheets tangled around her legs and a growing concern her head might split in half if she moved too quickly. She took deep breaths and attempted to will the room to stop spinning around her. She wanted to get up, use the bathroom, drink some water, but she was distracted by the feel of Mel pressed against her. She usually wanted to escape as soon as possible after a night of sex. And when she planned it well enough, her getaway was drama-free because whoever she was with needed to pack and check out of her hotel. But today was different. She lay still and enjoyed the small movements Mel made as she gradually stirred awake.

Pam had never missed this part. Had never wanted to stick around and hold someone, rest her palm on a lover's hip, bury her nose in rose-scented hair, synchronize her breathing with someone else's. But even after a night of mind-blowing sex, these small things—with Mel—seemed so important. She didn't need to panic. Everything else was still the same. Pam still had a distinct, specified time to leave. Next weekend Danny would be back at the inn. And her house's repairs should be done. Instead of the looming eleven o'clock checkout time, Pam had a few days to enjoy being with Mel. Even after hours with her the night before, Pam saw no indication they would get bored with each other physically any time soon.

If ever. Pam didn't mind, as long as her emotions were safe. They both wanted this kind of relationship. And they each seemed extraordinarily satisfied by the other. Mel knew some of Pam's past and enough about her present—maybe a little more than was comfortable— so Pam no longer faced a constant struggle to protect her secret failures or pretend she was the artist everyone seemed to expect. Yes, a casual, long-term affair might work, saving Pam the trouble of seducing tourists. And, even better, sparing Mel from the bother of flirting with any single lesbian who might stay at her inn. A win-win situation. Pam snuggled closer as Mel shifted and then sat upright.

"Ouch," Pam said, rubbing her temple where Mel's elbow had knocked her.

"What time is it?" Mel asked frantically, reaching for her alarm clock.

"Five," Pam said.

Mel checked the clock as if to verify Pam's statement and then rested back against the pillows. She pressed the heels of her hands against her eyes. "I have guests. I need to make breakfast. My God, I feel sick."

"Good morning to you, too," Pam said, resting her hand on Mel's bare stomach.

Mel peeked at her from behind her hands and gave her a weak smile. "Good morning. And I'm sorry I hit you. Not a nice way to thank you for an amazing night."

Pam leaned over and kissed her, trailing her hand up to cup Mel's breast.

"Don't start," Mel said, sliding away and sitting on the side of the bed. "I really do need to get up and try to serve omelets without throwing up on them. As soon as the room holds still."

Mel finally had some peace and quiet in the inn when her guests went out to dinner. Time to think, as she finished cleaning her kitchen. She still wasn't sure why she had pulled out of Pam's arms that morning, away from her kiss, when all she'd wanted to do was stay for an encore performance of the amazing sex they'd shared. For more kisses, more exploration, more orgasms. The sex had been great, and she wanted more. Wanted to make up for those lost years. But as she had slowly regained consciousness in Pam's arms—their breath, their bodies intertwined—she had panicked. Pam had softly nuzzled her hair, and Mel knew everything had changed. She had changed. Her friendship with Pam had definitely changed. She needed space to figure out who she was before she fell headfirst into this new world. Only yesterday she had started to consider the possibility of a purely sexual relationship, and suddenly she was in one. With Pam, who wasn't prepared or willing to offer anything more.

Unfortunately, the residual effects of too much tequila were keeping her from thinking clearly, let alone make life-altering decisions. She didn't know how she made it through the day. Her head didn't stop aching until dinnertime, and her guests were so cheerful and talkative she wanted to kick them all out of the inn. She somehow got beds made and laundry washed and picnic lunches packed. Pam was scarce all day, leaving for the gallery right after she helped Mel make breakfast.

"You're throwing those out?"

Mel turned to see Pam in the kitchen doorway, a pizza box in her hands. "Yes. I can't stand the sight of them," Mel said as she dropped the bag of key limes in the trash. "No way am I making them into a pie."

Pam laughed and put the box on the counter. "I missed you today," she said. She put her arms around Mel's waist and pulled her close. "Why don't we take this pizza and some sort of nonalcoholic beverage down to your room and have dinner in private?"

Mel leaned into Pam's embrace. The weight of a difficult day and the tension she had felt leading up to the wedding all faded in the strength of Pam's arms. She moved away before she got too comfortable with Pam's support. She had a few days, maybe another week or two, of Pam's company before Pam moved on to someone new. Pam didn't want or expect their relationship to consume Mel. To manipulate or subjugate her. She should follow Pam's lead and stop overthinking their affair. After all, Pam had done this before and would do it again. With someone else.

Mel shoved that thought out of her still-tender head. She'd be able to move on and find someone else as well. One of her future guests, a tourist, whatever. For now, this relationship was already miles away from Mel's previous one. She wasn't ignoring who she was or what she wanted. And what she wanted right now was to lock herself and Pam in her room, talk about her day, sit down, eat, replenish her energy with pizza and caffeine before she dragged Pam to her bed. She grabbed a couple cans of Coke and followed Pam downstairs to her bedroom. As long as she stayed strong and didn't get too close, she'd be just fine when Pam finally left.

Chapter Seventeen

Pam reached across the bed and came fully awake as her hand slipped over empty sheets. She sat up and stretched. After only a few nights with Mel, she had already changed her sleeping habits and had stayed on the right side of the bed rather than sleeping in the middle. The left side was untouched, the sheets still tucked in. Instead of the warm, rich colors of Mel's room, she was surrounded by pale lavender walls and the glint of morning light reflecting off the sea glass painting on the wall.

She stumbled out of bed and into the shower, blaming her edgy mood on the proximity of her painting. She was relieved to have a bed to herself again. Space and privacy. And to shower alone without jostling for room, getting shampoo in her eyes, knocking the soap off the shelf. She braced her hands on the back wall and let the hot spray land on her lower back. How many solo showers would it take before the memory of Mel's fingers tangled in her hair, Mel's lips trailing over her wet skin, faded away? Danny would only be here two more nights, and already Pam felt a sense of loss, a craving for Mel. She was an addiction, but merely a physical one. Spending time apart would break the habit.

Pam trailed down the stairs after Piper. She could hear Mel and Danny talking in the kitchen, but she went straight to the back door and let Piper out without stopping to say good morning. She had planned to sneak back upstairs after Piper's walk, but Piper made a beeline for the kitchen and Pam, again, followed behind. The smell of her favorite apple-and-cinnamon oatmeal was enough to push her past common sense and into Mel's presence.

She stood in the doorway, one hand on the jamb as she fought to keep from walking over to Mel and kissing her senseless. Mel was wearing one of her old painting sweatshirts and a pair of fleece pajama pants. She looked as young as her son as she sat at the kitchen table with her hands wrapped around a mug of coffee. Adorable.

"Knock it off," Pam scolded herself under her breath. Mel was sexy. Simply, objectively sexy.

"Hey, Pam," Danny said.

"Hey, Danny." He was diverted by Piper's enthusiastic greeting, so Pam had a few private moments to concentrate only on Mel. Hearing her voice, her laughter, brought Pam right back to the hours she had spent tossing and turning before falling asleep last night. Too hot, too cold. Window opened, window closed. Flipping restlessly until she had to get out of bed and straighten the sheets. She had told herself it was only the sex. A week of regular—okay, not *regular*, astounding—sex had spoiled her. But even taking care of that need, with the imagined vision of Mel's hands gripping her thighs and Mel's mouth on her, hadn't helped. What she really missed were the moments *after.* Sharing random thoughts, whispered words, intertwined fingers, until they dozed off. Dangerous. A few nights of sleeping alone would be good for her.

"Morning," Mel said with that intimate half smile Pam had seen so often over the past few days. "Want some breakfast?"

"Um, yeah," Pam said. She didn't have to be a mind reader to know Mel had missed her, too. She wondered if Mel had thought about her last night. In bed, alone, her hands sliding over her breasts and down…Pam somehow managed to stop the progress of Mel's imagined hand and step into the kitchen. "No, don't get up. I'll take care of it."

Mel and Danny resumed their conversation while Pam refilled Mel's coffee and poured a cup for herself. She dished up some oatmeal and poured cream over it and in her coffee. "You're going whale watching?" she asked in spite of her efforts to remain uninterested. She stood in the middle of the kitchen holding her breakfast.

"Sit down," Mel coaxed, waving at a chair.

"A friend of mine said gray whales migrate along the coast this time of year," Danny said as Pam took a seat opposite him. "I've never seen a whale."

"They're heading south to winter in lagoons in Baja," Pam said. Her thigh brushed against Mel's and she inhaled sharply. She shouldn't be here. She wasn't a good enough actress to keep her arousal off her face. Arousal, because of one simple touch. Focus on the whales. "But the migration doesn't get heavy until late December. You might see one or two this early, but don't count on it."

"You've seen them?" Danny asked.

Pam shrugged. "Lots of times. I found a great viewing spot on the cliffs in Ecola. It's off the main path, so it's private."

"We never went to the park when we came here for vacations," Mel said. "I've been meaning to go, so today's as good a day as any. I'll make us a picnic."

Pam put her spoon down. Mel's "us" sounded like it included her. She hadn't volunteered to actually take them to the park, had she? Taking Mel there alone, just the two of them, was fine. The thought of pulling Mel off the trail and pressing her against a pine tree, unbuttoning her jeans, was exciting. But going on a nature walk with Mel and her son? Not exactly what Pam had in mind.

"It'd be better to wait a few weeks. You'll have more of a chance to see whales."

"In a few weeks I'll have guests every weekend. I might not be able to spend a day away from the inn as easily as I can now."

Danny had been watching Pam and Mel's interchange with an expression Pam couldn't quite read. Shrewd? Questioning? But, then, he smiled and rubbed his hands together. "I'm feeling lucky today," he said, his face changing in an instant. Almost childlike again, like when he played with Piper. Pam couldn't keep up. "Do you have binoculars?"

Pam sighed. Until she got Mel out of her system, she'd just spend the day thinking about her if they were apart. She might as well go with them on what would probably be an unsuccessful whale-watching expedition. She'd let her hormones make the decision for her today. Just this once. "Upstairs. I'll need to bring Piper's leash, too."

"Then it's settled," Mel said, putting her half-finished coffee on the table and pushing back her chair. "I'll make sandwiches with the leftover chicken from last night."

"Finish your coffee then get dressed," Pam said. She stood and topped off Mel's mug. "I'll take care of lunch. I make a killer chicken salad."

Mel settled back in her chair and watched Pam rummage through her fridge. Danny even offered to help, and Pam put him to work chopping celery while she talked about whales and whale migrations and conservation efforts. Mel tuned them out and stared out the window while she sipped her coffee. She still felt prickly when Pam tried to help her, to take care of her. Defensive. Afraid she'd start to rely on Pam and stop relying on herself.

Mel put her coffee cup in the dishwasher and left the kitchen without interrupting the whale lecture. Danny seemed interested. And he liked Pam, but Mel wasn't surprised. Pam was still nervous around him at times—and after the brief revelations Pam had shared about Kevin, Mel was starting to understand why—but mostly, Pam talked to Danny as if he was an adult. No condescension, no dismissal of his opinions. She should be happy they got along. And happy she had Pam in her life as well. A sex partner, albeit a temporary one. So why did she feel so unhappy?

Mel got dressed quickly. Warm layers so she could remove some as they hiked through the woods. During breakfast, she had enjoyed the feeling of sharing a secret with Pam. Meaningful glances, the touch of Pam's thigh, the intimate smile on Pam's face. Shared memories. And last night, the sweet tension of being in the same house, but rooms apart. Her old fantasies of Pam—made much more pleasurable because Mel now had the remembered reality of Pam's touch to fuel them. Wondering if Pam was upstairs, thinking of her, too. All very exciting. Arousing.

And then Pam had offered to make lunch.

Just *lunch*. She wasn't taking over the inn. Not taking over Mel's life or even telling her how to hang a painting. Mel was silent while she drove them the short distance to the park. She had discovered the definite advantage of letting Pam take care of her in the bedroom. Over the past few days, she had been able to let go of some of her control and be the recipient for once. Enjoy the attention of a tender and enthusiastic…what? Lover? Friend-with-benefits?

Whatever Pam was to her, Mel still felt Pam's distance, her walls. She knew Pam's body, every beautiful inch of it. And she had learned about some of Pam's wounds, her difficulties with painting. But only glimpses. Pam had been talking easily since they'd left the house, but there was none of *her* in what she said. Never a comment about a lovely tree. Only a discussion about the shape of the Sitka spruce's cones and needles. Never a hint that she was moved or touched by something around her. Only a definition, a description of what she saw. Mel trailed after Danny and Pam as they left the parking lot and followed a dirt path into the forest. She should have been relieved by Pam's distance. How many times had she said she didn't want to lose herself in a relationship? So why did she feel so angry because Pam didn't want one, either?

"Wow, look!" Pam pointed toward a hill. "A peregrine falcon."

"Where?" Danny asked. "I don't see anything."

Pam handed him the binoculars. "See the tall, bare tree? Look at the tree to its left, about a quarter of the way down."

Mel squinted at the tree. She could make out the shape of a bird on one of the branches, but she had no idea how Pam knew what kind it was. She stood back and watched Pam and Danny standing on the trail, and her breath caught with the effort of keeping her face and movements controlled. She was outdoors, the wide expanse of ocean and huge trees around her, and she felt as stifled and suffocated as if she were trapped in a windowless room. She fought down the urge to scream. So many months of tears and effort and she had come full circle, back to a relationship of strain and silence. She wanted to talk to Pam about her conflicting desires, her desperate need to be independent vying with her insistent cry for intimacy, but Pam was the last person she could tell.

Pam finished describing the falcon's tapered tail and dark cap of feathers. They walked a few yards along the trail before she stopped again, to point out a flock of cedar waxwings. Mel faked an interest in the pointy-headed little birds. She was angry with Pam and she had no idea why. Mel felt her body coming alive after years of neglect and stifled desires. She bent down and picked up a fallen tree branch. She *felt* again. The rough bark and silky needles of the pine, the uneven path under her feet, the salty breeze off the ocean. Her shell had turned back into skin. With Pam's help. Pam had opened up a new world of sensuality for Mel, had filled a void after years of isolation.

But sex wasn't the only thing Mel had been missing over the years. Support, trust, a companion, a partner. Love. Pam offered some of them, but with limitations. She supported Mel and her efforts with the inn. She was fun company, a helpful friend. But Mel knew Pam was here for now, not forever.

Did Mel even want something deeper than what she and Pam shared, a real commitment, a lifetime of love? No. Not when she couldn't even let someone pack a lunch for her without panicking about her lost sense of self. Not yet, when she still had so far to go before she felt secure in her ability to take care of herself, her business, her goals and dreams—but, maybe, someday. Because pushing past her fear and trusting Pam completely in bed had been gloriously worthwhile. How much more rewarding would it be to push past her fears of committing to a loving partner? Could she find some middle ground between being fiercely independent and subjugating herself to a relationship?

Mel felt a wave of irrational jealousy as she watched Pam and Danny fight playfully over the binoculars. She liked seeing Danny and Pam form a tentative friendship. She liked it more than she'd ever admit to Pam because intuition told her Pam would freak if she thought Danny was getting attached to her. Getting close with Danny, like Pam had with Kevin, would be a sign of looming commitment, a warning to back off.

But Mel was jealous because she couldn't seem to break past Pam's barriers as easily as her son had. Years of hiding her sexuality and painstakingly keeping up the veneer of a false marriage had replaced her natural friendliness with a careful reserve. She wanted to find her way back to her real self, not swap her old lies with new ones.

Danny jogged ahead with Piper and they scrambled up a pile of big rocks alongside the trail. Pam stopped to examine the leaves of a bush growing alongside the path and Mel caught up to her.

"Come see what I found," Pam said. Mel stepped closer and looked at the waxy green leaf.

"Big deal, it's just a…oh!" Mel finally spotted the tiny green frog, no bigger than her thumbnail, nestled in the bend of the leaf. "How'd you find it?"

Pam shrugged. "I notice things. My grandfather taught me. He rarely went outside without binoculars and a stack of field guides."

Mel expected Pam to launch into a detailed account of the evolution of frogs, but instead she put her hand on Mel's back.

"Are you okay?"

Mel sighed, her tension and anger melting under the heat from Pam's palm, the gentle kneading motion on her tight muscles, the caress of Pam's breath against her neck. Mel stood in silence for a moment and let Pam's nearness reassure her. Mel's common sense might want her to keep her options open for future relationships, but her body still reveled in right now. She took a step back.

"It's hard," she said. "Hiding us from Danny. I spent too many years in hiding."

"Tell him if you want," Pam said. They started walking again, slowly following the trail Danny and Piper had taken.

"Tell him what?" Mel asked. Fishing. She couldn't ask Pam to define their relationship, give her some hope of something possible somewhere down the road. But she could find out how Pam would describe what they had, how she would explain it to Danny.

"That we're sleeping together, of course." Pam shrugged. So casual. "I'm fine with it, but be sure you think it through first."

"Think what through?" Mel heard the harsh notes returning to her voice. Question indirectly asked, question answered. Not dating, not a couple. She knew that already. So why was she still mad? "Whether I want to be honest with my son?"

Pam stopped again and faced Mel. "You told him you're gay, right?" Mel nodded. "So you're being honest about who you are. But you came out as an adult, after a lot of years in a passionless marriage. It's only normal you'd want to experiment a little, make up for lost time. Are you going to tell him about every woman you date? Every woman you sleep with?"

"No, I guess not." A fling with Pam, a string of short-term romances selected from her pool of single guests. How safe. How easy to keep her distance, avoid the threat that intimacy and openness posed to her individuality. She was blaming Pam for not wanting more, not offering even the hope of a future together. But was that part of the reason Mel had gone so willingly into her arms? Her physical attraction to Pam was undeniable. But Mel had been alone for so long. Was she isolating herself out of habit now? Accepting transitory flings because she was too scared to let anyone too close? Pam was supposed to be the one who kept up barriers, kept everyone at a distance. But maybe Mel was doing the same thing.

Pam tucked Mel's hair behind her ear. "Danny's a good kid. He's going to get attached to people in your life. I don't see any reason to give him the details of an affair unless it's about more than sex. He's your son, not your hairdresser."

Mel laughed along with Pam as they moved forward again, but she could feel the muscles in her jaw tighten as she forced a smile. Pam was right about one thing. Danny deserved to know if she had found a potential partner, someone who would become part of their lives. But she hadn't. She sat on a large rock to rest while Pam and Danny scanned the trees for some kind of wren Pam had heard. She knew what Pam wanted—just sex. Another limitation in a lifetime full of them. But Mel had stopped limiting herself when she bought the inn. Every day had seemed the same in her old life. A month had stretched to a year, had stretched to eighteen years. With little change, little growth, nothing to separate the days in her mind except for having a child and celebrating his milestones.

But that had changed last August. Since then she'd had some bad days filled with setbacks and doubts. And great days marked by hung paintings and a wedding and a water heater she'd installed on her own. Peaks and valleys. Dimension in a life that had once been so flat.

"Is ornithology class over yet?" she asked. Sex with Pam was definitely one of the highest peaks. Mel had no fucking clue how she'd climb out of the valley when Pam left. But she would. And she'd be stronger because of it. She stood and hooked her backpack over one shoulder. "I'm ready for lunch."

CHAPTER EIGHTEEN

Pam turned and saw Mel standing in sunlight as it filtered through the tree branches. Shadow and light. So very beautiful. "I'm hungry, too," Pam said. "Let's take the cliff trail on the way back."

Pam led the way along a narrow path through the forest, relieved they had to walk single file for a few minutes. Mel and Danny followed, making enough noise to scare off every bird in the county. Pam glanced back. Danny was trying to get at the bag of brownies in Mel's backpack, and she was fending him off with a tree branch she must have picked up along the way. Pam looked at the trail in front of her again, fighting to hide her smile and her shock at how relieved she was to hear Mel's laughter again. Mel had been so withdrawn most of the day, but not first thing in the morning. Then Pam had felt the energy of sex between them. The sex they had been denied the night before. The sex she was certain they both missed. Pam stopped when the forest gave way to a breathtaking view of the ocean. She never got tired of this place. She just wasn't accustomed to sharing it with anyone else.

Pam scanned the horizon with her high-powered binoculars. She wasn't surprised by the absence of whales off the coast. The day was perfect for viewing, with a fairly calm sea and an overcast sky that kept the water free from glare, but there wasn't a whale in sight.

"There's a seal," she said, handing the binoculars to Mel. She stood beside Mel and pointed out to sea, where she could just barely see the seal's head bobbing with the waves. She didn't touch Mel, but she leaned so her chin was near Mel's shoulder, her lips only millimeters from Mel's neck. Torturing herself. So close she could put out her tongue and trace the curve of Mel's ear, the way that drove Mel crazy. Pam liked knowing that about her. Liked the way Mel's breathing changed and the way she swayed toward Pam before she moved away.

"I can't see it," Mel said, handing the binoculars to Danny. "You try."

Pam saw the slight flush of arousal on Mel's neck when she turned around. She definitely saw a hint of passion in the smile Mel gave her while Danny searched for the seal. But she saw sadness, too. In Mel's smile, in her eyes. When Danny gave up on finding the seal, they walked the rest of the way to the picnic area in silence. Mel had something on her mind, but Pam didn't want to ask what it was. Because she thought she knew. She had hoped Mel would be satisfied with sex, with their amazing physical connection, without wanting more. But she had heard the dissatisfaction in Mel's voice when they had talked about Danny.

Of course Mel would eventually want more. Had Pam really expected them to keep things private and casual for long when Danny spent most weekends at the inn? Going on outings, making kites, sharing meals. No matter how hard Pam tried to keep her distance, she'd be sucked in. Even today, she had made an effort to be impersonal and unemotional. A tour guide. Talking about birds and trees and the park's history. But she had spent more time laughing and joking with Danny than actually teaching him anything. And more time thinking about Mel, trying to sneak a kiss or a touch, than was comfortable.

Pam brought them out of the woods, and they found a picnic table overlooking the beach. Mel set out the lunch while Danny alternated between hunting for whales or other sea life and watching a group of surfers who were attempting to find a wave large enough to ride. Pam sat in silence, as introspective as Mel had been earlier. She had been deluding herself about this being a casual, long-term arrangement. A convenient sexual relationship with no chance of change or growth.

Or ending. Pam didn't want it to end. But if Mel eventually wanted more, they'd both end up hurt. Better to get hurt now, before anyone got too close. Before anyone felt like the three of them were forming some sort of family. Pam knew too well how bad the pain would be if she and Mel let this go on too long.

"Hey, Pam,"—Danny broke into her uncomfortable thoughts— "I thought all seagulls were the same, just big white birds, but that one has darker wings. Are there different kinds?"

Pam latched onto the topic with relief, glad to be distracted before she really decided she needed to break things off with Mel. Because she couldn't do it yet. Soon, probably. But not yet. She thought she saw Mel roll her eyes as she launched into a discussion about the differing characteristics of glaucous-winged and mew gulls, but she kept talking. She was more comfortable focusing on the details of the plants and creatures around her than sifting through the mixed-up emotions she felt around Mel. Describing, identifying, naming. Until her mind was relaxed by the list of clearly defined birds or trees. Instead of confused by the pleasure and sorrow of being joined to this family for a very short time.

She certainly wasn't willing to travel down this road again since it would inevitably lead to heartbreak. But, for some reason, she was suddenly so willing to stand on it for a moment, holding Mel's hand, before she went her own way.

Pam switched her attention to five pelicans flying in a V-formation just off the shore. Even without binoculars, she could see the tiny ripples made by the tips of their wings as they flew with rhythm and precision mere inches off the water's surface. She pointed them out to Danny and was explaining ground effect, when a sense of déjà vu made her falter for a moment. The day had reminded her of something, and she finally made the connection. A county fair, a day of food and laughter and the bright flashes of amusement park rides. She had carried Kevin through the animal barns, talking to him about the sheep and goats and cows. She'd held him on a shiny carousel horse while he'd clapped in time to the music and waved at Diane every time they swirled past her. And when he had called for his mommy to help him throw a ring and win a stuffed bear, he had been calling to her. Only a week later, she was nobody to him. Because Diane had decided to leave, and Pam had had no way to stop her.

She stumbled through the rest of her pelican lecture and stood up, mumbling something about finding the public restrooms. She walked to the far side of the parking lot and lit a cigarette. Mel shouldn't tell Danny about their affair. Pam would be out of their lives soon enough, but this time she would be in control and walk away on her own. She leaned against a signpost and shut her eyes as she exhaled a long breath of smoke, trying to exorcise the memory that had thrust itself on her day.

"Mom said to tell you to put out the cigarette and come eat lunch."

Danny's voice made Pam open her eyes. She gave him a guilty smile and stubbed out her cigarette on the pavement before throwing it away. "I'm surprised she sent you. I've been under strict orders not to let you see me smoke."

"Yeah, I might think you look so cool I'll want to try," Danny said with a laugh. "Unlikely. I've seen the real lung from a smoker. Didn't look like it'd be good for my football career."

"Smart kid," Pam said. She started walking back to Mel, but Danny stopped her.

"Can I ask you something?"

"Sure, I guess," Pam said warily, hoping it was a question about birds. Or an interesting tree he had seen.

"Are you gay?"

Not a question about birds. Damn. "Yes, I am."

"So's my mom. But you know that already, don't you?"

"Yes, I do. She told me." Pam shifted her weight and glanced over her shoulder. She wished Mel would come over and rescue her. She should be the one to answer her son's questions.

Danny hesitated, as if unsure how to ask his next question. "Do you like her?"

"Are you asking whether I *like her* like her, or just like her?" Pam asked, buying some time before she answered. She had blithely told Mel to say they were just sleeping together, but now the phrasing seemed inappropriate. But she wasn't going to lie to him.

"Yeah."

"Something in between, I guess," she said. "I really like your mom. I like spending time with her. But, no, we're not in a serious relationship. We're very good friends, but not girlfriends." Pam stopped rambling. How many ways could she say it? *I'm involved with your mom, but I'm not planning to stick around, so don't worry about it.* Danny was a smart kid, and Pam should have known he wouldn't need to hear the words to pick up on the energy between them and be upset by it. But he didn't seem upset to hear they were something more than friends. He seemed...relieved? Happy?

"Okay," Danny said. He started to walk across the parking lot again, and Pam hurried to catch up. "I just thought you might be... dating."

"No. We're friends, that's it. She gave me a place to stay, and I'm painting some pictures for her inn. Friends." She emphasized the last word and Danny nodded as if he understood. They walked side by side in silence for a few steps.

"Because she's really great, you know," he said in a rush. "When she's not making you do stuff like sand the floors."

"I know," Pam said "And don't tell her, but I kind of like helping with her projects."

"Yeah, me too. And she's a good cook, most of the time."

"She makes great oatmeal." Pam halted again. "Wait, are you saying you *want* me to date your mom?"

Danny shrugged. "You make her smile. And I don't like to think of her being here all alone. Plus, I like your dog."

Pam laughed at his final sentence, but the rest of the conversation troubled her. They got back to the picnic table and Pam sat facing Mel and Danny. Mel smiled at her, appearing a little more at ease, and started chatting with Danny as if determined to put aside her earlier reserve. Pam was silent as they ate, half listening to their talk about the upcoming holidays. She had been so concerned about reassuring Danny because she thought he wouldn't want her dating his mother. To hear him admit he'd be okay with it, and to realize he must have picked up on something between her and Mel, was disturbing. She and Mel might only want a quick fling, but there was another person involved. Now when Pam left, she risked hurting not just Mel but Danny, too. She needed to end this affair before someone started to expect her to stick around permanently.

"What kind of bird is that?" Mel asked quietly.

Pam looked down in surprise to find she had been sketching on Mel's napkin. "A kingfisher," she said. "He's right over there, on the railing."

Danny twisted around to look at the long-billed, gray bird. "I want to be able to do that," he said.

"Perch on a railing?" Pam asked, putting down Mel's pen and taking a bite of chicken salad sandwich.

"Ha-ha. No, I want to draw and paint like you do."

Pam continued to eat while Mel picked up on Danny's topic, and the two of them eventually came up with a plan to have Pam give them a lesson.

"We can have it tomorrow in the studio," Mel said.

Pam sighed. Mel was going to get her on display in that studio if it killed her. "I'm not a teacher."

"We're beginners, so we won't know the difference," Mel said.

Pam looked at the two of them and wanted to say no. But it had been a day of nos. No whales, no don't tell your son about us, no I can't date your mother. This was a chance to say yes, to do something simple for them. But would it be simple to share her art without revealing too much of her private pain? Pam would have to find out.

"Sure, I'll give you guys an art lesson." No problem.

Chapter Nineteen

Pam set up her easel behind the two she had borrowed from Tia. She put a canvas on each one and then stood back to check the light. She shifted one of the easels closer to the window. A tall table held a few brushes with freshly cleaned downy bristles and soft-leaded pencils within arm's reach of her students' canvases. She put the palettes and trays of paint next to her own easel. This time, she would mix the paints herself, once she knew what Mel and Danny wanted to paint. She would be quicker to blend the colors, and they could focus on getting a feel for brush on canvas. A faint urge stirred inside when she unpacked the palettes and smelled the phenolic residue from their recent scrubbing. She'd resist the scent of oils, the graphite, the washed canvases. She'd mix paint for Mel and Danny, not for herself.

Pam fussed with the easels again, changing the angle so they wouldn't be able to see each other's paintings while they were working. And an easel for herself, just in case she needed to demonstrate a brushstroke or sketching technique. She was too excited about the lesson to be upset that Mel had finally managed to get her to at least *teach* painting in the studio. She had told Mel she wasn't an art teacher. But she hadn't mentioned how much she had wanted to be one. She had been offered a teaching job at her university after she received her Master's. Only a couple of advanced portrait seminars, but turning down the opportunity was one of her biggest regrets. But the university was Diane's domain, and she couldn't bear to have Pam overshadow her there as well. Pam had turned down the job and never again brought up the subject of teaching. Out loud, at least. Inside, she had always wished she had jumped at the chance to share her love of color and shape and texture with others, in such a direct way.

Mel and Danny came in just as Pam was about to move the easels yet again. She got them settled in front of their canvases and adjusted the height so they were comfortable. She kept her focus on the details of art. The lighting, the numbers on the oil tubes, the careful arrangement of tools. Safe and unemotional. The parts of painting she could share with others.

"Where's the paint?" Danny asked, picking up a brush and feathering it across the blank canvas. Pam took the brush out of his hand and put it back on the table.

"You'll get that later. First I want you to decide what you want to paint, and then we'll sketch a pencil outline of the scene."

"I want to paint the surfers we saw yesterday," Danny said.

"You are not going surfing in the ocean," Mel said.

"I said I wanted to paint a surfer, not be one. And why can't I?"

"Because it's dangerous. You could hit your head on a rock or get caught in an undertow."

"Aw, Mom, I know how to swim and—"

Pam snapped her fingers until she had their attention. "Can you argue about this later?"

"There's nothing to argue about. No way is he going to—"

"Mel? What are you going to paint?"

"The garden with the boat in it," Mel said, pointing out the window.

"Bo-ring," Danny muttered.

Pam sighed with relief when she finally got them to stop talking and start drawing. She was starting to rethink her earlier regrets about not taking the university job. Two students were difficult enough. She wasn't sure she could handle a whole class of them. Of course, this was nothing like a university class—this was fun, humorous, a way for a mother and son to bond. And while she could lecture about technique and stroke pressure and the properties of oil paints all day, she didn't think she'd be able to handle it for much longer if Mel and

Danny kept treating the lesson like family game night. She walked over to look at Danny's sketch.

"Not bad," she said. "But do you see how you're putting everything in this small corner of the canvas? Three-quarters of your painting will be sky. You could add some rocks here...Mel, why don't you come over and look at this, too?"

Pam drew light lines to section off the canvas. This she could do. Like when Lisa asked her opinion on a drawing, or when she analyzed pieces before accepting them in her gallery. Stand outside and judge someone else's work. Untouched and unmoved. "Pretend you're looking at the beach through a camera lens. If you shift a little to the right, you're going to get a more interesting scene. You'd have some beach curving around here, and a few pieces of driftwood..."

Pam continued to sketch as she talked about balance and composition. After a few minutes she stopped and sheepishly stepped away from the easel, bumping into Mel who stood close behind her. "Sorry. I don't want to tell you what to paint."

"Amazing," Mel said, her hand resting lightly on Pam's waist. "You re-created the exact scene from yesterday."

"Yeah, thanks," Danny said. "I could totally see what you were talking about while you were drawing."

Pam gave him back the pencil as if it were as hot as a beach rock on a summer day. Tempting to touch, but burning her when she did. "Why don't you add some more detail or make any changes you want. Mel, let's see what you've drawn." She studied Mel's canvas in silence for a few moments. "Um, why is the boat so...big?" she asked tentatively. She chose her words carefully. Mel had asked for a lesson, wanted to be taught, but Pam was wary of giving her opinions on a sensitive subject like art to someone she was sleeping with. She had learned two rules about art critique. Only give advice if asked. And never give advice to a partner, even if asked.

"Because it was so heavy to carry," Mel said. "I made it extra big to represent the enormous backache I had the next day."

Danny gave a snort of laughter and Mel grinned at him.

"Really?" Pam asked.

"No. I just drew it. I didn't realize I was making it bigger than it should be."

Mel's smile was beautiful. She looked impish and close to laughter. Completely at ease with herself and with any comments Pam made. Pam felt her body relax as she gestured at the garden she could see through the window. "Look at the proportions of that rock and rosebush compared to the boat." She tapped the rock Mel had drawn on her canvas. "Now, look at how differently you've drawn them."

"What about perspective?" Mel asked. "Aren't you supposed to make some objects larger so you can tell they're in front of other things? Maybe I wanted to show that the boat is closer to us."

Danny stepped around so he could see the canvas. "So it's like a mile closer?"

Pam covered her mouth, but not quickly enough to hide her laugh. She glanced at Mel's face to make sure she didn't seem hurt by Danny's teasing. Instead, Mel had joined in their laughter. She threw her pencil at Danny, and he made a show of ducking behind his canvas.

"Go back to your surfers, dude," Mel said. She picked up a new pencil and handed it to Pam. "Here, fix it so I can get to the coloring-it-in part."

"This isn't a paint-by-numbers class," Pam protested. Still, it would be easier to show Mel what she meant instead of explaining it. "But I'll help this time. It's all about creating the proper ratios."

Mel watched Pam's hand as she superimposed her version of the garden scene over the disproportionate one Mel had drawn. A series of lines and curves gradually took shape until the picture Mel had originally conceived in her mind was suddenly on the canvas in front of her. She could see the difference between her drawing and Pam's, and she *sort of* understood the lecture about proportion and perspective Pam delivered as she sketched, but Mel knew there was no way she'd be able to match Pam's talent. She must have some sort of spatial deficiency, but she didn't care. She could have watched Pam's fingers all day as they lightly gripped the pencil and effortlessly flew across the canvas. She wanted to toss the pencil aside and get those hands on her...

"Do you see what I did there?" Pam asked. Mel made a vaguely affirmative noise, hoping Pam hadn't expected a more detailed answer. Apparently she didn't because she put the pencil on the table and walked over to the paints. She squeezed some paint on two palettes and spent a few minutes blending them without speaking. Then she demonstrated a couple of brushstrokes on the sky portion of Danny's canvas.

"This first time, don't worry about anything but getting a feel of putting paint on the canvas," she said as she handed Mel her palette covered with dollops of color. "If you don't like the tone, blend it with a little black or white to make it darker or lighter. Or just layer a new color over the top. Let yourselves experiment right now, and then we'll start to add technique."

Mel dipped her brush in some white paint and tentatively spread it on her canvas. She painstakingly outlined the edge of the boat, wincing each time her brush crossed the pencil line Pam had drawn. She wanted to go out to the garage and get her painter's tape so she'd be able to paint a straight line, but she didn't think that would be what Pam considered experimenting. She smudged some gray paint over the white in an attempt to give the boat a weathered look and tried to concentrate on her efforts and ignore Danny's disparaging remarks about the gray blobs on her painting and his comments about how fulfilled and safe his surfers looked. The harder Mel tried to perfect her painting, the worse it seemed to get. She finally lowered her brush and opened her mouth to call Pam over to help.

She closed her mouth again without making a sound. Pam was at her easel, her palette balanced against her hip as if it were part of her body. Watching Pam, she could see what real concentration was. Focus. Absorption. She had seen Pam painting once before, when she'd created the picture of the storm's aftermath on the beach, but this was different. There was a sense of calm this time. Pam's body and mind seemed to know what they were doing and had taken control without the struggle Mel had witnessed that afternoon. But Mel could see the same intensity on her face, in her posture, as if some vision in her head had turned into reality and had completely blotted out the world around her.

Mel had seen this expression before. When Pam leaned over her, about to kiss her, and looked at her as if she was something to be treasured, memorized. As if she mattered. But maybe that intensity was only something Mel had imagined, something she wanted to see. She didn't interrupt Pam. Instead, she continued to stroke color on her canvas, some of her attention on her work and most of it on Pam.

Pam could sense when Mel's attention had turned on her, but she couldn't stop painting. She had covered her palette with bright colors, intending to doodle to give Danny and Mel some time to play with their paintings. But from the moment the medicinal smell of oils had hit her, the moment she had dabbed green and then yellow paint onto her canvas, she had been instantly drawn into the scene.

No need to sketch any guidelines or borders. She finished the smear of paint that was Danny's imagined kite, and she continued to fill the sky with swirls of color and movement, a chaos of tails and wings and flapping silk. She and Diane had taken Kevin to the kite festival the same year she had observed the little girl who now hung in Mel's dining room. She was recapturing the day, when she and Diane had shared a rare afternoon of closeness and freedom. When Kevin had laughed in delight at the riot of color streaming overhead.

But there were differences in this scene. The people Pam added to the painting were abstract, static dabs of color anchored by the flying kites. But the dark-haired boy holding the duck kite was definitely Danny. Mel clearly stood in the crowd of spectators and watched. In a moment of respite from her painting, Pam looked at the beach she had created, surprised to find Diane and Kevin weren't there. But she was. Behind Mel, blending in the crowd but unmistakably her.

Usually when she finished a painting, it was the imposition of her memories onto the new image that disconcerted her. Today the lack of memory tugged at her mood, drawing her away from the euphoria of completion and into the depressed state she had come to expect with her art. She wanted to curl up and cry, fling the painting against a wall and destroy it, slash paint across its surface until the picture was no longer visible. But she wasn't alone.

Mel and Danny were standing by their easels, their own paintings finished. They were waiting for her to continue the lesson, and Pam surprised herself by shaking off her pain and walking over to them as if nothing were wrong. But everything was wrong. Blended, mixed up. Past and present, her old family and this new one to which she didn't even belong, memories that existed yet didn't exist.

She came to Danny's easel first. She was too disoriented, too shaken to continue the lesson. She needed to make an excuse and leave the studio, but Danny's picture and his smug-looking smile as he waited for her comments were somehow enough to distract her from her jumbled thoughts. Enough to ground her in the present again. Surprisingly, enough to make her want to laugh. She tried to take in the painting as a whole, but she couldn't stop staring at the surfers. "This is…well, you have a good sense of color. The tones are well-balanced and…did you drip paint down here?"

She pointed at the surfers, black stick figures with bright white-and-red marks on their heads.

"Those are their eyes and mouths. See? They're smiling and having fun. Who wouldn't want her son to be one of them?"

"They look like zombies," Mel said with a snort. "Way to convince me."

"This is supposed to be art, not propaganda," Pam said. She had been pulled away from the trauma of painting too quickly. Back to lightness and fun. But she was okay. She'd get through it. "Let's see yours, Mel. Oh."

Pam searched for something positive to say about Mel's painting. "You paint in sort of a primitive style. And nice bold colors. We might want to try something more abstract next time."

"Ouch!" Danny said.

Mel put her hands on her hips. "So what I hear you saying is, I don't have any talent, but if I just sling some paint at the canvas, I'll have a slim chance of producing something decent?"

"Hey, if monkeys can do it—"

Pam held up her hand to stop Danny from finishing his sentence. "I'm not comparing anyone to a monkey. And there's much more to an abstract painting than random slashes of paint. Maybe we should stop for the day. You both did very well for your first lesson, although now your teacher needs a drink."

"Thanks, that was fun," Danny said, giving Pam an awkward one-armed hug. "I'm going for a walk on the beach before dinner."

He left the studio and whistled for Piper to join him as he headed for the beach access. "There's a girl about his age who lives a few cabins down the beach," Mel told Pam. "At least he's getting some exercise walking back and forth in front of her house. Now can I see your painting?"

"*Your* painting, if you want it," Pam said as she followed Mel to her easel. "I have some primary colored sea glass I could use on the kites. It might look nice in the rose-colored room on the third floor."

"Dragon fruit," Mel said as she stared at the kite painting. "That's the color of the walls. And you're right. This will be perfect. It's like a rainbow, and I don't know how you can make oil paint...*move* like this. It's so beautiful."

Pam stepped behind her, wrapping her arms around Mel's waist and leaning her chin on Mel's shoulder. Somehow, from this angle, it was easier to look at her own painting without being bombarded by too many emotions to process. Mel leaned into her embrace. Pam welcomed the physical jolt as it ran through her. Sex, bodies, sweat, touch. Smells that would be strong enough to wipe away the lingering scent of paint. She needed to get Mel out of here. Into bed.

"That's Danny, isn't it? Flying the green-and-yellow kite? You captured his posture even though there aren't many details on your people."

"I can paint in some zombie eyes and bright red smiles, if you want me to," Pam offered. Even as she joked with Mel, she considered her words. She had earned her reputation as an artist by painting portraits, but since Diane took Kevin away, she had never returned to them. Now the infrequent humans in her art were faceless, unfinished figures.

Mel turned in her arms and rested her forehead against Pam's. "Are you okay? I know painting is private for you, and Danny and I were here..."

Pam brushed her lips against Mel's, just a taste, a reassurance. "I didn't mind having you in here at all," she said. Not a lie, but not exactly true.

She kissed Mel again instead of saying what else was on her mind. That having Mel and Danny talk to her, ease her tension and bring her back to reality, had made this the least difficult painting she had completed in years. Whether she struggled to paint or failed to paint, she had always kept her efforts private. But not this time. The connection she felt with Mel, her son, the painting wasn't something she could bring up with Mel because it was too intense. Too frightening. Mel and Danny were too damned close.

Pam had always felt emotionally vulnerable after painting. Hypersensitive to touch, to smells and light, to even her breath moving in and out of her lungs. Just because she could feel her enhanced emotions while she was kissing Mel was no reason to think their attachment was deepening. It was simply a matter of proximity. Her body's reaction to Mel's hands as they slid around her neck and into her hair had more to do with the act of opening the channels so she could pour her feelings onto the canvas than with her feelings for Mel. Any attractive woman would have made her heart beat faster, or made her shift uncomfortably as she felt wetness seeping through her underwear. She had to believe that, or she'd have to leave right now. She lifted her head and rubbed Mel's upper arms.

"You're cold," she said. "You have goose bumps."

"Yeah, cold," Mel said. "I need to find a way to heat the studio. We have at least an hour before Danny comes back. We could go inside and warm up."

"My room?" Pam asked.

"Your room," Mel agreed, pulling Pam behind her toward the house.

CHAPTER TWENTY

P am sorted through the box and picked out all the sky-blue puzzle pieces before she started to fit them in place. Danny and Mel had started the puzzle the night before, after dinner, and they had completed the outline of the jigsaw puzzle. Pam had been tempted to join them, to continue the camaraderie she had felt during their painting lesson and the closeness to Mel that lingered from their lovemaking. But she had gone out instead, to check on the progress of her house and to meet with Tia about her upcoming art show fundraiser. Now Danny had gone back to Salem, and Mel was curled on the living-room couch reading some DIY books. And Pam worked alone on the puzzle.

"I was going to reface the kitchen cabinets, but since I sanded the doors I think they look pretty good," Mel said. "I might just refinish them instead."

Pam fished out a piece of half sky, half lighthouse and put it in place before she looked up. "It's cheaper to refinish," she said. Mel uncurled her long legs and propped her bare feet on the back of the couch. Who knew Black Watch plaid pajamas could be so seductive? Pam turned her attention back to the puzzle.

"And I'd rather spend the money on a fancy new stove."

Pam finished a chunk of sky before she glanced back at Mel. "Paint or stain?"

"I wanted to use a Mediterranean blue to pick up the color of the backsplash, but it might be too dark for such a small space. I'd like to do a color wash with a sponge to soften the tone and give the cabinets some texture."

Mel talked about glazes and base coats, and Pam tried to focus on her words. Instead, she found herself distracted by the way Mel kept pulling a lock of her hair toward her mouth as if she thought it was still long enough to suck. She was so fucking sexy Pam wanted to toss her on the ground and take her while she talked about sinks and ovens and drains…

"Why are you looking at me like that?" Mel asked. "I'm boring you with all of this, aren't I?"

"Not at all," Pam managed to say. "I'm listening. You were talking about installing a garbage disposal."

Mel continued her monologue about kitchen remodeling while Pam struggled to regain control. It was okay to find Mel sexy when she was *being* sexy. But to get hot because she was trying to chew on her hair while she talked about a garbage disposal? Pam had crossed a line somewhere, and she needed to find her way back to the safe side.

The puzzle forgotten, Pam looked around the living room. Puzzles, games, books, movies. Throw rugs and chairs and a sofa. Mel had turned the old house into a home. A place where her guests would feel cozy and safe. A place where Pam was starting to settle in and get too comfortable. And she was part of the home now, too. Not merely a visitor, she was present on the walls of almost every room in the house. Even the living room had a place reserved for her fifth commission piece. The blank space on the wall hovered over Pam, daring her to fill it and put her mark on this room as well.

"My house is done," she said, interrupting something Mel was saying about bread ovens.

"What?"

"The construction on my house. It's finished. Piper and I can move back home and let you have your room back." The work had been completed a week ago. Pam didn't mention that. Maintaining the weak illusion of having stayed this long because she'd had to, not because she'd wanted to, was comforting.

Mel took the index card she had been using to jot down notes and stuck it in her book, lining the edge up precisely to buy time before she answered. *Step one of ending the affair. Move out of casual sex partner's house.* She had been aware of this inevitability since their picnic in the park—even before that. And she had seen the change coming in Pam's eyes yesterday, when she'd resurfaced after finishing her kite painting. But Mel had convinced herself that leaving this dead-end relationship was necessary if she wanted to be more open to love. Necessary, but so damn sad. And so soon. She had hoped for a longer time with Pam. More sex, more companionship.

"You know I've enjoyed having you here."

"It's been fun for me, too," Pam said, her eyes still on the puzzle. "But you'll be full of guests soon. I can't keep shuffling between Danny's room and upstairs when he comes to visit."

"Of course not," Mel agreed. But sometimes she forgot. On nights like this one, when they spent time together and talked. Nights when it was easy to forget they were supposed to mean nothing more to each other than sex. Nights that seemed worlds away from casual.

Pam came over and sat next to her on the sofa. "Mel, Danny asked about us. When we were at the park."

"Oh?" Mel wasn't sure what bothered her more. That Danny had guessed before she'd had a chance to tell him, or that he had talked to Pam instead of her. "What did you say?"

Pam shrugged and took hold of Mel's hand. "The truth. I said we liked each other a lot, but we weren't dating or anything. More or less. I can't remember what I said. But he seemed fine with…everything."

"Well, he likes you. And I appreciate you being honest with him. I just thought we could keep it a secret until I was ready to talk to him," Mel said, silently adding, *Since it wasn't like we were hiding a serious relationship.* But she had been serious about Pam. She had tried to fight it, had tried to be fine with no hope, no promises. She knew that now, and of course Danny had been able to see it.

Pam scooted closer and wrapped an arm around Mel's shoulders, kissing her on the temple. "It's for the best, Mel. Our arrangement worked because we wanted each other, and neither of us was looking for anything more than sex. But it'll be better for Danny if I'm not around as much. If he doesn't get used to me being here."

Step two. The it's-for-the-best speech. But why did Pam have to hold her so tenderly while she said it? As if she heard Mel's thoughts, Pam's caresses slowly changed from tender to intimate. She gently cupped Mel's breast and stroked her thumb over her nipple. Mel gritted her teeth to keep from moaning, hating her body for so quickly responding to Pam's touch even when her emotions were a confused mess. Nothing was certain except she didn't want Pam to go. But what was the alternative? Move in together officially? They had both agreed to a purely physical, purely temporary relationship. Still, logic wasn't convincing enough to cool Mel's heated response. She turned her face away from Pam's kiss.

Pam sat back slightly. "What's wrong, Mel?" She kissed Mel's neck, dragging her soft lips along Mel's jawline. "We have tonight. And we don't have to stop seeing each other like this. I just won't be living here anymore."

Mel didn't answer, but she waged a small battle within her mind. She was acting like a teenager who was only starting to date. They had defined an adult relationship, and Pam was only sticking to the rules they had both agreed to follow. Pam had always been honest about where she was, and she couldn't be expected to change because Mel was opening up to the idea of forever. Mel turned back and allowed Pam to kiss her, but she was the one who pulled Pam's sweatshirt off and threw it on the floor. And she was the one who slid her fingers under the waistband of Pam's sweats and made her come within seconds.

Pam packed her things and moved out the next day. Mel had been silent all morning and left for the hardware store directly after breakfast. Pam had to take three trips to get all her belongings home. She had come with only a few clothes and necessities, but over the past few weeks she had gradually moved books and extra clothing and painting supplies into Mel's inn. She moved sluggishly through the process, throwing things haphazardly into boxes, lugging them to her car, moving out of the house as if fighting a strong current.

She took one last glance at the starfish mosaic before she shut the door firmly. Every painting had been a struggle. She felt like a salmon swimming upstream to spawn, leaping rung by rung up a fish ladder. Out of a long-ingrained habit, she filed away the image of the salmon, weakened but sailing upward. Fighting against the odds. Would she ever have the chance—or the desire—to actually paint it? If she wanted to, she needed to leave. Love and loss had taken away her art once. Pam opened the back door for Piper and got in the driver's seat. She only paused to light a cigarette before she backed out of the driveway.

CHAPTER TWENTY-ONE

Pam hurried back to her gallery after lunch and locked the door behind her. She went into the small back office and pulled a fresh canvas from the stack she stored behind the desk. She didn't know why she had continued the habit of storing unused canvases in various places around her home and gallery when she so rarely painted—well, at least until about eight weeks ago, when she'd started on the commission pieces for Mel's inn—but right now, two weeks since she'd moved home, she was glad to have a clean and prepared surface at hand.

Her haste was so at odds with the subject she had to paint that she almost lost her focus. Then the image rose up again, and she began squeezing colors onto her palette. She had been staring out to sea during her lunchtime walk, and she had almost stepped on a huge jellyfish lying like a puddle on the sand. Only Piper's sharp bark had alerted her in time to break her stride and avoid the creature. It had oozed along the beach, its movement imperceptible but for the telltale indentation behind it, revealing its path.

Pam quickly streaked a thin wash of Payne's gray over the surface to make a blue-gray ground for the painting. While it was still wet, she stippled paint over the base for the damp sand. Dry sand created a border along the bottom of the canvas, and the edge of a wave defined the top. She played with several blends of colors on her palette before she sketched the jellyfish slightly to the left of center, its trail leading off the canvas to the right. She couldn't reproduce the quivering blob with her heavy oils, but she visualized the sea glass in place before she even finished the early stages of painting. Pale blues and grays and clear, polished glass would bring life and lightness to the heavy mass of paint and imitate the glistening reflection of sunlight off the creature's surface.

Smudge this line a little. Yes, perfect. Pam's brush froze on the canvas. She held her breath and carefully finished the stroke before lifting the brush. Where had the thought come from? Where was her usual disconnect from the work? She was right there, watching the painting unfold, making adjustments so it matched her vision, holding both the painting-in-progress and the finished product in her mind. Instead of locking part of herself away and letting the painting happen. Almost against her will. Now she was present, making conscious decisions about the work. She slowly put her brush against the canvas again, exhaling through her mouth as she stroked across the painting. Seeing the paint as it spread, anticipating the next layers of color, visualizing the completed and sea-glass studded mosaic.

Pam's mind moved ahead even further, beyond the completed picture, and she saw Mel hanging the painting in what Pam called the Gray Room. She named the rooms by their colors, but Mel had taken to referring to them by their paintings. She had a Starfish Room, a Seascape Room, a Storm Room, a Kite Room, and soon she'd have a Jellyfish Room. Pam refused to use those terms out loud, but under Mel's influence she was beginning to secretly follow Mel's lead.

She had been unaccustomed to living with her art. Over the past years, she had put her paintings up for sale as soon as she had managed to finish them. But the daily exposure to the pieces while she had been living with Mel had worn away some of her discomfort. She hadn't spent a lot of time contemplating the paintings as they hung on the walls, but she had at least been able to walk past them without cringing. She had to admit that Mel's excitement with each new painting was a big part of the reason she was slowly allowing herself to accept inspiration when it came instead of fighting so hard to ignore it.

Pam stepped back from the easel and from the vision of Mel hanging the picture in her inn. She had seen jellyfish on the sand hundreds of times, but never before had she felt so compelled to paint one. Maybe she felt a kinship with the slow, shapeless animal. These past weeks with Mel had left her feeling as if she were crawling through sludge in an attempt to keep pace with Mel's explosion of growth. From her inn to her garden to her relationship with Danny, Mel was transforming at a rapid rate. Pam, by comparison, barely was able to drag herself from painting to painting, from isolation to an uneasy companionship. She'd settle back into her own pace as soon as she delivered the last of her paintings to Mel.

Or would she? Go back to her sluggish pace of one painting a year, when she had just finished her fourth in less than twice as many weeks? She had been so accustomed to denying herself this outlet, this way of expressing her pain. Her pain and vulnerability, those feelings too intense to express any other way than through her art. She had blamed Mel for forcing her to paint, but Mel had only asked. Pam had picked up the brushes, had let the images pour out, had slowly moved from expressing her pain to easing it.

She looked closely at every detail of her painting. Looked at every line, every texture, breaking it into sections as she analyzed her work. She made some small changes to the jellyfish's shape so it didn't appear so symmetrical. Darkened the sand in one area, so the contrast between wet and dry was more pronounced. She had fought Mel's positive interpretations of her paintings at first. Then she had started to see them through Mel's eyes. Indirectly, cautiously. Always on guard against the chance of being hurt again. But she didn't need the filter anymore.

Her vision was direct and clear, even through her tears. Seeing the painting objectively, but still investing all her emotion in it. Somehow Mel's courage as she rebuilt her life and her inn had helped Pam find the courage to stop denying her art. The return to being an artist had been a long one. Eight years followed by eight daring and complex weeks. The eight weeks she had known Mel. Pam wanted to share her tentative hope, the hesitant resurfacing of her abilities, with Mel. But she couldn't. She'd share this painting with Mel, but not the breach in her protective shell. Not the aching joy she felt as her desire to express and create broke free. Love had almost destroyed her, as an artist and as a person. Being in love, losing her love. How many decades would it take for her to get over Mel if they started a real romance and failed? Pam might never pick up a brush again. She had used up all her courage. She wasn't brave enough to take the chance.

❖

Mel slowly peeled back the blue painter's tape from around the window sash. The neat white trim contrasted nicely with the slate-gray walls. She had chosen colors with more depth for the third-floor rooms. Pam's kite painting hung next door, against a rosy background. Pam was delivering the painting for this room today. She had given Mel some suggestions for colors but wouldn't tell her what she had painted.

Mel stopped to admire the panoramic vista offered by the upper-level rooms. They shared a bath, but the view more than made up for the slight inconvenience. Plus, the two rooms worked well as a suite for families, and Mel had already booked the full suite several times for the following month. She sighed and turned away from the ocean to gather her scraps of tape. She was doing all this work for other people to enjoy the views and the rooms while she languished alone in her downstairs dungeon. She was lonely without Pam and Danny and nervous about her soon-to-arrive guests. She had come up with the idea of an inn so she could have more people in and out of her life. But a few days with Pam in her bed, in her house, sharing her world, had spoiled her. She wasn't certain she'd be able to live her whole life like this. She didn't think she'd be able to survive with only intermittent companionship, with no lasting closeness.

Her body, her senses wanted Pam. Pam, windblown and smiling after drifting through ocean winds, a storm replacing the calm sea of her eyes when she took Mel in her arms. The taste of her kiss, as wild and uncontrollable as the tides. The feel of her arms, so strong and comforting, as the crashing waves of release washed over Mel's body. Mel had spent so many years denying her body, and now she was tempted to keep their affair alive. But her instincts whispered a warning so quiet it was almost lost in the turmoil in her mind. She wanted more. She wanted everything. Sex, yes. Definitely. But love, too. Companionship and honesty.

Pam wasn't ready to give her anything but sex. And it was almost enough, but not quite. Mel had to keep searching, find a new path to the future she wanted. Pam had emotional limits because of her past, because she had been hurt, because of things Mel still didn't fully understand. But would the women Mel was going to meet be any more available? Travelers, passing through town before they returned to their real lives. Short days in which to find a spark of interest, to try to find someone who didn't fail when compared to Pam.

She heard footsteps on the stairs. Pam. Bringing her fourth painting. At this rate, she'd be done with the commission within the week. Without the business deal to link her to Pam, Mel doubted they'd see each other at all except for accidental meetings in town. She had been so excited when Pam finished the first mosaics. Now, she dreaded the final one.

"Wow, the walls look great," Pam said, walking sideways to fit through the door with the large painting. She turned it to face Mel. "The color will be perfect with this."

Mel stared at the jellyfish. She had seen the creatures on the beach but had never expected Pam to paint one. She loved it. "It's different," she said, unable to articulate what she meant. Pam had painted a *portrait*. Of a globby jellyfish, but it was a portrait. Her other paintings were distant, as if Pam was standing as far away as possible. This time, however, she had stepped close. Stared her subject in the eye—or whatever it was a jellyfish had. She had somehow captured nuance and subtlety in the heavy oils. Mel wasn't sure what this step meant for Pam, but she knew it was progress. Special.

Pam laughed self-consciously. She had become accustomed to Mel's enthusiastic responses to her work, and the implied criticism she heard hurt. This painting wasn't more technically proficient or conceptually interesting than her others. Mel had no reason to like it better, no way to know how different the *process* of painting had been. Why had Pam expected her to understand? "Saying it's different is like saying a blind date is an interesting conversationalist."

"I didn't mean *bad* different. It's beautiful and unique. You can see sunlight glistening on it. I just meant, well, I've never seen you get so close to a subject. So single-minded in your focus. You've changed."

"Whoa," Pam said, backing away. She wasn't changing, wasn't turning into whatever Mel suddenly seemed to see. Vulnerability shifted to anger in a second. The hint of her former creative spark was still too new, too fragile to share. She had needed Mel's praise somehow. Her appreciation of the painting. But Pam wasn't ready to have the focus shifted off the art and onto her as an artist just yet. Not until she had regained some control, some of her old ability to paint at will. Some proof that the tentative confidence she had experienced while painting had some foundation in reality. "Don't read too much into it. I saw a jellyfish and I painted it. You know what they say, sometimes a cigar is just a cigar."

"Careful, the trim is still wet," Mel said, pointing at the wall behind Pam. Her voice rose in pitch to match Pam's.

Pam stopped backing up and stood her ground. "If you don't like it, I can try to paint something else…"

"I like it. I want it in my inn, so don't try to replace it. I wasn't trying to offer a psychological analysis of you as an artist. I just meant the subject and how you treated it is different from the other mosaics."

"Okay," Pam said. She was reacting foolishly and she tried to calm down. Just because Mel made the observation about her focus didn't mean she was trying to interfere with Pam's creativity. Dissect it until it disappeared. "I'm sorry," she said. "I've been…a little edgy since I moved back home. I miss, well, I miss you. Having sex with you, I mean."

Mel rubbed her arms. "I miss it, too. The sex part. And I'm lonely here, but I'll be better this weekend when my guests come."

Pam carefully put the jellyfish mosaic on the floor. She wanted to take Mel in her arms, keep Mel talking about sex. Make some joke about her *trim* comment and lighten the mood. Strip off her clothes and initiate the new guest room. Because that's what casual sex partners did.

But she had to let go of the illusion. She and Mel were anything but casual. Mel had been the key to unlocking her old talent, her broken love of art and creation. And Mel was the one person with the ability to make Pam lose everything once again.

"You'll be fine. We'll both be fine," she said. She walked away from Mel and from her painting. From the only part of herself she dared to offer.

CHAPTER TWENTY-TWO

The soft *ding-dong* of an old-fashioned doorbell startled Mel. She had installed the electronic chime on her front door, choosing the homiest sound-effect option, but no one had activated it until now. Her guests. She was tempted to stay in the kitchen until they gave up and went away, but she reluctantly put her eggs back in the fridge and walked out to greet them.

"Hi, I'm Mel. Welcome to the Sea Glass Inn," she said, forcing a smile.

"I'm Angie, and this is my partner Sara and our friend Tracy."

Mel shook hands with the three women. Angie had called last month to make this reservation for the group—her first official guests, since the wedding had only booked because they'd lost their original venue. She should have been excited, eager to celebrate the momentous occasion of launching her inn, but she felt curiously empty inside, lonely without Pam. She had gotten attached too quickly, and just as fast, their relationship was over. She had lost part of herself by getting too close to someone, just as she'd feared.

"What a beautiful old house," Angie continued as Mel picked up one of the suitcases and started up the stairs. "After talking to you and hearing about all the renovations you had to do, I was expecting to be staying in a construction zone. But this place is gorgeous."

"Thank you," Mel said, with a smile that felt more natural than her earlier one. She felt a mix of shyness and pride at the praise.

"Is this the original molding?" Tracy asked.

Mel halted in the middle of the staircase. "It's original, but I had to fill in some big chips and replace some whole sections. Here, and here," she said, pointing to the repaired areas. The project had taken her hours. "The joins aren't very smooth. I did this section first because I thought people would be less likely to stop on the stairs and notice. I improved, though. You can barely tell what I replaced in the dining room."

Tracy laughed. "Sorry to call attention to it. I promise I'll go up and down the stairs with my eyes closed from now on. But you did an excellent job—that's very exacting work."

Mel was surprised how pleased she was at the compliment. She carried the suitcase into the first room and then showed Tracy to hers. All three of her guests immediately went to examine and praise Pam's seascape, and then the storm painting. She had originally planned to put Tracy in the Starfish Room, the room Pam had used, but she couldn't handle having a stranger sleeping in Pam's bed. Eventually she would have to fill the room, but not yet. Forgetting about Pam was going to be very difficult when Mel had these massive reminders in every room. She endured the few minutes of discussion about Pam, her gallery, and the other paintings. And the inevitable tour through the inn to see the other mosaics.

Finally, Mel herded her guests back into their rooms. She would get over it eventually. She would let go of the weeks of sharing a house, and then a bed, with Pam. As Mel went through the motions of showing her guests where they could find extra blankets and pillows, she told herself she needed to take a lesson from Pam and approach their relationship with logic and reason, not feelings. She had come to the ocean to start her own business and live independently for once in her life. But she had given Pam enough power to upset her equilibrium. To make her wonder what she could have done differently to keep Pam here. She knew the answer. Nothing. Pam hadn't wanted to stay.

Mel tried to refocus on her guests. "I can make a picnic lunch for you to take on your bike ride tomorrow. And if you're looking for a place to eat, there's a binder full of menus from local restaurants in the living room. Breakfast will be at eight."

"If you have time while we're here, I'd enjoy a tour of the house," Tracy said. "I've done a ton of remodeling in my old Victorian in Seattle. We could compare notes on painting techniques."

Mel hesitated in the doorway. She noticed Angie and Sara exchange smiles behind Tracy's back. The realization stunned her for a moment. Tracy was obviously asking to spend more time with her. Tracy was interested. *In her.* She felt flustered and was about to make an excuse to put Tracy off when she suddenly wondered what Pam would do. Pam would flirt and would casually make a date with Tracy because she was an ideal candidate. Only in town for a few days. Very pretty with her shoulder-length brown hair and long legs. Mel didn't feel an instant attraction, an irresistible pull, as she had with Pam. But maybe a sexual connection needed time. Maybe it didn't have to be so natural and overwhelming as it had been with Pam.

"I'd like that," Mel said. "Catch me any time you're free. And if you're nice, I might let you spackle something."

She left the room and her guests' laughter behind and went downstairs to the kitchen. She returned to the task of preparing the ingredients for tomorrow's breakfast, quietly shocked that she had flirted with a stranger. Awkwardly flirted, but flirted nonetheless. She hadn't done that for years. Since her crush on Danny's teacher. But she hadn't been free then, and her overtures had been hesitant and short-lived. This was different. She was free. Single. Anything could happen. She whisked a bowl of eggs and cream and vanilla for a batch of muffins and covered it with plastic wrap before putting it in the fridge. The dry ingredients were already sifted and ready, so in the morning, she would only need to blend them and add some fruit right before she baked them.

Her methodical approach to breakfast was soothing. She knew she looked efficient and in control as she browned sausage and peppers that she would add to eggs and bake in a casserole. The melon was already cut and macerating with lime juice and mint leaves. Steel-cut oats were sitting in the Crock-Pot, ready to cook overnight. But the steady and organized prep work she was doing was completely at odds with her jumbled thoughts. She hadn't expected to connect like this with her guests, but now that she was running the inn she wondered why she was so surprised. She was hosting people who chose to be in a more intimate bed-and-breakfast instead of an anonymous, large hotel. And by advertising her inn as gay friendly, she had inadvertently set up a convenient dating pool.

She paused in her cooking to answer the phone. A couple traveling with their two grandchildren wanted to stay for a few nights in January. She would put them on the third floor, in the Jellyfish and Kite Rooms with their shared bath. She carefully entered the information on the spreadsheet she and Danny had created for her bookings, and she was amazed to see how many rooms she had reserved for the month. And she was already getting enough calls to hint at a full inn for the summer.

Mel returned to the kitchen and stacked her dirty dishes in the dishwasher. She could see the growth of her business so clearly. Phone calls, booked rooms, painted walls. But when she looked at her personal life, all she saw was what was missing. She'd called Pam a mistake. Thought she'd lost part of herself during their affair. But her brief interchange with Tracy proved her wrong. What would she have done two months ago? Would she have been too embarrassed to be playful? Would she even have noticed Tracy's interest? Before the inn—before Pam—she hadn't seen herself as attractive, certainly not in a sexual way. Closed off, shut down, too old, too late. But not one of those phrases applied to her anymore. They never had, but she had believed in them anyway.

Scenes from her time with Pam flashed through Mel's mind. The floor, the bed, the shower, the rickety back porch. Mel smiled and felt her skin grow warm with remembered arousal. She had lost Pam but no part of herself. Every step she had taken since buying this inn had resulted in another lesson learned, and her affair with Pam was no exception. She had grown, had gained clarity about what she wanted and deserved, had opened herself up to new possibilities.

Why couldn't she have a full inn and a full life? A full inn meant nonstop work. And now it meant she'd have an opportunity for a date or two. She wiped down the counter before heading downstairs. Some transitory flirtations might be exactly what she needed to get over her obsession with Pam. She sure as hell wasn't going to sit around and wallow in self-pity.

Mel shut the door to her room and sat on her bed. Where she and Pam had spent their nights together. Near the rug where they'd shared their first citrus-scented kiss. No, she'd never be unaffected by her time with Pam. She'd probably never fully get over her. And she had a feeling Pam's unemotional and carefree approach to sex was only a veneer concealing a passionate and sensitive soul.

She had seen Pam's paintings—had seen Pam paint—and the discrepancy between her pictures and her words was clear. Pam managed to look at a beach, at a wave, at a jellyfish and take her subjects deep inside her. Hold them there until she connected them to something bigger and wider and deeper than what she saw in front of her. She claimed to be noncommittal, happy to play with shallow relationships and surface emotions, yet her paintings, her memories, her love for the son she had lost revealed only depth. But Mel couldn't force Pam to acknowledge any feelings she might have when she seemed so determined to keep love, art, and emotion out of her life. The very qualities Mel wanted more than anything.

Chapter Twenty-three

Pam parked next to Lisa's van in the high school's parking lot. She hurried over to help Lisa, who had crawled in the back of her van and was wrapping protective blankets around several crates she had transported. Pam took one end of a heavy crate full of sculptures and walked backward quickly as they moved out of the drizzly afternoon and into the auditorium. They repeated the trip three more times with crates of paintings.

"I have your booth right up front," Tia said, coming over to greet them. "Did you bring any of your own paintings?"

Pam had been anticipating the question. Tia asked her the same thing at least twenty times before every annual charity art show. Pam always answered the same way. No, but she would purchase and donate a few pieces from other artists in her gallery to sell at the fundraiser for a local animal shelter.

"Yes," Pam said, enjoying the shocked expression on Tia's face. "I brought three."

"Let me see!" Tia said, pulling at the lid of one of the crates.

Pam laughed. "They're in here," she said, indicating the box at her feet. She pried open the lid and slid out one of the paintings. Tia pushed her away impatiently, but her hands gentled as she took off the bubble wrap and felt that protected the picture.

"Oh, it's perfect," she said, propping the painting against the booth's wall and stepping back to admire it. Piper ran at the water's edge, chasing a seagull and leaving paw prints in the damp sand.

"A dog painting for the shelter! We'll have plenty of animal lovers here, so this will sell right away. Is this the price you're asking? Nonsense. Give me that pen and I'll just add a one to the front of this number. Next year we'll plan to have you do an entire animal series. My neighbor has a cat that would be so handsome sitting on a sand dune."

Pam unwrapped the other two paintings and set them in a row. She listened to Tia ramble on and wondered at her complete lack of panic when Tia talked about more paintings for the next benefit, although she hoped Tia would forget about the cat idea by then. She had shocked herself by managing to get three paintings done in a week. Mel's commission for the mosaics had forced her to create, and the habit seemed to be sticking. One minute she had been laughing as Piper struggled up the beach with a huge piece of driftwood in her mouth, and the next she had been dragging out her rarely used watercolors and splashing them onto paper. A remembered scene of the dog pawing at a crab in a tide pool quickly followed. And then Piper's daily, and invariably failed, attempt to catch a seagull. Pam had liked the feel of the paint, the fluidity it gave to the dog's movements, the hazy colors of the sand and waves.

For the first time in years, she had created with a range of emotions beyond the negative ones of anger and pain. She had been enchanted by watching Piper play, and she had captured the moment. Simple. Fun. Not detached—because why paint at all if she didn't care?—but not wounded by the process. And her first thought when she finished was an almost overwhelming desire to rush over to Mel's inn and thank her, to show her the paintings, to try to express what it meant for her to create even such a small thing, like these watercolors. She didn't need to see the pictures through Mel's eyes, to rely on Mel to show her the joy here. Pam could see it on her own. She simply had wanted to share them with Mel. But her relationship with Mel was anything but simple, and she had stayed home.

"Thank you," Tia said, grabbing Pam in a big hug.

"You're welcome." Pam gave her an awkward pat on the shoulder and stepped back when Tia released her.

"So is your girlfriend coming tonight?"

"Didn't we have this conversation already? She let me stay while my house was being repaired," Pam said. She could tell Tia was teasing, but she wanted to be clear about her relationship with Mel. To protect Mel's reputation in town. She turned away and started to unpack the sculptures. "It was damaged in the storm, remember?"

"Of course. And I noticed you wisely waited a week for the paint to dry before you moved back home."

Another gallery owner arrived, and Tia went to meet him, leaving Pam mercifully alone. She set several risers of varying heights on the booth's table and covered the whole thing with a shimmery, pale-blue cloth. She arranged a series of brightly colored enamel fish sculptures on the lower level of the platform. Yes, it was true. She could have moved back home weeks before she did, but she had waited. Until her feelings grew too threatening for her to stay any longer. She hadn't answered Tia's original question about whether Mel would be coming to the art show because she didn't know. But she hoped so. Especially tonight, she had a ridiculous urge to share her watercolors and the hesitant renewal of faith in her art with Mel.

Mel and Tracy ran across the dark parking lot and burst into the auditorium, laughing and shaking raindrops everywhere. Mel immediately scanned the brightly lit room in search of Pam and just as quickly scolded herself for caring whether or not Pam was here. The entire population of Cannon Beach seemed to have flocked to the art show. Mel wasn't surprised. She had learned there was little to do in the town on a Saturday night, especially in the off-season. After so much time alone and isolated in her inn, the masses of people, smell of popcorn and hamburgers, and colorful displays of art were a welcome sight.

Mel had found she liked having people at her inn, especially after spending two weeks alone, without Danny or Pam. Seeing her inn as a success, with satisfied guests and the beautiful, comfortable rooms she had imagined, had given her a personal boost in confidence. This morning she had leaned in the living-room doorway after she'd served breakfast, sipping her coffee and chatting with her three guests. And when Tracy had mentioned she wanted to give Sara and Angie a chance to dine alone, Mel had felt perfectly comfortable suggesting they get a pizza in town and go see the art show. She suspected Tracy's comment had been motivated not only by her wish to give her friends some privacy but also by her desire to spend time with Mel, and Mel liked that. Mel had even mentioned her marriage, and Tracy, rather than judging her as Mel had assumed everyone would, had commented on how brave Mel was to start over in such a life-altering way.

A woman with spiked blond hair and a color-blocked silk tunic separated herself from the crowd and came rushing toward her. Mel glanced over her shoulder to see if she was aiming at someone else, but the woman stopped directly in front of her.

"Melinda Andrews, am I right? Proprietor of the Sea Glass Inn? I'm Tia Bell, of the Bell Gallery."

"Mel is fine. And this is Tracy, a guest at the inn." Mel put her hand out, but Tia grabbed her in a bear hug.

"No formalities here, our small community is like a family. Tracy, welcome to Cannon Beach. Do you just love staying at Mel's inn? I've heard it's fabulous. Of course, I had a feeling from the beginning about you moving here, Mel. I told everyone I saw, 'This one's going to make it,' and sure enough, you did!"

Mel wasn't certain three guests constituted "making it," and according to talk Mel had heard at the local grocery store, no one in town had been very optimistic about her venture. But any sign of acceptance as a local was welcome. "Thank you. I—"

"I've been meaning to stop by and take a tour of your inn," Tia continued, apparently comfortable carrying on a conversation without assistance. "Oh, you should have a housewarming. It'll be a great way to meet your neighbors and spread the word about your business at the same time. Word of mouth is the best way to advertise, I always say. I'll plan the party for you—it's what I do. And you should join the arts commission, and I'll give you the schedule for city council meetings. I'm sure you'll want to get involved in your new hometown. By the way, rumor has it you have some of my dear friend Pamela's artwork in your inn…Whatever you paid for them, I'll give you double."

Mel was trying to figure out how she'd possibly have time to join every committee in town, and she slowly caught up to the last part of Tia's monologue.

"My mosaics are quite definitely not for sale, but I'd love to show them to you if you stop by for coffee sometime."

"Ah, a shrewd businesswoman. Just as I suspected when I heard you had snapped up that beautiful old house. Coffee and a tour sounds divine. I'll come by Monday at three? So *good* to have met you at last, Mel. And you too, Tracy. Now I must run. Enjoy the art show, and remember all proceeds go directly to our local no-kill shelter."

"Serve decaf," Tracy said as they watched Tia accost another arrival.

Mel laughed. "So she heard a rumor I have some of Pam's paintings? I have a feeling most rumors in this town start and end with her."

Mel and Tracy walked down the first aisle. Most of the booths were filled with paintings and sculptures, but there were plenty of crafts and holiday items as well. Mel had already met more locals than she had realized while on shopping trips in town, and she had an unexpected sense of belonging as she greeted new friends every few feet. She enjoyed being with Tracy as well. The occasional brush of their shoulders and their closeness when they'd lean in to talk over the noise of the crowd was pleasant. Mel didn't have the same instant reaction she did every time Pam came near, but she felt comfortable and happy with Tracy's companionship.

Tracy stopped to buy some stained-glass Christmas ornaments, and Mel wandered alone to the end of the aisle. She scanned the paintings in each booth as she passed, hoping to find a painting with colors to match her bedroom. She had almost asked Pam for yet another mosaic, but even the thought of sleeping with a glaring reminder of Pam in her bedroom seemed masochistic. And, someday, she wouldn't want an ex in the bedroom with her and a new partner. Mel came to the end of the aisle and was about to turn around and look for Tracy when she saw a painting of a dog with a piece of wood almost its own size in its mouth, running on the beach. The dog was unmistakably Piper, the style unmistakably Pam's. Mel walked over for a closer look at the series of watercolors.

Pam motioned for Lisa to come over and finish wrapping the bronze puffin she had just sold. She had noticed Mel the moment she approached the booth, had seen her smile when she recognized Piper. Pam had the ridiculous notion she had painted those watercolors just to see that smile. Creating for someone else. Something she hadn't done so completely since her portrait work. She had painted the commissioned mosaics for Mel, for the inn, but she had used subjects that inspired *her*. Had expressed emotions she needed to purge. Had converted thoughts—thoughts she couldn't put into words—into images.

But this new balance was something unexpected. Familiar, but lost for so long. Painting because the subject made her smile, infused her with a sense of wonder and appreciation for the world around her, but also because she remembered the look on Mel's face when she met Piper for the first time, connecting with another creature after being isolated for so long. And because she liked the way Danny dropped his young adult persona and became a kid again when he played with her dog. Pam had reluctantly sold the watercolors only minutes after the show had opened, but she had wanted to keep them. Give them to Mel. But Mel might have read more into the gift than Pam meant to say.

Pam stepped up behind her. She wanted to put her arms around Mel's waist, whisper in her ear how much she had missed her, drag her out to her car and *show* her how much she had missed her. She stood there, feeling awkward and out of balance. She only missed the sex, not Mel herself. But if that were really true, she'd have no problem touching Mel, suggesting a night together. Instead, she was tempted to hide under the table until Mel left the booth. But they lived in a very small town. She couldn't avoid seeing Mel forever. She cleared her throat and Mel turned to face her.

"These are lovely. I didn't know you painted with watercolors."

"Depends on the subject," Pam said. She couldn't stop herself from stepping closer. Inhaling, searching for the scent of roses. "It's good to see you again."

"You, too," Mel said. "How's your house?"

"Good as new," Pam said. Partially true. The walls and roof were fixed, the new patches fitting seamlessly with the old. But the house wasn't right. The bed was cold. The sheets smelled wrong. The walls were empty. Pam hadn't noticed those things before. "I saw a different car parked outside your inn. Your guests must have arrived."

Someone approached them before Mel could answer. A customer. Pam sighed, irritated by the interruption.

"There you are, Mel," the woman said. She moved next to Mel, their arms just touching.

"Pam, this is Tracy, one of my guests. Tracy, Pam's the artist I was telling you about." Mel didn't move away as she made the introductions.

"Nice to meet you—I love your mosaics. They're perfect for the theme of Mel's inn."

"Thank you," Pam said stiffly. Not a customer, but one of Mel's clients. Obviously wanting to be something more. She was looking at Mel with the same kind of longing Pam guessed had been on her own face only moments before. She wondered if this woman was sleeping in her room, with her starfish. Or was she sleeping in Mel's room? Did she really need to stand so close to Mel? Pam was tempted to get the bronze puffin back and drop it on Tracy's foot. Put her out of the mood for romance.

"I'd love to buy one of these for Danny's room," Mel said. "Are all three sold?"

Pam nodded, dragging her gaze off Tracy and her thoughts off whatever the two of them might be doing together. She was the one who had told Mel she should experiment, play the field. She just hadn't expected her to start with her very first lesbian guest. She wasn't surprised this Tracy woman was interested in Mel. Who wouldn't be? Mel was sexy. Beautiful and strong and talented and interesting. And sexy. Pam had hoped to have more time than this. Time to get used to seeing Mel around town, being her friend. Time for her urges to fade. The need to touch her, the desire to feel her naked body pressed so close. Time for Pam to be able to think of Mel with another woman without wanting to scream. Maybe she'd drop the puffin on Tracy's head instead of her foot.

"They are, but don't worry. I'll paint one for Danny," Pam said. Her surprise at the ease of her offer momentarily replaced her uncalled-for jealousy. She had fought against taking Mel's original commission, but now she had no qualms about agreeing to produce a watercolor for Danny. An image of him and Piper scaling big rocks at the park slipped easily into her mind. She filed it away. She would paint it tomorrow.

"He'll love that," Mel said. "And I'll be sure to donate the money I'd have spent to the shelter."

"Cool, they can use it," Pam said. An uneasy silence followed while she wondered how she could get Mel alone again.

"How about getting that pizza now?" Tracy asked. Her voice sounded overly bright, as if she had picked up on the uncomfortable dynamic between Mel and Pam.

"Sure," Mel said. "Nice to see you again, Pam."

Mel got through dinner at Fortuna's and managed to pay enough attention to Tracy to keep up her end of the conversation. Her wandering mind often returned to Pam, though, and her unreadable expressions when Mel first turned and saw her and when Tracy walked over. Pam had stood so close, desire and promise blended together in the curve of her smile. And Pam had never failed to deliver on that promise. But Mel hadn't been able to read Pam's reaction to Tracy. Jealousy or anger? Or, even worse, indifference? There had been plenty of other women in the auditorium, so no doubt Pam had been able to find company of her own. Mel had no question about her own reaction to the thought of Pam being with someone else. She didn't like it at all.

A strong wind had blown the rain inland, and the evening was cold and clear by the time Mel pulled her Honda into the inn's driveway. She got a couple of beers out of the fridge, and she and Tracy bundled in heavy coats and sat at the top of the stairs leading to the beach.

Mel leaned against the back gate and relaxed into the intermittent talk and companionable silence. The ocean was invisible but so present she could feel the constant drone of waves inside her. High tide. She could tell just from the sound of the surf. She enjoyed Tracy's company, liked talking to her, and was surprised by how much they had in common. But the energy of the tide fueled the restlessness that had been growing inside her as the evening progressed. So different from the night when she and Pam had kissed for the first time.

She breathed deeply, pulling herself out of the past and into the present moment. Trying to forget the day she and Pam had sat in this very spot and shared a pizza and wine. When they had talked about Mel's past and the clouds and the approaching storm. But she couldn't forget because her thigh rested against the cold metal ashtray Pam had used. And the ocean breeze stirred up the smell of stale smoke. And the waving blades of sea grass that caressed Mel's hand felt as soft and centering as Pam's touch had been when she had reached out to comfort Mel. The wind brought tears to her eyes and made the muscles in her face tighten in the cold.

Tracy reached over and gently traced Mel's hand with her index finger before she slid their palms together and tightened her hold. Mel was aware of the soft comfort of Tracy's grip, the growing warmth of skin on skin, the pressure as Tracy's thumb gently massaged the top of Mel's hand. This was what she wanted. Connection, intimacy, someone who was able to talk about relationships and dating without breaking out in a nervous sweat. Tracy leaned forward and kissed her, her lips asking a question Mel answered with a yes. She kissed Tracy back, a part of her rejoicing because after so many years she felt sexy. Desirable. Hopeful. And too aware. She hadn't thought about those things when she had kissed Pam because Pam consumed her. And then she *was* those things.

Tracy pulled back with a sigh. "The artist?"

Mel didn't have to answer. She figured her feelings had been obvious from the moment she had shown her guests to their rooms and told them who had painted the mosaics. "I'm sorry."

Tracy gave her hand a squeeze and, then, released it. "Don't be. I had a feeling, but I had to try. To see if I could kiss her out of you."

Mel laughed. "I was hoping you could, too."

"Do you want to talk about it?"

"No," Mel said. She was tempted. Pour out her heart, share the feelings she had for Pam. Feelings that insistently grew stronger, more intense, even though she tried to fight them with common sense. But if she talked about them with anyone, it should be with Pam. "Thank you, though."

"I'll let you be, then." Tracy gave her a quick kiss on the cheek and stood up. "I had a fun evening, even considering how it ended. Good night."

She went back to the house and Mel stared after her. The inn's lit windows gave it a soft, welcoming look, and the glazed stones in the meandering path glistened in the diffused light. The old house had been stubborn, but Mel had made it adapt to the fragile vision she had carried in her mind. She had tried to endure her marriage by pretending to be a straight and happy wife. And she had tried to do the same thing with Pam, pretending to be satisfied with a no-strings relationship. No more. She hadn't compromised on any part of the dream she had held for her new home. She certainly wasn't going to settle for anything less when it came to love.

CHAPTER TWENTY-FOUR

Pam stepped out of her office on Tuesday afternoon and saw Mel standing by the window. Her hair was windblown and her cheeks red from the cold, as if she had been on the beach only moments before. She seemed miles away from the silk and hair spray Pam had noticed on her first visit to the gallery. When she turned and saw Pam in the doorway, her smile was different as well. Back in August, Mel's expression had been self-conscious, hopeful, sexy. But, since then, she had been tested and had succeeded. Now her smile was easy and confident. Breathtaking. Pam saw no trace of the tentative outsider Mel had been in the summer. She looked at home. In the gallery, in the ocean town, in her bulky jacket and faded jeans.

"Hi, Pam," she said, walking closer. "I need to talk to you. Come for a walk with me?"

"Sure. Lisa, you'll be okay without me here for a bit?"

"Oh, I think I can manage," Lisa said without looking up from her crossword puzzle. Pam could guess what she was thinking. Of course she'd be okay. She'd been running the gallery single-handed all morning while Pam had sat in her office and stared blankly at the tax form she was supposed to be completing. The numbers had made no sense, and the only figures she had been able to see were Mel and Tracy tangled together in Mel's sheets. She grabbed her coat and followed Mel outside.

Mel crossed the street and led them to the beach. She was silent on the short walk, and Pam's daydreams of Mel stopping by for a quickie in her office faded away. She let Mel set the pace of their meeting and didn't ask the questions she had burning in her mind. Mel was obviously a woman with something serious to say. Never a good thing. Pam saw no reason to rush into whatever trouble was ahead.

Mel climbed up to sit on a large tree trunk, which was weathered and smooth from the ocean's waves. Pam sat next to her and hugged her coat tighter against the chilled breeze. Mel stared out at the ocean for a moment, her chin-length hair whipping across her face. Finally she turned to face Pam.

"I lied. To you and to myself," she said, brushing her hair out of her eyes and tucking it behind her ear. "After all my claims to want an open, honest life, I lied. I told you I didn't want a serious relationship, that I was opposed to marriage. The truth is, I didn't like my marriage. I didn't like who I was in my marriage. But I believe in love and commitment, and I want those things in my life."

Pam felt the crashing ocean waves competing with the beating of her heart. Of course she had known Mel needed forever. As much as she had tried to convince herself Mel was like her—a player, able to separate sex from any emotional attachment—she had always expected their relationship wouldn't be enough to satisfy Mel. And Pam had let her own feelings get out of control. She had gotten involved with a woman who had come here to settle, to make a home. And she had needed to get away before Mel trapped her in the life she was building.

She had been too late, though. Mel had already trapped her. Pam wasn't satisfied with their few nights together, the few weeks they had lived in the same house. She wanted more. And if she were given months to be Mel's lover, years to be her friend, Pam still wouldn't be satisfied. She'd never get tired of Mel or bored with her. Better to stick with tourists, strangers. Because an hour or two, a night or two, was always enough. And when they left, they didn't leave a hole in your heart. An aching for more. Yes, Mel ought to have someone who loved her, was committed to only her. Forever. Not just because Mel wanted it, but because no woman could possibly be satisfied with only a brief moment in time with her.

"You deserve those things," she said. She brushed her fingers through Mel's unruly hair and cupped her cheek. "And I believe you'll find them. But not with me."

"I won't accept secrecy or being used," Mel said, raising her hand to cover Pam's. "We'd be good together. We balance each other. And I love every part of being with you. Your talent, your sensitivity, your body, your touch. But I'm offering a whole relationship. I won't settle for less."

Pam shook her head and withdrew her hand. "I care about you. More than I should. But what you want—it's just not who I am."

"I think deep inside you want the same thing. You're just afraid of it." Mel leaned over to give Pam a kiss. Her mouth lingered for a moment, and then she pulled away and stood. "Good-bye, Pam."

Pam could hear the sadness in Mel's voice, and she saw determination in her posture as she walked down the beach toward her inn, the waves breaking at her feet. Pam wanted to run after her, to convince Mel to resume their halfhearted, comfortable arrangement. But Mel was forcing her to give more than she had. She said Pam was afraid, and she might have been right. Mel had been brave enough to survive when her world shattered, to rebuild her life from scratch. Pam was too broken to match Mel's courage. She could get through, day by day, but only if she protected herself from the chance of being hurt again.

❖

Mel pushed against the wind's current as she made her way back to the inn. She had stopped just short of telling Pam she loved her, but she knew what she felt. She should be sad, brokenhearted, because Pam wouldn't accept her love, but instead she only knew a sense of lightness, as if the breeze might pick her up and fly her like a kite. She had stood up for love, for what she wanted and deserved, and somehow that mattered even more than having her feelings reciprocated.

Each receding wave seemed to erode the wall of regrets she had built around her. Regrets over how she had lived her life. The choices she had made. She was finally ready to move forward and stop reliving the past. She had hoped Pam would choose to join her, but she wasn't ready. Mel was finished with changing herself to meet other people's needs. Her love wouldn't ever go away, but eventually it would ease. Until then, until she found someone who was willing to accept and support the person she truly was, she would be fine alone. With her inn, with Danny, with her new friends and community.

❖

Pam arranged her brushes in an orderly row, from slender ones with fine-tipped hairs to a couple of thickly bristled ones for background work. She spent another half hour searching through boxes for a fan-shaped paintbrush to add to the lineup. Finally, she faced the canvas she had set up in the entryway to her home, the only place where she could find the clear morning light she needed.

Until Mel's starfish painting, Pam had kept her house free of art. Separate from any creative impulse she might have. She had painted her mosaics in the gallery, locked alone in her office as if she were hiding a dirty secret. Then Mel had asked her to paint, and she had needed to capture the starfish immediately, no time to drive into town and shut herself away. And she had gone on to paint in Mel's house, in the studio with Mel and Danny there to see her. Coming to life, coming out of hiding.

Even her house was showing signs of emerging from a long hibernation. Paints and brushes were near at hand, covering her tables and countertops and no longer stuffed in boxes, in closets. She had even hung a few paintings she had purchased over the years and stored in her office. By other artists. Each step had been difficult, but it had brought light and color back to her empty walls. She had been patient with the small successes, nurturing her budding creativity as if it were a frail child. But now she was ready to paint something of her own, hang it on her wall, live with it.

She had brought out the half-finished painting yesterday, after her talk with Mel. Hiding in the back of her closet for years, moving with her from home to home but never completed or displayed on a wall. She had taken it out as a reminder of how much pain relationships caused. As a warning not to give in to her foolish heart and go running back to Mel. Pam brushed her fingers over Kevin's face. She had started the portrait only a few days before Diane left. She had never wanted to finish it. Until now.

Pam started with the background—the park near their house, where Kevin loved to play. The swings and slide, the grass and sandboxes. She worked quickly, filling in details she had left out during the early stages of painting. Eight years later, and she was still sore inside. Falling in love, being a family, losing her family had been too much to take. She couldn't risk having it happen again. She had no choice but to stay here alone. To go back to occasional one-night stands with women who were only passing through town. To suffer the longing every time she'd go into their small town and run into Mel, and Danny, and the inevitable woman who wouldn't be stupid enough to let Mel get away.

Pam wanted to be that woman, and she was well aware of the immediate advantages of accepting Mel's offer of a relationship, a partnership. But how would she survive when it inevitably ended? After just a couple of outings, a few conversations with Danny, Pam had let her guard down long enough to care. And Mel. A handful of nights together had only left Pam wanting more. Had made her fall in love. Pam touched up the details of Kevin's face in the picture. His curly hair, the pink of his toddler cheekbones. She had vowed to avoid love forever. Mel had somehow made her lose sight of her promise and the reasons behind it.

But Mel wasn't Diane. Diane had been jealous of her art. Painting had defined Pam—and it was slowly starting to again—and she had felt constrained by the constant need to hide her talent, downplay the joy and pain of creating, stifle those unexpected urges to sketch and capture moments on paper. But Mel had encouraged and supported her, had eased her transitions between the worlds she created and the one she lived in.

Because Mel understood what it meant to give up part of your soul to please another person. Pam paused and braced her left hand against the wall. Why hadn't she seen it before? How different Mel was from Diane. How different she would be in a relationship. Pam had been so wrapped up in protecting herself against Mel and what she would take from Pam if she left. Pam hadn't given Mel enough credit, hadn't fully appreciated what she'd *bring* to her.

Mel insisted she'd never lose herself in a relationship again, never lose sight of her needs, her dreams, her desires. And Pam knew she'd never want her partner, her lover to suffer those losses. Mel would offer support because she had lived without it. She'd cherish and encourage her partner's dreams because her own had withered for so long. She would share without forcing compromise, love without demanding change. She had lost her identity in her marriage and had fought bravely to rediscover it. She was strong and confident because she'd earned it. She had climbed out of her dark place on her own, not by stepping over Pam or anyone else. Instead, she had reached out and pulled Pam along with her.

Unlike Diane. Who had built up her own shaky self-confidence by expecting Pam to downplay her talent, hide it. Pam had tried to do whatever it took to keep her happy, to stay in Kevin's life. Even after Diane left, Pam had continued to deny her art, had almost stopped painting completely. As if punishing herself for failing Kevin. She hated being separated from him, hurt so deep inside she wanted to crawl out of her skin sometimes. But how long would she have survived with Diane? Starving her soul?

Pam stopped painting and stared at the canvas. She picked up a different brush and leaned close, adding fine lines to the portrait. Coppery hair slightly mussed so it looked natural. Delicate strands, wispy and out of place, because he loved to run and play and explore. She switched brushes again, swirling a flat one through the oils on her palette, darkening the flesh tones for the shaded areas of Kevin's neck, his chin, alongside his freckled nose. To give his face depth. Her hand was smudged with oils, her short fingernails green like the grass she'd been painting. She felt the brush handles, so comfortable to hold. Wood. Smooth and fat, or delicate and narrow.

But as she worked, she felt connected through the brushes to the humid summer day at the park. Sand sifting through her fingers. The metal slide so hot to touch. Kevin's small hand tight in hers as they stood in line to get ice cream. The air filled with the sweet scent of cottonwoods and vanilla-infused waffle cones. She breathed deeply. The narrow entryway was heavy with the smell of linseed oil. For years, she had barely survived on the empty air in her sterile house. Now the scent of paint, of living, nourished her. But she craved other smells, too. Roses and citrus and freshly baked scones. Cinnamon and apples and the verbena she'd planted next to Mel's back door.

On a flash of inspiration, Pam tossed aside her small brush and chose a wider, fatter one. She squeezed some paint onto her palette and mixed rapidly, impatiently rummaging through her tubes in search of the right shade of red to add to the mix. Once she was satisfied with the color, she made broad strokes across the canvas and transformed Kevin's pale yellow shirt into a bright orange one he had loved. The sweeping strokes eased some of her tension. The vivid color brought back a series of memories. She had focused so often on the moment of loss and had too often forgotten the three years of happiness he had brought to her life.

Pam finished with Kevin's eyes, adding depth and brightness, blinking tears out of her own eyes when she stood back at last. A little paint on canvas, a few details and brushstrokes, and she had managed to put some of the pain of losing Kevin behind her while allowing the good memories to resurface. Pam put down her brush and palette. She had made a start on dealing with the past. Maybe it was time to look forward to the future.

Chapter Twenty-five

Pam carried a blank canvas out of the laundry room and found Piper curled in a ball under the easel she had set up next to the dining-room table. She bent down to scratch her dog's ears before she set the canvas in place. Brushes arranged in a neat row, trays filled with scrunched tubes of paint lined up, a clean palette. She had everything she needed. Except an idea.

She stared at the white canvas and let her focus soften. A memory of painting the starfish surfaced. Her first commission piece for Mel, and an emotional battle to paint. Back then, the unpainted canvas had seemed threatening, a temporary respite in oblivion before the painting was finished and she was jolted back to the pain of real life. A foolish illusion of beauty and permanence, when all Pam had known was abandonment and grief. Now the pain of losing her son was like the distant roar of the ocean waves instead of a battering storm. Always with her, in the background of her mind, it no longer eclipsed the joy of having been his mother for a few short years. His portrait hung on the wall near her, out of hiding. And someday, maybe, she would try to mend her relationship with Diane enough so she could see him again. But today the blank canvas was full of possibilities, of promise for the future.

When she'd painted portraits, she'd always had a model. Landscapes and seascapes had been places she had seen, noticed, and felt compelled to paint. She'd always been driven by what she'd seen. Only after she had finished a painting would she recognize the emotions behind the composition, so she'd never minded when people read her paintings in a different way than she did. All that had mattered was getting the image out of her head and onto the canvas.

But now, for the first time, Pam wanted to paint emotion on purpose. Now she was trying to choose the subject to fit the message she wanted to express. And, more than anything, it mattered to her that Mel would be able to see the love Pam wanted to convey. She ran through her memories, searching for something to paint. The inn in its various stages of disrepair and renovation. The studio where Pam had sketched her garden design for Mel and Danny, where she had given her first art lesson, and where she hoped to paint for Mel and her guests. Or Mel, herself. Priming walls, laying floors, creating the geometric pattern of the garden path. Sitting on the steps leading to the beach with her arms wrapped around her knees and her eyes looking back at her past even as she stared at the ocean.

Pam's mind came to rest on the unsuccessful whale-watching trip in the park. She had felt like part of the family with Mel and Danny. It had scared her then, but now she could only hope for more opportunities like it. For a lifetime of them. She remembered Danny's hesitant questioning, his awkward approval of Pam as a partner for his mom. She thought of the kiss she and Mel had stolen, the night they had spent together. Even now, her body responded to just the memory of Mel between her legs, as if she were being physically touched. Pam had tried to fight against the sense of family and love she'd experienced that day. But now she was ready to embrace it, to ask for more. She just couldn't find a picture, an image to pull out of the memory and capture on canvas.

Maybe because she didn't want to recapture the day itself. Pam quickly plucked a few tubes of paint off the trays and squeezed color onto her palette. She wanted to paint a future that hadn't happened yet, a memory she and Mel and Danny had yet to make. She hurried to draw a gray whale breaching, breaking free from the ocean for one brief moment of weightless joy. She sketched the shape, the motion, before the vision disappeared. Once she had caught the broad outlines of the painting, her sense of urgency eased and she slowed down, even stopping to look up a photo in one of her nature guides to check the accuracy of her whale's flippers. She didn't need to hurry, didn't need to rush through the process or be afraid of the finishing point.

Pam layered more paint over her initial outline. She softened and arced the lines of the rectangles and triangles she had thrown on the canvas to give shape to the whale. She used a heavy hand for the ocean, thick paint to depict the weight and pull of the sea. She gave energy to the twisting, arching movement of the whale by lightening her touch when she painted the spray of droplets surrounding the creature. The motion was Mel bursting out of the secretive, unfulfilling life she had led and into an expressive, public, challenging new career.

Through her brush, Pam could feel the courage it must have taken for Mel to break free and start over. But more than bravery, Mel had shown a deep kindness, an expansive desire to offer to other people the same freedom she sought for herself. Pam had watched the first guests at the Sea Glass Inn find an oasis of acceptance in a world that didn't always offer it. And Pam believed Mel would beat the odds and make her inn a success. She would continue to provide a haven for many more people in the future. And Pam wanted to be part of it.

Swirling winter clouds mirrored the ocean waves. Pam stepped back to check her work, to make sure the heaviness of the sea and sky didn't overwhelm the whale's breach but, instead, emphasized its power. She felt the same power moving through her as she painted her feelings for Mel. Her break from the past hadn't been as sudden as Mel's. But her hope, her happiness, were as complete. She had healed slowly and quietly. As she'd silently sanded the floorboards in Mel's dining room after she'd painted her storm. As she'd dug yards of sod out of the backyard. As she'd licked a lazy trail of lime juice off Mel's neck…

Mel—and Danny—had given her the full feeling of being part of a family again. But Mel gave her the same encouragement and respect she offered her guests, without any of the jealousy and manipulation Pam had known with Diane. Mel had made sacrifices for her son, and she obviously wanted him around as often as possible, but Pam knew she had never tried to discourage him from staying in Salem with his dad. Mel's generosity of spirit, her ability to empathize with other people, gave Pam the courage she needed to make the final break from the pull of her past and trust someone again. If Mel would take her back. If she could understand the message Pam was trying to paint.

Pam sat cross-legged on the floor in front of the painting, next to Piper. She idly rubbed her dog's belly with one hand while she sifted her other through the box of sea glass. She hadn't searched for new glass for years, and she let her thoughts wander to isolated beaches she could visit with Mel. She concentrated on smaller pieces of glass for the drops of water around the whale. Mostly whites and blues to match the ocean, but also some multicolored chips of glass that would catch the light and add interest to the neutral tones in the painting. Brown for Piper, green and yellow for Danny's school colors. A coppery-gold glass so a small part of Kevin would forever be in the painting. And peach and sea-foam green for Mel, because those colors reminded Pam of walking into the inn and finding Mel sitting in a patch of sunlight, caught between an ending and a beginning.

Pam carefully cleaned her brushes and palette and stowed all her supplies in the laundry room. She was torn between the desire to rush over to Mel's and show her the partially completed painting and the self-protective need to avoid the rejection she might face. The whale wasn't complete without its mosaic of glass shards, and Pam wouldn't take it to Mel until she had given the painting its full meaning. She grabbed her heavy coat and opened the back door for Piper. A walk on the beach would keep her mind off her upcoming attempt to talk to Mel. Unless, of course, her walk took her past the Sea Glass Inn.

CHAPTER TWENTY-SIX

Mel crawled along the studio floor on her hands and knees, dragging the pan of latex paint and glaze with her. A row of freshly sanded cabinet doors were lined up on a drop cloth. She had painted them a bright blue, and now she applied an off-white color wash in long strokes. She liked the striped pattern the stiff bristles made on the base coat, but she had to be careful to keep her brushstrokes long and even. She sang a song as she worked, something from a CD Danny had played countless times on his last visit. She didn't know the group or most of the lyrics, but she couldn't shake the song from her head.

"Those aren't the right words."

Mel started at the sound of Pam's voice. She glanced over to where she leaned in the doorway and then looked back at the door she had been painting. An arc of glazed drops cut across its surface.

"You made me mess up," Mel said, reapplying the wash before the drops could dry. She had been hoping to see Pam. Last night, she had even considered going to Pam's house and taking back her assertive speech, promising she'd be willing to just have sex with no strings. Her weakness where Pam was concerned annoyed her, and she heard it in her voice. Plus, she had imagined several scenarios bringing them back together, but in none of them was she singing loudly and out of tune with old sweatpants on and blue paint in her hair. She hoped her irritation at Pam's unexpected arrival would help her keep a distance and keep control.

"Sorry," Pam said, stepping into the studio. "Can I help? Not that I think you need…I was just offering, but…"

Mel gestured at a bench near the windows. "There's an extra brush over there."

Pam knelt next to Mel and dipped her brush in the wash. She swept on the glaze with long sure strokes. Mel watched her hand move, her fingers flexing with the brush as if it were part of her. "Why are you here?"

Pam didn't look up. "I brought the fifth painting."

"Oh, I see." Pam had finished her commission. She had come to tie up loose ends, to be free from Mel and their business deal. She couldn't think of any small talk, so she continued painting in silence. Pam seemed satisfied with the quiet, and between the two of them they quickly finished the remaining cabinet doors.

Pam stood up. "These are going to be beautiful in your kitchen," she said. "I love the muted color."

"Thank you. And thanks for your help," Mel said. Pam would probably want to drop off the painting and collect her check without sticking around, but Mel had to be a polite host. "Would you like a cup of coffee?"

"Coffee sounds great," Pam said. "I'll get the painting out of my car and meet you inside."

Mel wasn't sure if she was more surprised by Pam's willingness to stay or by her friendly smile. She got a pot of coffee going and then went into the living room where Pam was unwrapping the painting. She set it on the mantle and turned to Mel.

"What do you think?"

Mel stared at the whale breaching, its mottled gray coat and the blue sky and waves accented by the sparkling spray of tiny sea glass chips. Mel could feel the powerful joy Pam had managed to convey with simple stones and tubes of paint. No matter how many of Pam's paintings Mel would be privileged to see, she'd never look at one without the same feeling of awe she had experienced on that long-ago August day. When she had first spotted the seascape and had been startled and amazed by Pam's talent and drawn to the artist behind the brushstrokes.

Since then, Mel had learned about Pam. Pam didn't just depict emotion in her paintings. She lived it, experienced it. Whatever she felt moved through her and spread outward, onto the canvas. The whale was Pam breaking free, resurfacing as an artist. Mel knew Pam's struggle, knew she had been weakened by pain until even lifting a brush was too much effort. And she knew the profound release Pam must have felt as she painted this gravity-defying creature. What Mel didn't know was where she fit in Pam's new future.

"Well?" Pam prompted.

"I've been wrong before," Mel said. "I've looked at your paintings and wanted to see something hopeful even when it wasn't what you meant people to see. I'm afraid to interpret it the wrong way again."

"Mel, I painted this for you. I know how you see my art, what you find there even when I'm too scared to admit it to myself. You won't be wrong."

"Then I need to hear you say it," Mel said, still facing the whale, unable to look at Pam. "I see what you painted, but I need to hear the words."

Pam stepped close enough to touch Mel, but she kept her hands to herself for the moment. "I love you," she said. "I love you because you wanted to learn how to hang a painting by yourself. Because you make sanding and digging and installing water heaters seem like fun. And because you gave me back my art."

Mel released her held breath when Pam finally touched her. Simply rested her palms on Mel's hips, against her worn cotton sweatpants. And it felt suddenly, explosively right. Pam was touching her like she was supposed to do, like she was meant to do. No chasing after an attraction that wasn't there from the first moment. No one else's hands should be where Pam's were. Where they belonged. Just as suddenly, Mel felt all her regrets vanish. Lingering regrets about her past, the choices she'd made, the way she'd lived her life. She wouldn't change any of her past decisions even if she had the chance because they suddenly had a meaning, a purpose. Because they had brought her here, into this house, into Pam's arms.

"I love you, too," Mel said, turning to face Pam without pulling away. The words were too simple to convey the gratitude, the happiness, the elation she felt. She slid her thumb along Pam's jawline, her hand into Pam's hair, pulling her close and kissing her. Pam had to use her art to say things she couldn't put into words. Mel knew her kiss would do the same thing. Would tell Pam everything she needed to know.

Pam pulled Mel's hips against her as they kissed. She was torn between arousal and an overwhelming urge to weep in relief. The journey had been so long, so lonely, so exhausting. But Pam needed to stop looking back at the past. She slipped her hands under the waistband of Mel's paint-smeared sweatpants and felt the much more fascinating texture of her lace panties. A tantalizing promise, a hint of passion. She pushed Mel backward, not breaking their kiss, until they bumped into the sofa. Pam stripped off Mel's sweatpants and nudged her into a seated position. She straddled Mel's hips.

"I want you," Pam said, taking Mel's chin in her hands. "All of you. I want to listen to you talk about your inn every night. What you repaired, what you painted, how much laundry you did. I want Danny to be best man when we have our wedding in the garden we made. I even want your damned guests to wander through my studio while I'm painting."

Mel laughed. A perfect song. Relaxed and happy. Pam slid off Mel's lap and knelt between her knees.

"I want…you, too," Mel said, her voice catching as she lifted her hips so Pam could pull off her panties. "I want to trip over your easels and hunt for sea glass with you and—oh, yes, that's nice—have your paintings covering all my walls."

Pam heard Mel's voice falter to a stop as her fingers gently wound through Pam's hair. No more words were necessary. Pam had been so afraid to trust another person with her heart and her emotions and her creativity. But Mel would take care of them, cherish them. And Pam would do the same for Mel. Simple as that. Their future was a blank canvas, but Pam wasn't scared of it anymore. She and Mel would paint it together.

Mel struggled to control her breathing, determined to make this moment last a lifetime. Pam's mouth on her, their bodies and souls connected. Mel had fought against losing herself in a relationship, losing her identity again. She glanced at Pam's mosaic. This painting represented everything strong and beautiful about Pam. Her talent, her sensitivity, her honesty. But it didn't overshadow the wall Mel had painted, the fireplace she had tiled, the wainscoting she had stained. The mosaic didn't eclipse Mel's more practical expressions of creativity. It enhanced them. Mel turned her attention back to Pam and her increasingly insistent tongue. She closed her eyes and gave in to the irresistible force of her orgasm. Finally, after so many years, she was home.

Chapter Twenty-seven

Pam turned her sketch pad so it was horizontal and separated the large page into several panels with light strokes of her pencil. She drew an outline of the cove in each square. The pine-covered bluff, the distant lighthouse, the jagged basalt formations.

"I guess I shouldn't have been so worried about him drowning," Mel said.

Pam glanced at Mel. She sat low in her folding chair, one long leg draped over its canvas arm. An interior design magazine was propped open on her lap, and her mouth curved in a half smile. Pam reached out and rubbed her hand along Mel's thigh. She loved the lack of interruption between desire and action. Loved being able to touch Mel, hold her hand, kiss her so freely, with no need to hide or suppress her desire. Loved the way Mel's smile deepened at her caress.

With effort, Pam shifted her attention to the beach in front of them. Danny lay on his stomach on the hard-packed sand. He braced his arms and swung up to a crouched position on the surfboard and then stood with his knees bent.

"He'll be in the water soon enough," Pam said as Danny repeated the motion several times. She felt a pleasant rush of pride as she watched how fluid his movements were. "He's a natural. See? There they go."

Danny turned and waved before he picked up the surfboard and waded into the water with his instructor. Mel waved back and then took hold of Pam's hand where it rested on her leg.

"Ouch," Pam said. Mel appeared at ease, but she tightened her grip on Pam's hand as they watched Danny visibly struggle against the incoming waves. "Honey, I can either hold your hand or draw Danny's lesson. Not both."

Mel hesitated. "Draw," she said, releasing Pam. "But tell me again how safe this is."

Pam shook her fingers to get the blood flowing again. "It's very safe. Danny is an excellent swimmer, and Jeff is a great instructor. I've known him for years, and I wouldn't have recommended this if I didn't believe Danny would be okay." Pam wanted to reassure herself as much as Mel. She had grown so close to Danny over the past months, since she and Mel had told him they were together. Pam already felt like part of their family. No, she already *was* part of their family. She watched Danny paddle toward the shore with a wave. "Besides, look how much fun he's...oh, well, everyone falls a few times before they figure out how to balance."

Mel gave a small gasp, but it turned into a relieved-sounding laugh as Danny's head resurfaced behind the wave. "Be sure you draw a picture of him falling, but don't you dare tell him I laughed."

Pam looked at the paper in front of her. She still felt a brief hesitation before each new drawing or painting. A moment of worry, followed by a breath of relief and wonder as the picture in her mind poured onto the page or canvas. Maybe she'd always feel this way, with each new creation. She didn't mind. Somehow it seemed right, seemed fitting to appreciate what it meant to paint because she knew what it meant when the painting stopped. Art had been effortless when she was younger, and she had hoped to find her way back to that place of ease and simplicity. But the moment of struggle only added dimension and depth to the process.

Today was meant to be fun, though. No deep artistic contemplation necessary. Mel laughed as Danny flipped off his surfboard again. He popped back to the surface and waved at them with no sign of embarrassment or concern before he climbed on the board once more. Pam quickly filled in each panel with a picture of him, in the style of the graphic novels he loved. She drew him practicing on the beach, lying prone as he paddled through the waves, toppling off the board when he met his first wave. And, because he was his mother's son and wouldn't give up until he succeeded, a picture of him riding a wave all the way to shore.

Mel cheered as Danny returned to sea for another ride, a big grin on his face. "See?" Mel said, leaning over to give Pam a kiss. "I told you everything would be all right."

About the Author

Karis Walsh is a horseback riding instructor who lives on a small farm in the Pacific Northwest. When she isn't teaching or writing, she enjoys spending time outside with her animals, reading, playing the viola, and riding with friends.

Books Available from Bold Strokes Books

Sea Glass Inn by Karis Walsh. When Melinda Andrews commissions a series of mosaics by Pamela Whitford for her new inn, she doesn't expect to be more captivated by the artist than by the paintings. (978-1-60282-771-4)

The Awakening: A Sisterhood of Spirits Novel by Yvonne Heidt. Sunny Skye has interacted with spirits her entire life but when she runs into Officer Jordan Lawson during a ghost investigation, she discovers more than just facts in a missing girl's cold case file. (978-1-60282-772-1)

Murphy's Law by Yolanda Wallace. No matter how high you climb, you can't escape your past. (978-1-60282-773-8)

Blacker Than Blue by Rebekah Weatherspoon. Threatened with losing her first love to a powerful demon, vampire Cleo Jones is willing to break the ultimate law of the undead to rebuild the family she has lost. (978-1-60282-774-5)

Another 365 Days by KE Payne. Clemmie Atkins is back, and her life is more complicated than ever before! Still madly in love with her girlfriend, Clemmie suddenly finds her life turned upside down with distractions, confessions, and the return of a familiar face. (978-1-60282-775-2)

Tricks of the Trade: Magical Gay Erotica edited by Jerry L. Wheeler. Today's hottest erotica writers take you inside the sultry, seductive world of magicians and their tricks-professional and otherwise. (978-1-60282-781-3)

Straight Boy Roommate by Kev Troughton. Tom isn't expecting much from his first term at University, but a chance encounter with straight boy Dan catapults him into an extraordinary, wild weekend of sex and self-discovery, which turns his life upside down, and leads him into his first love affair. (978-1-60282-782-0)

Silver Collar by Gill McKnight. Werewolf Luc Garoul is outlawed and out of control, but can her family track her down before a sinister predator gets there first? Fourth in the Garoul series. (978-1-60282-764-6)

The Dragon Tree Legacy by Ali Vali. For Aubrey Tarver time hasn't dulled the pain of losing her first love Wiley Gremillion, but she has to set that aside when her choices put her life and her family's lives in real danger. (978-1-60282-765-3)

The Midnight Room by Ronica Black. After a chance encounter with the mysterious and brooding Lillian Gray in the "midnight room" of The Griffin, a local lesbian bar, confident and gorgeous Audrey McCarthy learns that her bad girl behavior isn't bulletproof. (978-1-60282-766-0)

Dirty Sex by Ashley Bartlett. Vivian Cooper and twins Reese and Ryan DiGiovanni stole a lot of money and the guy they took it from wants it back. Like now. (978-1-60282-767-7)

Raising Hell: Demonic Gay Erotica edited by Todd Gregory. *Raising Hell*: hot stories of gay erotica featuring demons. (978-1-60282-768-4)

Pursued by Joel Gomez-Dossi. Openly gay college student Jamie Bradford becomes romantically involved with two men at the same time, and his hell begins when one of his boyfriends becomes intent on killing him. (978-1-60282-769-1)

The Storm by Shelley Thrasher. Rural East Texas. 1918. War-weary Jaq Bergeron and marriage-scarred musician Molly Russell try to salvage love from the devastation of the war abroad and natural disasters at home. (978-1-60282-780-6)

Crossroads by Radclyffe. Dr. Hollis Monroe specializes in short-term relationships but when she meets pregnant mother-to-be Annie Colfax, fate brings them together at a crossroads that will change their lives forever. (978-1-60282-756-1)

Beyond Innocence by Carsen Taite. When a life is on the line, love has to wait. Doesn't it? (978-1-60282-757-8)

Heart Block by Melissa Brayden. Socialite Emory Owen and struggling single mom Sarah Matamoros are perfectly suited for each other but face a difficult time when trying to merge their contrasting worlds and the people in them. If love truly exists, can it find a way? (978-1-60282-758-5)

Pride and Joy by M.L. Rice. Perfect Bryce Montgomery is her parents' pride and joy, but when they discover that their daughter is a lesbian, her world changes forever. (978-1-60282-759-2)

Timothy by Greg Herren. Timothy is a romantic suspense thriller from award-winning mystery writer Greg Herren set in the fabulous Hamptons. (978-1-60282-760-8)

In Stone: A Grotesque Faerie Tale by Jeremy Jordan King. A young New Yorker is rescued from a hate crime by a mysterious someone who turns out to be more of a *something*. (978-1-60282-761-5)

The Jesus Injection by Eric Andrews-Katz. Murderous statues, demented drag queens, political bombings, ex-gay ministries, espionage, and romance are all in a day's work for a top-secret agent. But the gloves are off when Agent Buck 98 comes up against The Jesus Injection. (978-1-60282-762-2)

Combustion by Daniel W. Kelly. Bearish detective Deck Waxer comes to the city of Kremfort Cove to investigate why the hottest men in town are bursting into flames in broad daylight. (978-1-60282-763-9)

Ladyfish by Andrea Bramhall. Finn's escape to the Florida Keys leads her straight into the arms of scuba diving instructor Oz as she fights for her freedom, their blossoming love…and her life! (978-1-60282-747-9)

Spanish Heart by Rachel Spangler. While on a mission to find herself in Spain, Ren Molson runs the risk of losing her heart to her tour guide, Lina Montero. (978-1-60282-748-6)

Love Match by Ali Vali. When Parker "Kong" King, the number one tennis player in the world, meets commercial pilot Captain Sydney Parish, sparks fly—but not from attraction. They have the summer to see if they have a love match. (978-1-60282-749-3)

One Touch by L.T. Marie. A romance writer and a travel agent come together at their high school reunion, only to find out that the memory of that one touch never fades. (978-1-60282-750-9)

Night Shadows: Queer Horror edited by Greg Herren and J.M. Redmann. *Night Shadows* features delightfully wicked stories by some of the biggest names in queer publishing. (978-1-60282-751-6)

Secret Societies by William Holden. An outcast hustler, his unlikely "mother," his faithless lovers, and his religious persecutors—all in 1726. (978-1-60282-752-3)

The Raid by Lee Lynch. Before Stonewall, having a drink with friends or your girl could mean jail. Would these women and men still have family, a job, a place to live after...The Raid? (978-1-60282-753-0)

The You Know Who Girls: Freshman Year by Annameekee Hesik. As they begin freshman year, Abbey Brooks and her best friend, Kate, pinkie swear they'll keep away from the lesbians in Gila High, but Abbey already suspects she's one of those you-know-who girls herself and slowly learns who her true friends really are. (978-1-60282-754-7)

Wyatt: Doc Holliday's Account of an Intimate Friendship by Dale Chase. Erotica writer Dale Chase takes the remarkable friendship between Wyatt Earp, upright lawman, and Doc Holliday, Southern gentlemen turned gambler and killer, to an entirely new level: hot! (978-1-60282-755-4)

Month of Sundays by Yolanda Wallace. Love doesn't always happen overnight; sometimes it takes a month of Sundays. (978-1-60282-739-4)

Jacob's War by C.P. Rowlands. ATF Special Agent Allison Jacob's task force is in the middle of an all-out war, from the streets to the boardrooms of America. Small business owner Katie Blackburn is the latest victim who accidentally breaks it wide open, but she may break AJ's heart at the same time. (978-1-60282-740-0)

The Pyramid Waltz by Barbara Ann Wright. Princess Katya Nar Umbriel wants a perfect romance, but her Fiendish nature and duties to the crown mean she can never tell the truth—until she meets Starbride, a woman who gets to the heart of every secret, even if it will be the death of her. (978-1-60282-741-7)

The Secret of Othello by Sam Cameron. Florida teen detectives Steven and Denny risk their lives to search for a sunken NASA satellite—but under the waves, no one can hear you scream... (978-1-60282-742-4)

Finding Bluefield by Elan Barnehama. Set in the backdrop of Virginia and New York and spanning the years 1960–1982, *Finding Bluefield* chronicles the lives of Nicky Stewart, Barbara Philips, and their son, Paul, as they struggle to define themselves as a family. (978-1-60282-744-8)